D0191949

How to Repair a
Mechanical
Heart

J.C. LILLIS

HOW TO REPAIR A MECHANICAL HEART
Copyright © 2012 by J.C. Lillis

Cover design by Mindy Dunn
Cover illustration of linked hands by Andrea Sabaliauskas

ISBN: 978-1-514632-77-2

Follow the author on Twitter (@jclillis) and on her blog (www.jclillis.com).

For my mom and dad

1»

SIM AND CAPTAIN CADMUS huddled close in the crystal spider cave, their secret hearts thudding with untold passion.

I scroll down fast, my own secret heart thudding more than I want to admit. Plastic Sim shoots a plastic glare of judgment from his perch on the gooseneck lamp clipped to my bedpost. I know what he's thinking, but I can't help it. Replace "Cadmus" with "Brandon" and this fanfic graduates from terrible to tolerable in 0.3 seconds.

Abel doesn't have to know.

Summoning all his courage, Cadmus gently touched the arm of the cerulean-haired android, his breath hitching in the eerie, dim light of the cave. "Hey, Tin Man," he rasped. "Don't take this the wrong way, but...I think I love you."

My kneecaps tingle.

Sim's smooth, impassive face betrayed no emotion, but his mechanical heart glowed blue in response. "Captain," he intoned. "I would like to reciprocate, but my sensors tell me—"

"Screw your sensors," said the captain, just as he had before, the day their ship first crashed on this red planet of terrors. His brawny hand massaged the android's thigh. "Who cares what they think? Who cares what anyone thinks?"

"That is a useful perspective."

1

I pull my laptop screen closer. I grab Plastic Sim and clutch him to my chest, like Gram with her blue moonstone rosary beads.

A crystal spider bayed in the distance. Cadmus knew it was now or never. Sim's silver eyes glittered, the red sensors on his collarbone pulsing in the dark. Cadmus let his rough fingertips trail down Sim's face, wanting to kiss him and be him all at once, and in their warm electric closeness the android smiled and murmured—

"Someone get the door, willya?"

I slam my laptop shut. Plastic Sim clatters to the floor, right by the suitcase I packed and re-packed three times. Five words from Dad downstairs and I'm back to the real me: a dumbass on solar-system sheets, sneaking forbidden *Castaway Planet* fanfic and putting off leaving for a six-week trip I sincerely should have said no to. I wriggle out of bed and rescue Plastic Sim, slip the action figure in the pocket of my cargo shorts.

Then a different downstairs voice:

"May I come in?"

I freeze with my hand on the suitcase.

Footsteps shuffle; the front door whines shut. I hold my breath. It can't be him. It was Dad doing an impression, or the hot new weatherman on Channel 12. If there's a God and he still likes me even a little, he wouldn't let this happen. Not when I'm already freaked about this trip.

"Brandon?"

Mom downstairs. I picture her peeking around the banister, still in the funny apron she wore to make our pancakes this morning. *If God wanted me to cook, why did*

He invent restaurants?

I clear my throat. "Yeah."

"Come on down, okay?"

I hear the visitor again: *Oh Kathy, did you make this awesome wreath?* and *Greg, how's that garden?* My mouth goes sandy. This is happening. If I were Natalie I'd find a way out of this; Mom would knock on my door two minutes later and I'd be halfway down the street with my earbuds in and my fists jammed in my pockets, the fire escape ladder still swaying from the windowsill.

I pull in a breath. It hurts.

"Be right there," I yell.

I yank on my favorite *Castaway Planet* shirt—blue with red letters, freshly ironed with the Steamium I got for graduation—and trudge downstairs. My suitcase bumps behind me. The living room smells normal, like syrup and coffee, except there he is on the flowered couch with his wide white smile and the rumpled curls that make the girls check *The Thorn Birds* out of the library. My teeth clench. Mom and Dad perch on either side of him, like benevolent henchmen. A breeze from the open window ruffles Dad's bonsai on the sill, three snow-rose trees with tiny perfect leaves shaped like teardrops.

"Look who stopped by," says Dad.

"Hey, Brandon."

"Hi, Father Mike."

"Congrats on graduation."

"Thanks."

"He was out here visiting Mrs. Trugman, and he came by to give you a blessing for your trip," says Mom. "Isn't that nice?"

Father Mike power-shakes my hand. "Bec's mom mentioned it to me at the potluck, and—"

"She did?"

"Yep. Wow, so just the two of you..."

I unclench. Thank God. If my parents found out Abel was coming too, they'd lock me in a windowless tower. He met them once and the next day I heard Mom on the phone with Aunt Meg saying "I'm just glad they're not in the same school—can you imagine?" They don't know thing one about our vlog. When I disappear to record new posts with Abel, they think I'm strumming Coldplay covers at open mike night with a couple other guys from the Timbrewolves.

"Just the two of us," I nod.

"And I think it's great," Father Mike says. "Nothing like a drive across the country to clear your mind, you know? Make you think about things a whole new way."

"That's what we thought," Dad nods.

"You and Becky were always so close."

"Still are. They still are." Mom smiles.

Father Mike sips from Mom's Grand Canyon mug. "And I understand you're going to some—what, fan conventions, right?"

"For *Castaway Planet*."

"Wow. Great show. I catch it now and then."

"Yeah?"

"Sure, sure. Love its vibe. Sort of retro sci-fi, a little campy, but a really powerful allegory, you know?" He tilts his head and nods at me. "I think everyone feels lost on a scary planet sometimes."

He wiggles his fingers to illustrate *scary*. I think I'm supposed to smile.

"Father Mike, would you like some blueberry pancakes while you're here? There's leftover batter."

His blue eyes crinkle. "That would be excellent. Thanks, Kathy."

"Greg, can you help?"

4

"Hm? Oh! Yes, sure."

Don't leave me don't leave me I say with my eyes but of course that's the point, and they vanish into the safe yellow kitchen. They have no clue. When I met with Father Mike before Christmas for an informal counseling session, they asked me how it went and I blushed and muttered *fine*. I could have told them about the stuff he said, could have blamed my leaving St. Matt's on the creepy "must-read" book he lent me. But I kept quiet. Because under their sweet candy shell, I know they're bitter enough to agree with him.

I fix my eyes on the family-photo wall. Mom and Dad at senior prom, wedding at St. Matt's, me and Nat mugging in pirate hats, the four of us on Sunset Beach in matching white shirts and chinos.

"How've you been, bud?" he asks me.

"Fine."

"Still miss you on Sunday."

I nod.

"I see those great parents of yours in the pew all by themselves."

I look at the floor.

"It's been what—four, five months?"

"I guess."

"That's a long time." He holds up a hand. "I'm not judging. I just think you must feel lonely. We miss that guitar of yours in folk group."

My face burns. He steps up to me and puts his hands on my shoulders. He's wearing a blue polo shirt tucked into khakis and he gives off a childish smell, like Wonder bread and school antiseptic.

"Brandon, I want to tell you something, okay? Something I maybe didn't make clear enough when we talked. Can you look at me?" I can't meet his eyes. I settle on his

5

left nostril. "The Big Guy upstairs still loves you. He understands what it's like to be a young boy, these swarms of strange feelings filling up your heart..." He knocks a fist into his chest. "He's on your side, you know? And as long as you pray for the strength to live life the way he asks, he will give you that gift. I know he will. I kinda have an 'in' with him."

He grins and nudges me, and when I don't do anything he nods until I nod back. I hate giving in. I want to be casually profane like Nat is when she comes home from Bennington and tries to shock us with stuff from her Theology of The Simpsons class. I want to say *I left church for a reason, and I'm not coming back.* But when Father Mike walks in a room I'm ten years old again. I'm traveling the altar midway through Mass, lowering my brass candle snuffer over one, two, three flames while he watches from his big chair with a gentle smile, making sure I've got everything right.

"Can I give you a quick blessing?" he asks me.

"Okay."

He thumbs a cross on my forehead and starts in with this intense *Lord, defend Brandon* prayer. I wonder if this is a stealth exorcism. Plaid flashes in the kitchen doorway and I know Mom and Dad are listening in, hoping to God it does the trick but ready to set their jaws and keep loving me if it doesn't. I don't know which makes me feel worse.

"Amen?" he says.

"Amen," I whisper.

"That was really nice, Mike." My parents slip back in the room reverently, like he's just made me a saint. Mom hands him a short stack of pancakes on my favorite blue plate.

"My pleasure."

"You just worry so much. His first trip without us,"

says Dad.

"Well, he's a man now. He needs independence. He'll make good decisions, I know it."

He winks at me.

"I have to go," I say.

Mom and Dad descend on me. Hug from Mom, shoulder pat from Dad, desperate last-minute directives from both:

"Call us every night."

"*Always* lock the door."

"Be good to Becky."

"Don't let her drive on back roads. She's not as experienced as you."

"Remember what we practiced: slow down for trucks, conservative on turns—"

"He knows, Greg."

"And don't blow your savings on food, all right? Mom stocked the RV for a reason."

"Okay."

"And can you do me a favor, sweetie?" says Mom.

"Sure."

Please rewire your brain circuitry so we can go back to normal.

Mom doesn't say that, not out loud. Instead she goes to the lampstand and pulls out an old *TV Guide.* David Darras smolders on the cover in his Sim costume, the same picture I used to keep under my mattress and take out at night for inspirational purposes. Iconic white suit, pale silvery skin, ice-blue hair. Mom gives the cover a shy smile and tucks a blonde curl behind her ear. It weirds me out. I never thought she paid attention to *Castaway Planet.*

"If you do meet David Darras," she says, "can you get this signed for me?"

"Oh, the perfect man." My father does a dreamy sigh.

7

"Will you shush!"

"Brandon, it's time you knew. Your mother has a crush on an android."

They all crack up, Mom and Dad and Father Mike the loudest of all. Coffee sours in my stomach. If a nice little anxiety disorder wasn't programmed into my motherboard, I'd say *So do I* and watch them implode. Instead I take handshakes and back-slaps, one more ten-dollar bill from Dad in case of emergency.

"Brandon?" says Father Mike.

"Yep."

"Remember everything I said."

"I will."

The Sunseeker's parked at the end of the driveway, gassed up and gleaming like it's waiting for Dad's hiking gear and field guides, Mom's plastic bin of nonperishable snacks, Nat's heavy black boots and graphic novels. I lug my stuff down the walk and shove it all in. My suitcase, my guitar, the pouch with my savings and graduation cash, the Phillies duffel bag I've had since I was nine. When the RV door clangs shut, I hurry to the bushes at the edge of our yard, kneel down in the dirt, and throw up as quietly as possible under the lowest branches. Then I pop two mints and slip Plastic Sim in my shirt pocket, where I can see him. I have a twenty-minute drive to turn back into the person Abel thinks I am, and I need all the help I can get.

2»

ABEL MCNAUGHTON LIVES in a house that's like ninety percent glass. It's across the river on the west shore, halfway up a mountain in a development where you can't see houses from the road, just pine trees and gated driveways. The McNaughtons have custom-made redwood gates that are never closed; the one time my parents picked me up here, my mother said the gates were an awful waste of money and weren't redwoods an endangered species? She had a lot to say about the house, too: so much glass, too hard to keep clean, and any lunatic could walk right up to it and see into all your business.

I spot Abel as soon as the house comes into view. The fourth wall of his bedroom is one big window, so it's like I'm seeing him on a giant TV. Black silk robe, pajama bottoms with neon squiggles, white hair a spider-plant mess. When we did our season finale recap three weeks ago he'd just re-bleached it; he used too much gentian violet and loved the surprise purplish tinge. "It'll fade in a day, but whatever," he'd said, shrugging on his vintage *Purple Rain* shirt to match.

I shift the Sunseeker into park by his mom's neglected petunia bed. Abel doesn't notice me. He's standing in the doorway of his walk-in closet tossing clothes at a huge black bag, and the fact that this is probably the first and only packing he's done all week makes me want to deliver an athletic kick to the seat of his pajamas. He's talking to himself. At least I think he is. Then I see this big tanned hand shoot out from the closet, wagging Abel's acid-yellow Jesus vs. Mothra tee. Abel grins and yanks the guy into view—tan and tousled, shiny green shorts, a bad bicep tattoo I guarantee says something stupid in Chinese. Of course they start kissing, because even though Abel and I are just business partners I know exactly the kind of business he gets up to when I'm not around, and now they collapse on the closet floor and all I see are four feet nuzzling and I know they're whispering sexy things I can't imagine without feeling unzipped and turned inside out.

HHREEEEAAOONNNNK. *Crap.* I lift my elbow off the horn, but it's too late.

Here comes Abel. He's creeping up to his window like Elmer Fudd hunting wabbits, shading his eyes in the late-morning sun. He points down at me, and then he rips his robe open and does a goofball shimmy, pale belly pressed to the glass. My eyes squinch shut. I see the cover of the book Father Mike gave me, the clean blond boy thrusting a fist in the air: *Put on the Brakes! The Cool Kid's Guide to Mastering Sexual Temptation.*

Come in, Abel mouths. He makes a frantic camera-cranking gesture. *Vlog post. Now!*

I gesture back. *Aren't you busy?*

He wiggles his fingers above his head and patters them down on his shoulders. Greenshorts is getting in the shower, I guess. I climb out of the Sunseeker, hoping that wasn't some obvious sex code for *five more minutes.* I don't want my cover blown.

Abel and I met last October in a *Castaway Planet* fan forum. I was **shytown** with the Sim-in-the-snow icon, he was **x_offender** with the shopped icon of Cadmus in a Speedo. This was right after I had The Talk with my parents and word spread at school; I hadn't gotten any black eyes or hot-pink FAGs on my locker, but guys I'd known since kindergarten were suddenly keeping their

10

distance or talking to me in a weird stilted way, as if I were an alien whose friendliness might just be a cover. Nights when I wasn't on Bec's couch picking at popcorn and snickering at telenovelas with her, I was shut up in my room, hiding out in the forum with other Casties. The Abel thing happened fast. I wrote a rant about the "deep and irrefutable stupidity" of Cadsim fanfic after Episode 4-14, he thought it was funny, we spent a few days chatting about *Castaway Planet* and old sci-fi B movies, and then we figured out we lived twenty minutes from each other and he asked me to co-run his vlog with him. He sent an actual invitation to my house on cream stationery with a plea in fancy script: *Abel McNaughton requests the honour of your collaboration on "Screw Your Sensors," the Internet's third most popular Castaway Planet fan vlog. Please please please be my awesome business partner!!!*

No guy ever called me awesome before, so the lies started pretty much the second I hopped up his marble front steps. I told him I'd been out for six years instead of two weeks. My parents were one hundred percent fine with me, just like his. Aftershocks from twelve years of Catholic school? None at all, and I'm certainly not a freak who has panic attacks in Dairy Queen bathrooms after a guy tries to kiss me. I even invented a tragic heartbreak to shield me from his matchmaking: some pre-med sex god named Zander, who had me dreaming of a picket fence and two adopted kids before he dumped me for a bartender and ruined me indefinitely for all other men.

If Abel found out about the real me, he'd start gazing down from a lofty throne of pity, so I have to be careful every second I'm around him. I keep it cool and mysterious, like Sim. His dry little comments. His ease in his own synthetic skin. His decision to cut out his evolution chip, so he could enjoy nice safe friendships without all the terrors of falling in love.

I wind my mechanical heart and open his door.

***

"You ready, partner?" he says.

"We're unveiling now?"

"We *have* to. The girls've been trolling us all morning. Wait'll you see."

Abel and I hunch in front of his laptop at the glass kitchen table, next to a stack of cruddy glasses and plates I very much want to scrub. He's crunching Cookie Crisp from a china bowl that probably cost more than my car. His limited-edition Plastic Cadmus grips the pocket of Abel's robe with his super-ripped hero arms and I side-eye him; even three inches tall, Cadmus is a smug bastard. No one's home besides us, as usual. Abel's dad's at Mercy fitting someone with a new heart, his mom and little sister are in Boston on their book tour, and his brother Jacob's at some school in New York for musical geniuses with bad attitudes.

"Don't worry. You look *lovely.*" Abel slides on his shades with the red steel frames, an exact replica of Cadmus's. "You've got that cute all-American khakis-and-flip-flops thing going on. You're like Volleyball Ken."

I sip my water. "Now with Eye-Rolling Action."

"Do I have sex hair?"

"Ew."

"Brandon, seriously. Wait'll you meet Kade. Best five days of my life!"

"Please spare every detail."

"Cynicism gives you blackheads. Studies show."

I tip my chin at the laptop. "Let's *go.*"

He grins and hits record.

"*Bonjour,* fellow Casties." He musses his hair and turns on his best news-anchor purr. "It's your two favorite re-cappers, coming at you live from my kitchen on May the twenty-ninth, a day that will forever live in infamy. Say hello to my distinguished fellow commentator, Brandon—"

"Hi guys."

"—currently obscuring his cute little abs with the *baggiest Castaway Planet t-shirt* in recorded history."

"It's comfy."

"What are you hiding under there?"

"Secrets. Many secrets."

Abel rips off his shades and cocks an eyebrow. I let out a snort. I picture a handful of strangers watching this at home, thinking my secret is cool and mysterious like a jagged scar across my chest, and not dull and heavy like *I gave up church but not the angst.*

"Anyway, guys." Abel pops one last Cookie Crisp. "Today we unveil that Super-Secret Summer Spectacular we've been teasing y'all about, 'cause we know how our fifteen fans like, follow our every move and have shrines and shit."

"My shrines are bigger." I grin.

"Whatever. Here's the deal. You real fans who come here and watch our episode recaps every week are A-plus, right, 'cause you love *Castaway Planet* as much as we do and you've got more than ten brain cells to your name. But as we all know, there's one faction of the fandom..."

"One very vocal faction."

"...that is, and we say this with love, STONE COLD CRACKERS WITH A SIDE ORDER OF CRAZY FRIES. I am referring, of course, to—"

He plunks Plastic Cadmus in front of the camera. I do the same with Plastic Sim.

"—Cadsim shippers."

I perform a cartoony shudder.

"Guys, I don't know if you're following our ginormous flamewar with Miss Maxima and her minions at the Cadsim fanjournal." Abel sighs. "The slash fiction was bad enough, but these rejects have been calling it canon since the crystal-spider-cave episode, and that we *cannot* abide. Look, maybe it's semi-tempting to think they had secret sexytimes when they're stuck in the cave and there's that 'meaningful look' and the fadeout, but people? Captain James P. Cadmus is a blazing hot male specimen who can kill a sixty-pound alien spider with his bare hands, and Sim is a freakin'-damn ANDROID—"

"Who's way too good for Cadmus."

"That statement is too ludicrous to acknowledge," Abel huffs, petting Plastic Cadmus's plastic head. "Anyway, our feud with the crazypants Cadsim girls? Officially ends this summer. We at the Screw Your Sensors vlog have made a wager. Hold up the CastieCon tickets, Bran."

I fan them out. Abel explains the bet, which basically goes like this: we hit the six tour stops the *Castaway Planet* convention makes this summer, go to the Q&As with all five main cast members plus the showrunner, and ask them what they think Cadmus and Sim did in the cave scene after the fadeout. If a majority of them agree that no hookup happened, the Cadsim girls have to run an all-caps disclaimer on every one of their fanfics, *forever.*

"Brandon, tell them what it says." Abel slides me a printout.

"PLEASE NOTE: A legitimate Cadsim hookup has been definitely disproven by the cast and creator of Castaway Planet, as well as professional Internet gods Brandon Page and Abel McNaughton. I freely admit I am a dingbat with zero respect for canon or for Cadmus or Sim as characters;

14

I just want to see hot boys get it on. Read at your own risk."

"That's right. However, on the extreme off chance we lose? Miss Maxima, the Queen Bitch mod of the Cadsim community, will select a scene from one of their rotten little fanfics and we'll act it out *on camera—"*

"—Within. Reason." Why did I say yes to this?

"Right. Strictly first base, pervs. We're gay but not for each other." He scrolls through the Cadsim fic archive on his phone. "For instance, we won't do the one where Dr. Lagarde plants a 'sex chip' in Sim's brain and he and Cadmus do it in a hammock."

"For crap's sake." I facepalm.

"Nor will we perform the futurefic where they're back on Earth and get *stuck in an elevator* during a blackout."

"Or any other elevator fic."

"Or hurt/comfort fic."

"Or alternate-universe steampunk fic."

"So we better make *damn* sure we come out on top."

"Sim likes the top."

It just shoots out. I feel my ears redden; when I slip and say something flirty, it sounds like an elephant trying to bark.

Abel cracks up and stops the recording right there. He hits *upload* before I can object.

"On that note, Tin Man," he says. "I have a little...*surprise.*"

He reaches in his robe and rummages. My left leg starts jittering. Last time Abel surprised me it was my birthday, and he slipped a special card under my windshield wiper: Sim's head taped to a cutout of a gym rat in a leopard thong.

This time it's just a small silver envelope.

"Open it," he sings.

"What is it?"

15

"A lock of David Darras's hair."

"Wha—"

"Open it, doof."

I unstick the flap. Inside are three more tickets on heavy silver paper. Two robots waltz in silhouette between an embossed P and F.

"What's this?"

Abel bounces in his seat. "I totally splurged," he squees. "You, me, and Bec have VIP tickets to the Fourth Annual Castaway Ball! At the Long Beach con! *With special guests David Darras and Ed Ransome!"*

My stomach twists. The thing about Darras barely registers. Stories from the Castaway Ball pop up in fandom all the time. Dance-floor dramas, bathroom gropings, afterparty orgies in smoky hotel rooms.

"Why—" I force a Sim face. Indifferent, slightly amused. "Why would we do that?"

"Well, clearly we're going to win the bet, so you won't be making out with me anytime soon. *However,* I thought a whole ballroom of hot dorks in cosplay would be a lovely consolation prize." He presses Plastic Sim to my lips, making a loud smoochy sound. "We're going to find you a Sim, my dear. And get you over that Zander douchelord, like *finally."*

"Oh." Panic flushes through me. I knew he'd pull something like this; he's tried to set me up with three different guys since January. "That's...nice, but—"

"Nope! No more excuses." Abel waves Plastic Sim like a magic wand. "Befoooorrre the stroke of midnight at the nerd prom, yoooooou, Brandon Gregory Page, will meet a beautiful boy on the dance floor and break the sinister spell of celibacy with the Kiss of True Love. Or True Lust. Whatever."

Put on the Brakes!, Chapter 4: **Celibacy and hap-**

16

piness—can they go together? You bet! You can still have a full and fulfilling life while obeying a special call to abstinence...

"Thus it has been decreed," Abel proclaims, "and therefore on this life-altering journey, you, Brandon, will be my project, and I shall help you—"

"—Stop dressing like a frat boy?"

Abel and I turn around. Bec's grinning in the doorway with her suitcase and the bowling ball bag she keeps her camera equipment in. Just seeing her makes me exhale. She looks pretty and practical: cargo pants, blue tank top, no makeup on her round freckled face. Her curls are forced into two stumpy braids, and she's got on the faded rainbow friendship bracelet I gave her when we were fourteen. Her Zara Lagarde action figure clutches her belt loop, little plastic machete tight in one fist.

"*Mon petit pamplemousse!* Love the braids." Abel blows her a kiss. She blows one back on her way to me and we fold into a hug. It's so easy. We look like brother and sister—some brown-haired blue-eyed Dick and Jane in a kids' book from the fifties—and she feels soft and friendly as Mr. Quibbles, my old stuffed penguin I would die if she told Abel about.

She tosses an arm around my neck. "So what's Abel decreed for you?"

"Nothing," I mutter.

"*Everything*," Abel says. "Life. Love. Sex. Rebirth."

"Ooh. Can I have some?"

"We can all have some, Rebecca." He raises Plastic Sim's arm and traces a cross on her forehead with it. "We can *all* have some."

She snorts. "Did you make special brownies again?"

That Kade guy's shuffling around upstairs. I hear him at the railing now: *Abe...seen my shoes?*

17

"Hold please, Bec." Abel tosses me Plastic Sim. "Brandon can fill you in on his renaissance while I dress my boy."

He bounds upstairs, humming the *Castaway Planet* theme. Bec's smile snaps off. She sticks her hands on her hips and looks me up and down.

"What's wrong?" she says.

"What? Nothing."

"Bullshit. You ironed your t-shirt."

"I did not."

"Your shorts look ironed too."

"I couldn't sleep."

"Are you pussing out on this trip?"

"How mad would you be?"

"Um, furious?" She grabs the front of my shirt. "I *cannot* be in my house this month, Brandon."

"Why not?"

"My mother and sister are hosting a book club. Eight choir ladies plus wine spritzers plus a stack of Amish romance novels."

"Ugh."

"What's the problem?"

I slide her the tickets to the Castaway Ball and fill her in, the whole terrifying find-me-a-guy plan. Between the lines, I appeal to her time-honored status as my best friend. The one who knew I was gay a year before Nat talked me into coming out, the one who buoyed me up with sensitive grace and good humor through the parent talk and the Father Mike meeting and the dark nights of the soul when I lay awake at 1 a.m. pondering the existence of God and praying for a sign that he was real and sympathetic and still pretty much okay with me.

She cracks up laughing.

"You have to help!" I smack her arm.

18

"How?"

"Tell him I won't be over Zander for another year. At least."

"Oh, Fake Zander? I don't—"

"Shhh!"

"Whatever." She grabs a pear from the fruit bowl and takes a big messy bite. "You can't stay fucked up forever, can you? You need to start putting yourself out there and getting humiliated like the rest of us. Only then will you be a Real Boy."

I glower at her. "What kind of friend are you?"

"A heartless one." She drops a sticky kiss on my cheek. "I love you, though."

"Aww! Ken and Skipper."

Abel's grinning in the doorway. Two tanned hands knead his shoulders and he pulls in Greenshorts, who isn't Greenshorts anymore because he's got on frayed army pants and a white V-neck that's a little damp and clingy. His light brown eyes and skin are fanfic-flawless and he's all lean muscle. I imagine a conversation with him, a one-sided ode to 12-minute workouts and wheat-grass shakes.

"So Kade, this is Bec, our lovely and amazing camera-person—she's only a moderate *Castaway Planet* fangirl but she's putting up with us anyway. And, uh, you've seen Brandon online."

"Uh-huh." Kade squints at me, stifling a yawn. "You hook up with this one?"

"Noooo. No no no. Tell him, Brandon."

"Not my type," I say.

"Obsessed with his ex," Abel whispers to Kade.

"Right, right." Kade grins. "You don't do guys with baggage."

"I merely assist them. He's my summer project."

Kade looks me over again and elbows Abel. "Babe," he stage-whispers.

"Hm."

"He looks like that dude from the movie."

"Which one?"

"The one we watched at the party. That hit man with amnesia—"

"The main guy?"

"No no no...the *little* dude." He drops his voice low. "With the...ears?"

"Oh my God." Abel snorts, raining cute smacks on his shoulder. "Brandon, don't listen. He's *awful!*"

My ears burn like Kade's thrown a hot spotlight on them, but he's already jumped to the next thing: kissing Abel in a place I never thought about, the spot where the strong line of his jaw curves up to meet his earlobe. Abel kisses him back like no one else is in the room. When Kade turns his back, his thin t-shirt gives me glimpses of more tattoos I suspect are inversely proportional to intelligence, including a chicken with wings of fire and NO REGRETS spelled out in barbed wire. Bec traps me in this tractor beam of pity that's deeply unnecessary since I couldn't care less who Abel's playing Perfect Boyfriends with, so I cross my eyes at her and grab the laptop again.

Abel's got the Cadsim fanjournal bookmarked. I hop on to see if Miss Maxima and the rest of them are smacktalking us yet. Abel loves it when they do; he thinks it makes us famous. I still remember when Jimmy Gilver called me a dillhole in third grade, so I'm pretty weirded out when I read:

cavegrrl94: DEATH TO BRANDON & ABEL!!!

murklurk: They will lose this bet. SO HARD.

mrs.j.cadmus: B & A are pathetic, srsly. love is alien to them.

murklurk: Yeah, really. Even Sim knows more about it than they do.

Miss Maxima: Don't worry, girls. Pride goeth before a fall. In six short weeks their smug jaded mugs will be onscreen, acting out one of our very best Cadsim fics in exquisite detail. I can't wait to see their stupid lips moving closer...closer...*closer*...

"I want a picture!" says Bec.

I fold down the screen. For a second I think she wants to snap one of Abel and his guy the way you'd photograph a pair of zoo otters who won't stop doing adorable things, but then she tosses her camera to Kade and they're pulling me in front of the huge silver fridge, nudging me between Bec and Abel. Kade directs us: action figures in fists, arms around each other. Abel makes big jokey kissy lips next to my face. I stiffen and curse the brain defect that made me say *yes* when he tempted me with those CastieCon tickets his parents bought and begged me to sign up for six weeks of his company. Personal space invasion. Toast crumbs in the butter. Nonstop matchmaking. Maybe I can ditch him at a rest stop, run off to some mountain village where the yurts are far apart and everyone stays inside whittling and no one cares if you just want to be alone.

Good idea, bud, says Father Mike. *You can still stop this.*

The camera stops flashing. I shut my eyes. White halos dance in the dark. Abel hooks Plastic Cadmus to the rim of my ear and leans close, whispering in his best space-captain rasp.

"Let's get started, Tin Man," he says. "I can't *wait* to see how you drive that thing."

CastieCon #1
Cleveland, Ohio

3»

"THIS RV," Abel declares, "is like, nine months pregnant with *awesome*."

I'm up in the cab of the Sunseeker, zoning out to Kings of Convenience and powering the RV down the last strip of highway before Cleveland. Behind me, Abel and Bec are recording our first on-the-road entry. I hope they leave me out of it. I spent three hours in a Pennsylvania truck stop today while Abel tried on stupid hats and fed five hundred quarters into a gumball machine to get a gold plastic medallion with a dollar sign on it, and now I just want to space. I'm Sim in the cockpit of the U.S.S. Starsetter, my default setting switched to NAVIGATE and the sensors in my collarbone blinking red, scanning the skies for hidden dangers.

"Check it out, Casties. There's a rug shaped like a pinecone and a duck lamp that quacks and I don't know what's in these rustic moose-head pillows but they're really super-comfortable...Hey, Bran!"

I knock my head against the backrest. "What?"

"Whatcha thinking about up there?"

"Eternal damnation."

"Hot." He's in my face with Bec's camera now, his white hair teased up and experimented on. He looks like Edward Scissorhands rolled in flour. "You're so Cadmus when you drive an RV. Look guys, he's got that non-chalant 'I-only-need-one-hand-on-the-wheel' thing—

"Uh-huh."

"It's true! All you need are six inches and a bomber jacket. Ooh, ooh, do the Cadmus line from the pilot, okay?

C'mon, I'll set you up." He stiffens his back like Sim and puts on some phony robot voice. *"Captain, we appear to be veering off course. My navigation sensors indicate—* that's you, Bran. Say it!"

"Screw your sensors!" I roll my eyes.

"Mm. You're not *quite* projecting 'sexy desperation,' but we'll work on it. Hey, tell our fifteen fans where we're headed."

"The Robot's Bookshelf."

"Guys, we are *seconds* away from our pre-convention appearance at this sci-fi bookstore where they're having an essential CastieCon geek gathering and Brandon's going to talk to a B-O-Y, and—"

"What?"

"That's your assignment tonight. You converse in public with a boy. You've heard of them, right? They're like girls, but with penises?"

Father Mike's going to pepper my subconscious with Leviticus 18 in another second. I turn up the music and Sim myself steady. "Boys do not interest me, Captain."

"Right. Here, this could be you, are you ready?" He fumbles with his phone and reads off the screen. *"Sim felt his steely resolve slowly melt away. He could taste the hot manly tang of the captain's lips—"*

"Will you quit it?"

"Running his nimble silver tongue over his perfect teeth, he—Hey!"

I snap his camera shut. Abel blips the Cadsim fic off his phone's little screen and thunks his boots up on my dashboard, grinning. His cheek is smudged with powdered sugar and Plastic Cadmus chins the rim of his jeans pocket, as if there are crumbs and sticky change in there and he's desperate to escape.

"Donut hole?" We stop at a red light. He wags the bag

from the Donut Hut in Clarion. "You know you want one."

"No thanks." I smell cinnamon. My mouth waters. "Why do you have to read that fic out loud?"

"Um, because it's hilarious?"

"Huh-uh. There's some deeper neurosis here."

"I love it, actually. It speaks to me."

"I knew it."

"Well, who *doesn't* love a good mpreg?"

"A what?"

"Sim gets man-pregnant? Gives birth to twins during a tornado?"

"I'll pretend I never heard that."

"Here, I'll read you the wedding one—"

"NO."

"But Xaarg's the minister!"

"I will end you."

"Where's your sense of humor?"

"Zander took it."

He chugs some root beer and summons a massive belch. "You know what?" A smaller belch follows. "You could learn a lot from this android-learns-to-love fic."

"I've already loved. He dumped me for a—"

"—bartender, and he was pre-med, and he read *Ulysses* for fun and caught salmon with his bare hands and played basketball with albino orphans—"

"You're just jealous 'cause your boyfriend works at Sub Shack."

"He's a *sandwich technician*. And at least he's present tense."

"Whatever." I craft an expert left-hand turn. "I'm not talking to a guy tonight."

"Why?"

"I just...need more time."

"Brandon. This is dire. Don't hold out for Mr. Candlelight Romance." His cheeks bulge with donut. "You wait too long and soon you'll be seventy-five and you'll live all alone in a sad fourth-floor walkup that reeks of loneliness and takeout chow mein, and then you'll wish you listened to me."

"What's wrong with chow mein?"

He lobs a donut hole at me.

"I mean, I'd rather have moo shu pork, but—"

"Can I punch you? Like for real?"

Dad's GPS breaks in: *Arrive at destination.* I wave Abel quiet and bump up into the bookstore parking lot, looking for a spot I can ease the Sunseeker into without breaking a sweat. I've got this swervy carsick feeling. It's the Zander talk. Can Abel tell it's a lie? He's too smart to be fooled forever.

"Whoa..." Abel says.

My knuckles go white on the wheel. "What?"

"A-plus park job."

"Oh. Thanks."

"You did that one-handed."

"I did."

He toys with Plastic Cadmus. "I've been like, covertly admiring you all day. I'd crap my pants if I had to drive one of these."

I sneak a glance at him. It doesn't compute, Abel scared of a thing that's like walking for me. RV driving's just geometry and physics; it's Dad in the seat beside me with his tall can of BBQ chips, guiding me through highway merges and practice park jobs in empty lots. You get into a rhythm on a long straight road, and after a while you forget you're hauling something huge and scary behind you.

"It's easy." I shrug.

"Really?"

"Well, I'm kind of amazing."

"Confidence. Excellent." He stands up and stretches like a cat. "Just what you need tonight."

"Okay, but I swear I'm not—"

He kicks the Sunseeker door open, like in the pilot episode where Cadmus breaks into StarPort 38's android-storage locker and steals Sim from his charging dock. He turns to me, holds out his hand with a grave stage-glare. Bec watches, grinning, shrugging on my Phillies sweatshirt. Abel's got on a candy-striped polo shirt and his new truck-stop hat with Punxsutawney Phil on it, and right above the fly of his dark designer jeans is a big ironic belt buckle that shouts PRAISE THE LORD.

"C'mon, shake your circuits, android," Abel quotes. *"Your freedom is waiting."*

***

To enter The Robot's Bookshelf, the three of us duck under a droopy *Welcome CastieCon Attendees!* banner and squeeze through an archway wound with silver garland and blue plastic lights shaped like spaceships and stars. The owners are huge *Castaway Planet* geeks, you can tell. Dr. Zara Lagarde's favorite album is playing (Janis Joplin, *Pearl*), they've got the snack bar stocked with Cadmus's favorite jellybeans (cinnamon), and the backdrop to the small stage is this giant blown-up photo of sunflowers, like the ones in Cadmus's visions of his Earth childhood.

"Sim scanned the room, rusty heart creaking in his plastic chest," Abel narrates, reading off his phone. *"Before him, men flirted in the shadows, their nuances painfully foreign—"*

"What is that?" I know I'm blushing. I've read this one at least three times.

"'Sex and the Single Droid' by cavegrrl94. It's relevant." He exchanges five dollars for a packet of jellybeans. "Carry on."

"Let's find a table," I tell Bec.

As he roamed the crowded room, he realized he was ill-equipped to choose a man for himself, at least from the selection before him. He turned to Captain James Cadmus, who blazed with raw masculinity in his tight black t-shirt and aviator shades.

I tilt my head at Abel. He slams back a fistful of jellybeans.

"Captain,' Sim said. 'Help me choose a male with whom to converse.'" He pecks my shoulder with his index finger. "That's your cue, Tin Man."

I pick a table in the corner made from parts of a theme-park rocketship, painted retro-aqua to look like the U.S.S. Starsetter. There's no chance I'm talking to a guy, but I scan the room to humor him. Few dozen AV-club types, some with gawky girlfriends. *Castaway Planet* is supposed to have a big gay following, but none of them seem to be here tonight.

"Captain: clarification." I eyebrow him. "I should flirt with a random straight guy?"

"No! No flirting. Just talking. I mean, look at these sweet untainted boys, they sleep on *Star Wars* sheets. What could be less intimidating?" He elbows Bec. "Rebecca: can he handle it? Yea or nay?"

"I'm pulling for him."

"All right, Mr. Roboto." He bangs Plastic Cadmus on the table like a gavel. "Put your antenna up."

My stomach crackles.

"You find an appropriate specimen," I stall, "and I *may* oblige."

Abel surveys. Disgustingly, he cracks an ice cube

between his teeth.

"Him." He points. "With the blue Chucks."

"Unacceptable."

"Pourquoi?"

"He's barn owl-y."

"Fine. Mr. Inkblot T-Shirt?"

"Pretentious."

"So? I love pretentious people!"

"Why?"

"They try so hard to be interesting, you don't have to do any work."

"Next."

"Argh! Fine. Mr. Sensitive Ponytail. Reading *Dune*."

"He looks weird."

"He looks awesome. Go talk to him."

"About what?"

"Keep it show-related. Talk Season 5 rumors. Bitch about the cliffhanger. Bet he thinks Cadmus is really dead."

I shoot Bec a *save me* look. She shrugs.

"All right," I say. "I'll talk to *him*."

Abel brightens, until he sees where I'm pointing. The guy's got on polyester pants the color of gravy, glasses thick as a telescope lens, and a baggy blue t-shirt with the *Castaway Planet* logo on it. I'd put his age at sixty, maybe sixty-five.

"Outstanding," Abel says. "You think you're funny? Grandpa it is."

Old Guy weaves between tables with two white cups on a red plastic tray. He sets it carefully on the two-top in the corner, where a white-haired lady in a matching *Castaway* shirt waits for him. The little gold cross around her neck glints in the red light of the bookstore's OPEN sign. He pours two creamers in one cup, stirs it, and presents it to her with a flourish. They smile at each other. Their smiles are the same. They look like my parents will in about twenty years.

That's what a real marriage looks like, says Father Mike.

"Aww. Ancient fandom geeks." Abel melts, clutching his heart. "I shall name them Lester annnnd..."

"Gladys," Bec says.

"Perfect. Lester and Gladys." Abel shakes his head. "Wow. That's what I want someday. Don't you guys?"

Yes yes yes, I want to say. The *yes*es gather thick in my throat; I swallow them down and blink up at a string of stuttering star-lights.

"Not really." I shrug.

"*Look* at them! They're like little salt and pepper shakers. One breaks and the other's useless."

"'Scuse me." Bec hates soulmate talk; has since her dad left. She gets up from the table. "Bathroom."

"Brandon—"

"Shh! Look."

I point to the stage. Someone's at the mike: this doughy college-age guy with kind apologetic eyes, thinning blond hair, and a black t-shirt printed with constellations. He looks familiar. I don't like to stereotype since I'm probably a bigger *Castaway Planet* nerd than half the room, but I can almost see his high school notebooks, and the margins are filled with sketches of supergirls in metal bikinis.

"Hey there, Casties." Sheepish nice-guy wave. "I'm Bill. Welcome to the CastieCon Kickoff Party."

We clap. Abel kicks me under the table.

"So—ah." He takes out some inkstained index cards and clears his throat. I flash back to traumatic oral book reports in grade school. "Four seasons ago, a crew of misfits on the run crashed their spaceship on a tiny

31

unknown planet and became the unwilling lab rats of a merciless and childish omnipotent being known only as Xaarg. Since then, *Castaway Planet* has captured our imagination and sparked debate week after week. From the rash bravery and grim humor of Captain Cadmus to the, um, deeply human struggles of the elegant android Sim, these characters have become our second family. Good thing we don't have to spend Thanksgiving with them, though. Right?" He looks up like he expects a laugh. When he doesn't get one, he clears his throat again and shuffles the cards.

"He's kind of adorbs," Abel whispers. "Don't you think?"

"No."

"C'mon, he's all awkward-turtle."

"Sh."

"Like he just won a tech award at the Oscars—"

"I'm trying to listen."

"So anyway, guys," Bill taps the last index card. "There's a trivia contest in twenty minutes, 30% off DVD sets and novelizations, and don't forget to partake of the goodies at the snack bar or we'll have to, ah, *cast* them *away*. Any questions, I'm your go-to guy. Yes? You sir."

He's calling on Abel.

"Can you come to our table? We have a question."

"Sure thing."

I smack his arm. "What're you *doing*?"

"Talk. Just chat a little. You need your wheels greased."

"I told you—"

"Heyyy, Bill!"

Abel makes introductions. Bill smiles and shakes his hand. I hide mine under the table; they're already slick with sweat.

"What can I do for ya?" he says.

"Brandon, tell him your question." He whispers to Bill

across the table. "It's a really good one. We wanted a *Castaway* expert to weigh in."

"Wow! Well, I'm flattered. Shoot."

Bill turns his postcard-pool eyes on me. I get that hot sick feeling I got at Abel's birthday party in March, when his spinning bottle stopped at me and I feigned a speck in my contact lens. I know who he reminds me of. Ryan Dervitz. Sci-Fi Club treasurer, Timbrewolves tenor, my first and only near-kiss. I see him in his sweaty white dress shirt and khakis, behind our school after we sang "Life Is a Highway" for Parents' Night. One second he was smiling like normal, flicking a lightning bug off my collar, and the next he was filling my whole field of vision with his pale freckled moonface. His lips only made it to the corner of my mouth before I shoved him away, leaving him limp and baffled against the brick wall while I booked it down the street and shut myself in the Dairy Queen men's room, Father Mike muttering in my ears the whole way.

Bill smiles politely. "So...ah, what's your question?"

I can't talk. My clothes feel see-through.

"It was about Sim." Abel jumps in, shooting me death rays. "We're debating if he should've stayed human after he got his evolution chip in Episode 2-14."

"Whoo, excellent question. Hmm." He bongos the table. "What do you think, Brandon?"

Ryan never looked me in the eye again. We used to talk baseball and debate classic *X-Files* episodes in sixth-period study hall, but he suddenly had reams of algebra homework that required total concentration. I'd watch him scritch his pencil nub across his notebook, factoring quadratic trinomials with dark broody passion. I never knew I wanted to kiss him back until it was way too late.

"*Brandon.*" Abel kicks my shoe.

I know what's happening. Red splotches spreading, one on each cheek. I want to vanish.

Abel glares. "I'll tell you what I think," he says. "I think when Sim was 'human' it was one freaking excuse after another. That whole arc was one long whine about how inconvenient feelings are and how it sucks to know you'll never know everything, like, *we get it.* Stop being so emo about it and get on with things, you know?"

"I guess," Bill says. "I thought it was sad, though. How he went back to being—"

"A total bore?" Abel stiffens his shoulders and tilts his head. "Captain Cadmus, might I suggest some seventeenth-century poetry to distract your mind from existential torment?"

His robot voice is still dumb, but the dim lights here contour his face in Simlike angles and shadows. I get this quick fanfic flash: his strong hands gripping my wrists, slamming me up against a spider-cave wall.

Put on the Brakes!, Chapter Five: **Ask God for the strength you need to flee temptation. And then don't walk away—run!**

I try to shoo the words away. They scuttle into unreachable corners of my mind, prodding me with tiny sharp claws.

Don't run, I tell myself. You idiot. *Don't listen.*

My chair's already screeching back.

"Brandon?"

Abel charges after me. Grabs my arm by the bakery case. He does it like it's nothing, like he doesn't even realize his hand is there, and meanwhile my arm is zapping hot panicked messages to my brain: *he's touching me I'm being touched don't move don't breathe act normal be Sim.*

"What is *with* you?" says Abel. "You can't string two

words together?"

"I—"

"Practice! You need practice!" He shakes my shoulders. "What happens when we're at the Castaway Ball and you see a flawless guy in a Sim suit and he starts walking over? What then?"

"I run from the weirdo."

Abel gives me a *why-must-you-be-you* sigh. Whatever. Used to those. I got them a lot from my parents after The Talk: *Why him? Makes no sense. He likes the Phillies. He can tie twenty-six different kinds of knots.*

"We'll get you back in the saddle. You *may* require more intensive intervention than anticipated." Abel plucks a free lanyard from the basket on the bakery case and hangs it around my neck ceremonially, like we're in a Hawaiian airport. "By nerd prom night, you'll be ready for greatness again. Trust me."

He gives me a kiss on one cheek and goes for the other but I jump back. I can't help it.

His eyes narrow.

"You okay?" he says.

"I—You smell weird."

"I do?" He sniffs his pits and shrugs. "I like it."

Across the room, Bill drums the table and drifts away, probably wondering what kind of curricular adaptations I needed to graduate high school. I touch the spot where Abel's lips brushed my cheek.

Careful, says Father Mike.

Then I see Bec.

She's standing by the DVD display, holding up her phone and giving me The Look—the same one she gave me the night her sister and mine got in a parking lot catfight at the DQ. Teeth clenched together, eyebrows bunched. Our standard code for *something's really wrong.*

4»

BEC PULLS US DOWN a quiet aisle. My insides rumble. What if Dad looked up *Castaway Planet* and found our vlog? He'd know Abel was here. He'd know I lied, and he'd flip in that scary-calm way I can't handle at all. Bec's dad used to roar like a chainsaw; mine makes tiny snips that bleed you so slowly you don't notice until you're weak.

I picture him on the deck he and Mom built together, adjusting his brown plastic eyeglass frames and depositing guilt in my voicemail. *Lying, huh? You know, you might not believe this anymore, but there's actually this crazy thing called 'right' and 'wrong.'*

"Okay." Bec holds up the phone. "So I was reading the Cadsim fanjournal—"

"—And someone hates us," says Abel. "Boo hoo, like that's even—"

"Just look!"

We huddle on either side of her. The little screen shows a post with two words: **HELL BELLS** in red all-caps. She taps it and a blurry picture of Abel pops up. Not a regular photo. A screencap from the post we put up on our vlog this morning. He's holding our action figures up to the camera and whoever capped it took a lot of care to catch him in an ugly moment, with his open mouth looming over the head of Plastic Sim.

Abel lets out a cartoon gasp and clutches my arm. I yank away and lean closer.

Under Abel's photo is a comment from the person who posted it. I don't recognize the username. **hey_mamacita.**

Her icon freaks me out: a statue of an angel with a halo made of knives.

She says:

tick...tick...
BOOM.
brandon & abel: we see you boys.
operation hell bells has begun.
any Cadsim girls wanna get nasty?
YOU KNOW WHERE TO FIND US.

"Whaa—?" Abel shakes his head.
"You don't know her?"
"I don't think so."
"Read the comments." Bec scrolls down.

cavegrrl94: JFC NOT AGAIN.

illumina: OMG batshit hell bell creepers. someone should warn A&B, for real

simbeline: mamacita u guys are out of ur minds. u crossed the line like a hundred miles back. it's not cool when it gets so personal

mrs.j.cadmus: whatever its what they deserve!!!

murklurk: Maxie, do your job. Ban her already.

Miss Maxima: hey_mamacita, this is your FINAL warning. Not to defend the horror that is Brandon and Abel, but this Hell Bells thing is hella creepy and you know it. I know where you live and if you and your minions don't stop cluttering my community with your utter psychosis I swear I WILL MURDER YOU IN YOUR SLEEP.

37

"Oh my fucking goodness," says Abel.

A shiver slides up my spine.

"What *is* this?" says Bec.

Abel explains the reference. The ring of silver bells Xaarg rattles when he's launching a new nightmare for the castaways doesn't technically have a name, but most fandom geeks call them the Hell Bells. "I don't know what it has to do with us, though," he says.

"You've never seen them talk about it?" I scan the comments again.

"Nope. Why would I?"

"You're on here more than I am."

"Just to laugh at the fic. Never seen word one about this." Abel taps his lip and studies the screen. A slow smile stretches across his face. "I don't want to alarm you guys, but this *might* be awesome."

"I don't like it," I say.

"Why not? I bet it's a secret snark community with some hilarious vendetta against us."

"God, no."

"Virtual voodoo dolls. Desperate plans to overthrow us. 'We'll blow up the RV! Assassinate them at the ball!'"

"Don't say that."

"Relax. It's a joke."

"Then how come they're freaking out?"

"They're being drama queens, I guarantee you. It's fandom, Bran. Getting butthurt over nothing is practically a sacrament."

It's a sign, says Father Mike. **God's telling you something.**

"It's probably nothing." Bec touches my arm.

"Yeah, I mean who *cares* if they're talking shit about us?" Abel pops more cinnamon jellybeans. "Least we got 'em talking."

"Right. Yeah."

"We should get in on the trivia game or something."

Pearl is over; a new album starts. The Beatles. The party's loud and the music wafts in and out of my consciousness, like in the morning when the song on your alarm clock drifts into your dream.

"Bran," Abel says. "You want to be on my team?"

The aisle feels hot and narrow. *Rubber Soul.* I'm ten again, riding home from Disney in the Sunseeker, sitting up in the cab with Dad while Mom reads an Agatha Christie with her Mickey ears on and Nat broods in the loft scrawling postcards to potheads. Dad's St. Christopher medal dangles from the rearview, scattering splinters of light on the ceiling. Somewhere in North or South Carolina the CD changer calls up "In My Life" and Dad turns all sad and tender like when he watches *Field of Dreams* or drinks too much Miller Lite at the Donnellys' Super Bowl party. "Someday you'll be sitting here behind a wheel, and your family will be back there," he says to me, just the thought of my future making him smile, "and you'll feel like this, like everything is exactly the way it's supposed to be."

I look up. Bec and Abel are staring.

"I don't feel good, you guys," I say. "I think I need to go."

***

I sit in the Home-N-Garden lot where we're stealth-parked for the night, sipping Dad's generic antacid on the pull-out metal steps of the Sunseeker. A warm wind sifts through my hair and skips a crushed beer can across the empty parking lot; in the distance, it rustles the tarp on the garden center's koi pond and the white rose bushes that look like my father's.

On the ride back from the bookstore I made my first *I'm-fine* call to Mom and Dad.

Liar.

Down the street, a church points its sharp white steeple at the moon. I've never been inside it, but I know what it smells like on a summer Sunday—old-lady perfume and new-baby powder and the sweet creamy scent of memorial carnations. I miss a lot of stuff about church. Strumming "Morning Has Broken" at the 6:00 Folk Mass, flipping pancakes with Dad at Sunday socials, laughing with everyone at the jokes Father Mike would crack as he read off the weekly announcements. I feel bad that the stuff I miss doesn't have much to do with God, that I don't miss the prayers or the psalms or that quiet time after Communion when Father Mike said *the Big Guy Upstairs* could read our hearts.

I never liked that idea, even when I was younger and the idea of God seemed simple. I'm not optimistic enough to trust in a kind and merciful higher power like my mother does, so it's almost more comfortable to doubt one exists at all. In my strongest moments I become Sim. Programmed for poetry and logic, destined for a scrap heap, no Bible verses rattling out of context in my head and no possible reckonings or afterlives to worry about. And then I pass a church or see a priest on TV and I'm back where I was when I was twelve, sweating every swear word and boy crush and offering up a guilty rushed prayer. Just in case.

"The android felt himself slowly awaken."

Behind the RV door, Abel's reading Bec a bedtime story.

"Desire surged through him, flooding his processors. He remembered the day he and Cadmus jumped into the Red River, the current making helpless marionettes of their

bodies."

"That's...actually not bad," I hear Bec say.

"It's murklurk," Abel says. "So tragic, when bad pairings happen to good writers. Listen to *this...*"

I make my arms a nest and rest my head inside. Father Mike finds me in the dark, like he did when I was thirteen and he caught me and Mark Tarrulo coughing on cigarettes in the church basement. He'd pull out the same I-am-calm-yet-concerned voice he used on me then.

You're worried, aren't you? Operation Hell Bells? C'mon.

Abel reads, *"Cadmus released the remnants of his fear. He pulled the android close in the dim amber light of the cave, searching his face for the sign that said yes, our time is now, I want you too."*

Brandon, God sends us signs. It just takes courage to read them.

"Sim felt his features respond, arrange themselves into the happiness he had seen so often on the faces of others..."

Do you really think He's happy with you? You spend all year doubting Him, and then you run off to nowhere with a boy?

"'I want to stay here with you,' Cadmus whispered. 'The two of us. Here together. Alone.'"

Come home, bud. Just come home.

I choke down the last swig of antacid. It tastes like chalk and the cherry cough drops at the bottom of Gram's purse. I think about Lester and Gladys. What their house must look like, a queen-size bed that's always made and a dinner table with a clean white tablecloth and walls hung with history: science fair ribbons, woven crowns from old Palm Sundays, framed photos of their sons at every age.

You won't have that now, says Father Mike. ***Don't kid***

yourself, kiddo.

I go into a windup with the drained antacid bottle, aim at a wood-slat wastecan. I want contact, a Louisville Slugger *crack.*

I miss by a mile.

5»

"Fellow Casties: *We have arrived.*"

We stand on the amazing technicolor carpet of the Fairlee Hotel in Cleveland, in front of a life-size cardboard cutout of Bree LaRue and a pull-down screen with a fanvid flickering on it. Abel's costume of the day: Cadmus shades, skinny jeans with sky-blue hightops, a red puffy vest over a tight black shirt he stole from Kade.

Bec's camera is rolling.

As more fans in costumes and logo shirts flood the Q&A room, Abel motormouths about some tragic new Cadsim fic called "The Passion of the Droid." I'm only half listening. *We're here.* And when you're a weird and awkward and paranoid person at all times, CastieCon is the happiest place on the planet.

It's like, a baseline level of freakiness is expected here, right? So unless you're disemboweling goats in the vendor hall, no one gives a damn who you are or what you're doing. You want to spray your hair blue like Sim's? You'll fit right in; ten others beat you to it. You want to dress like Xaarg at a biker bar? Girls will take photos with you, fondling your black studded jacket. You can talk to vendors about bad paint apps on action figures; you can openly geek out when two writers sign your second-season finale script; you can join a panel debating if Castaway Planet is a real place or all in their head. And when you're waiting for a Q&A and you see a fanvid on the screen—set to "Hallelujah," for crap's sake—no one will judge you if you get a tiny bit choked up.

"Bran." I jump. Abel's poking me. "What do you think?"

"About what?"

"We're taking bets on why Bree LaRue's late to her own Q&A."

"She burned her hand on her curling iron," says Bec.

"She couldn't find the down button on the elevator," says Abel.

"She's pissed she got no screentime in this fanvid." I grin.

Abel glances up at the pull-down screen and glares at the clip they're showing. It's from this season's cliffhanger. Ed Ransome as Cadmus, bloodied and bitten, buckling beside the giant spider he's just killed. Sim runs over in slo-mo, drops to his knees to check the fresh bite marks on Cadmus's neck. The music fades slightly to lift up the line: *If I die, Tin Man, you're the new me. Promise.* Abel performs a shudder and screws one eye shut.

"I can't look." He groans. "This whole scene like, *wounds* me."

"Whatever. Xaarg'll save him—"

"DON'T EVEN."

"—because he's his daa-aad."

Abel facepalms. "I hate that theory."

"We know."

"Super-lame. Super-derivative." He vacuum-breathes like Vader. *"Cadmussss...I am your fatherrrr..."*

"It's foreshadowed, though."

"Don't you dare bring up 2-17."

"Xaarg's been watching him *his whole life?*"

"Clearly a lie! Intimidation tactic."

"I dunno." I shrug, basking in the indignant-fanboy back-and-forth. "I'd be happy if my TV boyfriend was a possible demigod."

"He's already a demigod. FYI."

44

Abel sticks out his tongue and we bust out laughing like a pair of fourth graders. Onscreen, Cadmus is using the spider corpse as a grim translucent footrest, telling Sim knock-knock jokes about Xaarg and his henchmen to prove he's totally fine and definitely not at all almost-dead. Ed Ransome's great in this episode, so great I almost get why Abel loves him.

"Brandon?"

"Yeah."

Abel blinks at the vid. He leans in and whispers, "I don't really love cinnamon jellybeans. I just eat them to, ah...feel like him."

"You do stuff like that?"

"Kinda sorta constantly." Abel peers down at the smiley face doodled on his left shoe. "Sometimes when I do something brave I feel like I'm cheating because I was being him in my head the whole time. I get so into it that I'll catch my reflection in a window and for a second I'm surprised I look like me instead of him." He side-eyes me. "Did I say that out loud? God, I swear I'm not a nutbar!"

I nod with quiet reverence. It's like when I was five and found out Danny Zurick liked peeling glue off his hands, too. "S'okay."

"You won't tell?"

"I've got four Sim playlists on my phone."

"Dork." He smacks me, laughing. "You know, I had this horrible dream the rumors were true and they killed off Cadmus."

"Don't even worry."

"But just the idea."

"I'm the same. Like in 3-11, when the Henchmen took Sim apart—"

"—and he kept saying *Status: All systems destabilized* in that creepo Exorcist voice? Oh babe. I know."

"I needed counseling. Ask Bec." I turn to her, but some jerk in a Cookie Monster t-shirt is chatting her up. He has these super-sincere liquidy blue eyes and his dark hair is flat and shaggy at the same time, like the plastic hair on those Lego people. I want to step in and save her but then Abel's hand is squeezing mine and I have to keep my face Sim-still and pretend I'm a regular human who has tons and tons of casual palm-to-palm contact with guys who share my specific fanboy neuroses.

"Bran." Abel smiles sideways like Cadmus.

Smile back. Don't be a freak.

"Yeah...?"

"Dude in the TEAM ANDROID shirt is *eyeing you up.*" He leans close and cups my ear. "Glance to the left and be subtle!"

"I—"

Some guy in a dark suit saves me, shoving through the crowd with headset clutched to ear. People start whispering. The weird Hell Bells thing makes a sinister *ting* in the back of my mind. I try to breathe myself calm. We're not assassination candidates. No one takes shipping that seriously.

Right?

Father Mike, tossing me marshmallows at the youth group campfire. ***Okay, poll time, guys: If you died today, do you think you'd go to heaven?***

The worried guy's onstage now, hands locked behind him, introducing Bree LaRue with a film of sweat on his forehead. Everyone's chattering, grumbling, pulling out cameras. Abel grabs Bec's cam from her and hits record.

"Okay, people! This is it." He holds the camera too close. "Cadsim ladies, hold your gloating till the end, mmkay? I know Bree-Bree's on record as a shipper, but it's not over till we get her on video, and plus she's all moony-eyed over that Cash Howard guy from *Husband Hunt* so she's not exactly the brightest bulb on the—"

"People!" Worried Guy makes a time-out gesture. "Here she comes, okay? Let's be a little quiet for her."

The pull-down screen rolls up, and someone female comes stalking out from behind the black curtain when the audience cheers and hoots for Bree LaRue, but for a good ten, fifteen seconds my brain thinks there has to be a mixup.

Because the person onstage? That can't be her.

***

Bree LaRue plays Defense Officer Leandra Nigh, and if you've ever seen an episode of *Castaway Planet*, the thing you remember about her is her hair. It's shiny and blond in a synthetic, display-only kind of way, like the loose curls presented for worship in shampoo commercials. The person onstage has something entirely different on her head. I'm not sure how to describe it. Did they ever make black shag carpeting back in the seventies? It's like someone cut a circle out of that and made themselves a skull cap.

Abel pokes me, his mouth an O.

"I think it looks kind of good," whispers Bec.

Bree LaRue is wearing wrinkly jeans and tall black boots and a St. Tropez t-shirt with an orange stain on it. Her eyes are bloodshot. She steps up to the lip of the stage, yanks the mike off the stand, and starts twisting the cord around her wrist.

"Heyyy, kids," she mutters.

No one breathes.

"So what's new?"

Silence.

"I got a haircut. Like, obviously." She ruffles it with one hand. "Certain people aren't gonna be happy with me, but I say fuck it. You know? *Wigs exist.*"

Worried Guy edges closer to Bree, rubs his thick hands together. "Okay, guys, let's start with some questions. Who's got a good one for Miss LaRue?" He turns to her. "Is that okay? If they ask?"

"That's why I'm here."

A whisper runs through the audience. Then a red question paddle goes up, slowly, to the left of the stage.

"What's your favorite color?" some girl says.

Bree LaRue stares at the base of the mike stand. She screws up her mouth and hocks a wad of spit at it.

"Blue," she says. "That's as good a color as any, right?"

"Yeah. Definitely..." The girl's wearing an electric blue jacket like Leandra Nigh's. She looks like she wants to disappear. I want to hug her, even though Nigh is like my eighth favorite character on *Castaway Planet* and the person onstage bears zero resemblance to her. I glance at Bec and we shake our heads.

Question paddles pop up faster.

Fiftyish guy in Xaarg hat: "If they killed you off, how would you want your character to die?"

Bree LaRue swigs from her steel sport bottle. "Spontaneous combustion sounds good."

Pink-haired girl in black halter top: "How are you different from Nigh?"

"Uh, I guess because she's always an optimist. Even when it's incredibly, *unbelievably* stupid to be."

"Who does Nigh belong with: Cadmus or Dutch Jones?"

"Whoever doesn't dick her over."

"What's your favorite episode?"

"Eh. What's the one where Xaarg sends that swamp monster after us and I almost die?"

48

Someone yells out, "3-16!"

"Yeah, that one. I got to scream a lot." She throws back her head and releases an unholy screech, loud enough to chill the collective blood of the Social Media conference two ballrooms over.

Everyone freezes. The guy chatting up Bec breathes *holy shit.*

Abel leans close. "Omigod," he hisses.

"I know."

"We were there, Bran. We were there when Bree LaRue melted down in Cleveland. *Historic.*" He puts his hot hand on my back and my body goes stiff, like metal bolts are tightening all my joints.

Onstage, Worried Guy's talking to Bree in the low soothing tone that cops use when someone's about to jump off a ledge. His hand reaches out for her mike. She snatches it back, squints into the crowd: "More questions! Cough 'em up, come on! How much did you guys shell out for this?"

"Should I ask?" Abel mutters.

"Just wait."

"Come on, pry me open, people!" Bree LaRue crows. "I *know* stuff, okay? Tom Shandley has a third nipple! David Darras fucking hates Lenny Bray! The writers stole the whole plot of the season finale from a fanfic writer and didn't give her credit!"

Someone behind us whispers *career suicide.* I just stare. I can't close my mouth.

Abel grabs the question paddle.

"Not yet!" I tug his sleeve.

"They might shut her down, Bran."

Worried Guy points. "Guy in the vest. Go!"

Abel touches his chest. "Me?"

"Yes. Come on."

49

"He's cu-ute." Bree LaRue stumbles sideways, shielding her eyes with one hand. "Aww, look at his hair. And the chin! He's like Laurence Olivier, and a cockatoo. Like if they had a baby?"

"Hurry it up," Worried Guy tells Abel.

Abel clears his throat a million times. Bec leans closer with the camera. His hands quiver, just a little. Stage fright? Unexpected.

Sort of cute.

"Hi Miss LaRue I'm Abel and this is Brandon and we're here representing the Screw Your Sensors fan vlog at screwyoursensors.blognow.com?"

"Super, honey. Ask the question."

"Okay, so we're having this debate with some other fans—"

"Oh. Perfect."

"—and we wanted to ask you." He takes a deep breath. "That scene in the season finale where they're trapped in the crystal spider cave and Cadmus is like 'it's so quiet in here it could swallow up all your secrets' and Sim is like 'yes Captain...quite' and then Cadmus puts his hand on his arm and they look at each other and it fades out, do you think they did anything in the cave for real or is it all just fanwank?"

I have this sudden sick vision of losing the bet with the Cadsim girls; Abel's lips coming at me with a camera pointed at us. I cross my fingers tight.

Bree LaRue cocks her head. "Cadmus and Sim."

"Yes."

"Were they..." She claps her hand to her heart and bats her eyes. "...*together*."

A female voice in the crowd goes, "So cute it hurts!"

"I said that once, didn't I?" Bree LaRue shoots the girl a rueful smile.

"Yeah."

I scan the crowd. The girl's wearing a fake sunflower in her hair and a homemade Cadsim shirt, a manip of them holding hands above the words YES, CAPTAIN... QUITE. Bree LaRue rolls her eyes and makes a jacking-off motion. Abel jabs my ribs.

"You think it would work? Like for real?" Bree scratches the back of her head like she's trying to make it bleed. "'Cause here's what I'm thinking would happen, like, it looks good on paper 'cause they're both beautiful and everyone loves to see pretty with pretty, but then Sim wouldn't know what to do like, mechanically or anything, and Cadmus would get bored in five seconds because that's who he is and guys like that never ever change and one day Sim would be at some stupid convention at some *stupid* hotel and Cadmus would call him up at six a.m. and say hey, you know that girl I said was just a friend? Yeah, well, we're in Barbados right now drinking rum-frickin'-swizzles in a hammock, and when we get back can I come by and pick up my things? Sorry baby. *You knew this would happen.*"

I see this is all about Cash Howard dumping Bree LaRue and I should be sad for her, but I picture him shirtless in a hammock and oh God. Once I was watching his *Husband Hunt* season with Mom, tuning out his dumb words and staring at his abs. They were almost obscenely gorgeous in a soft and classical kind of way, like he'd just touched fingers with God and waltzed off the Sistine ceiling. Mom was knitting pink and blue blankets for the Genesis Pregnancy Center. Her needles stopped clacking and I caught her watching me watch him, and then her ears turned pink and she said *Sweetie, why don't we watch Cooking with Carlene instead?*

"I'm really sorry," Abel says.

"Aren't you sweet," Bree says.

"It sucks. Happened to me once, too."

She leaps off the stage when he says that. Like literally leaps, the way a jungle cat would, and lands hard on her feet right in front of us. The crowd hushes. She steps closer and brushes her hand across Abel's cheek. Cameras flash and I start to absorb it: Bree LaRue is twelve inches away from me. She's a real person, with farm-girl freckles peeping through her face powder and a Band-Aid on one finger.

"Why can't I just be with a guy like you?" she whispers.

"I'm gay," says Abel.

"Exactly."

She smiles sadly. More camera flashes. Then Worried Guy steps down, helps her back onstage. She wobbles when she stands. The spindly heel of her left boot has snapped right off. We glance around and Abel spots the heel on the floor, a few feet in front of us. I grab it and hold it up, but she just gives a shrug and a vague wave: *What's the point? Hopelessly broken.*

"Miss LaRue?" Abel calls.

"Yeah."

"That was a no...right? To the Cadsim question?"

"Step back," Worried Guy says. "She has to go to her room."

"Yes it was a no, honey. God. Sim is completely asexual." She's being escorted out now, limping with dignity like Blanche DuBois in that *Streetcar* play our school did last spring.

Over her shoulder, she adds: "And he's frickin' *lucky!*"

6»

WE SETTLE THE SUNSEEKER at tonight's free campsite, the parking lot of a 24-hour SavMart a couple miles outside Cleveland. I crank the old generator and Abel whips up Mac-in-a-Minit and canned chicken, crooning *I miss you*s to Kade on speakerphone while he arranges food on paper plates and snips fake parsley sprigs from one of Mom's wall wreaths. While we scarf down dinner, we upload the Bree LaRue video evidence for the Cadsim girls, with a header that's maybe more gleeful than necessary: BRANDON & ABEL = 1, CADSIM SHIPPERS = 0, in sparkly purple text.

Then Abel's like, "Change your shirt. I'll call the cab."

"We're going out?"

"What'd you think we were going to do? Play WordWhap?"

"Where are we going?"

"We have to celebrate. Victory Number One!"

"Isn't that kind of ghoulish?"

"Uh, no. Trust me, this'll be the turning point of Bree LaRue's career. She should thank Cash Howard for making her interesting." He unzips his bag, chucks a shirt at me. "If they write her off the show she'll be in some Lars von Trier film within a year. Guaranteed."

"I was just going to—"

"Stay here, stagnate, watch *Castaway* on your phone. Forget it." He pulls on a Blondie t-shirt and zips up his fake python cowboy boots. "We're gonna stir shit up. You and me."

I know what he's up to. I scramble for brilliant

excuses. Migraine. Tainted cheese powder.

"Jesus, will you relax?" he says. "I'm putting your boy renaissance on hold. You don't have to talk to anyone but me."

I don't trust him. "Bec, will you come?"

"Nope." She has her flip-flops kicked off and she's eating rice crackers and reading *Blankets* again. "Too hot. You're on your own."

"What if someone breaks in?"

"I'll blind them with spray cheese."

I uncrumple the shirt Abel threw me. It's hot-pepper red with SEX BOMB on the front in army green. The O is a grenade at a jaunty tilt, the sex bomb in mid-hurtle toward its target. It's so ridiculous I have to smile.

"I wore it the night I met Kade."

"At that astrophysics lecture, right?"

"Put it *on*." Abel gives me a shove. "You dress like you want to disappear."

Don't do it, says Father Mike.

What if I did?

That isn't you. I know you better.

I close my eyes, dig my nails into my palm until it hurts.

"I'll go," I say.

But I don't put on the shirt.

***

The sign on the red door says THE EDGE OF HEAVEN in chipped gold curlicue letters. Underneath is a ragged flyer for the Cleveland OutPride Film Festival, stapled over a mural of two male seraphim doing something distinctly unholy.

I think of Bec white-robed and pink-haired in her

punk-angel costume two Halloweens ago; Mom with cat ears stuck in her mess of blonde curls, snapping pics in our front hall. *Closer, you two! How about a hug?*

"This okay?" Abel taps the door. "It's not too cheesy, is it? Guy at the hotel said it was chill."

"I've never been in a bar," I blurt.

"Seriously?"

"I mean, yeah, I *have*. Just not this kind."

"I know, right? Poor you. Zero gay bars in Blanton." Abel sticks his hands in his hair and expertly messes it up. "Whatever; it's not like Rocky Horror. They don't harass virgins."

My face gets hot, but then I realize he means bar virgins, not actual virgins. I make a big show of opening the door. "Shall we?"

Inside, dim rosy light and that sad-sweet smoke machine smell I remember from our freshman-year production of *Godspell*. The bartender is short with a wiry gray mustache and he's got on one of those cowboy shirts with pearly snaps instead of buttons. White Christmas lights frame the bar in back of him, which is decorated with a dirty rainbow flag, vintage seashore postcards, a little kid's card that says *I love grampa* in green crayon, and some gold-framed photos that confuse me. Guys dancing shirtless with glow sticks, wagging huge fake penises on parade floats, singing karaoke in sequins and wigs—should I like this stuff too? Take it seriously? I'm supposed to belong here. I should at least smile and not stand here like an idiot in my flip-flops and cargo shorts.

But you don't like that stuff, do you?

Abel gets us two brown-bottle beers with a fake ID and we snag a table in the corner, near a red velvet couch where a skinny guy in a tank top is chatting up a hot guy in a suit. The jukebox plays that tinny old song Abel loves about riding on a metro. He cracks our bottles open with his keychain and slides one over.

"It's Hammerclaw." He starts tapping at his phone, shoulders perking to the music. "You'll like. Trust me."

I check the room for cops and take a sip. The beer tastes different from Dad's; it's thick and smoky and makes me think of beef jerky, though it's probably not supposed to.

"To Bree LaRue." I lift the bottle.

"To Bree LaRue, and her beautiful bitterness, and the sound of a hundred Cadsim shippers sharpening their pitchforks." He clears his throat and reads off his phone. *"Bree LaRue's stupid opinion should be disqualified immediately, as she was clearly under the influence of illegal substances."*

"Oh Lord."

"droidluv95 responds with a drabble, in which *Sim rips off Cadmus's shirt and moans hotly in his ear, 'Captain: rumors of my asexuality have been greatly exaggerated.'"*

"Ha!"

"Our good buddy Miss Maxima adds, *Keep the faith, true believers. She may be lying on purpose! Odds are they're planning the first Cadsim kiss for sweeps week.* God, they're a special kind of stupid, aren't they?"

I get an idea. I arrange my best heartbroken-cynic face, which is kind of like my Sim face but with broodier eyebrows.

"You know," I say, "what Bree said is totally true."

"Meaning...?"

"Asexual people *are* the lucky ones." I shrug with careful nonchalance. If I deliver this just right, he might leave me alone for the rest of the trip. "Sim's got the right idea, you know? It's just easier if you never have to think about it. Plus I already lost the only romantic gay guy in

Pennsylvania, so I'm screwed anyway."

"Uh-huh. Nice pose." He takes a swig of Hammerclaw. "Don't hold it too long or you'll freeze like that."

"It's not a *pose*."

"Then that's just sad."

"Makes sense to me."

"Right. 'Cause everyone else is all meaningless random hookups in men's rooms."

"Maybe not everyone, but—"

"Ew. *Brandon*. Do you write NOM propaganda in your spare time?"

"Look at you, though."

"What about me?"

"What's your number? Like, fifteen? Twenty?"

He straightens and flutters his eyelashes. "Five, since you asked so *politely*, and I was safe every time, and three I actually dated. And FYI, asshole, I never once cheated."

"Right."

"I haven't!"

"You're a unicorn, then." I shrug and *take a pull* of Hammerclaw, the way tough guys are always taking pulls at their beers in the detective novels Dad reads. I'm coming off like a jerk, but it's too late to backtrack. "Just think I'm better off alone."

"Don't be a doof. Think of everything you'll miss! Don't you want someone to mock bad movies with? And like, skinny-dipping and diner eggs at midnight and snowball fights and come on: first kisses? How great are they, right?"

I peer in my bottle and wish I was a genie who could vaporize and hide inside. *Ryan Dervitz*. His moonface pale against the school's dark brick. The shock of his soft lips brushing my skin. The little-kid crack in his voice when he yelled after me—*Hey! I'm sorry!*—and I just kept running and running.

"Can we not talk about that?"

Abel looks surprised. "Why?"

"It's too...um."

"What?"

"Sacred."

"Effing Zander." He shakes his head. "That guy. The sex must've been—"

"Spectacular." My leg jitters. Can he tell I'm lying? I picture it with Sim, how it would be to lie with him under cool white sheets. "Like, intergalactic."

"Did you kiss him first or did he kiss you?"

"I don't—"

"I'll tell you about my first time with Kade. We were at his parents' pizza place at two a.m., and they have one of those kiddie rooms with the plastic balls, and—"

"I don't want to know."

"Whatever! Just tell me one place you did it."

"In the silken softness of beach sand, under three alien moons."

He squints. "Is that from a Cadsim fic?"

"Yep."

"You asshat."

He cracks up and kicks me under the table. Abel has perfect teeth, which is annoying, and now I can't unsee the Olivier/cockatoo thing. He does kind of look like an old-timey movie actor. Broad rounded shoulders, strong straight nose, subtle chin divot, green-gray eyes that are probably capable of smoldering under the right circumstances. And the white hair does look feathery. I never looked at it for this long. I wonder what it feels like. If it's soft and floaty or stiff with mysterious product. If I touched it—

"Oh my God."

He's staring at the bar. His jaw cranks open.

"Ohhhhhhh, *shit*."

Hell Bells.

My skin prickles. I keep my eyes on my beer.

"What?" I whisper.

"This is it. It's fate, Brandon."

"What's fate?"

"Don't. Look."

"Who is it?"

"That guy."

"*Who?*"

"Him. Team Android Shirt! From the Q&A."

"Ugh, you scared me."

"You should be scared. He could be your destiny—*don't look!*"

"You said we'd forget that stuff tonight."

"Yeah, but this is too perfect!...Omigod. Omigod, he sees you."

"So?"

"You have to talk to him."

"I don't, actually."

"Yes. *Yes.* After the Bill Debacle? Prove you can do this."

"My knee hurts."

"What are you, eighty? Here, drink the rest of this. It'll help your personality."

"I'm going to the bathroom."

"Don't do that! He doesn't want to think about you peeing."

"I don't care what he thinks!"

"He's getting his drink...Oh, Brandon, a Kamikaze? He's a total Cadmus." He drains the beer, slams the bottle down. "Trust me, Tin Man. You need this."

Abel gets up and cracks his knuckles. I say *no*, I feel like I say it a hundred times but he isn't hearing. He's loping to the bar with that casual Cadmus swagger and lighting up a smile and the guy in the black Team Android t-shirt—cute, with wavy blond hair and multi-pierced ear—smiles back right away. I watch them talk, my heel hammering the floor. It's so stupidly easy for him. He could do this any day of the week. Maybe he'll change his mind, keep this one for himself.

The guy looks over. He nods and gives me a little wave. I wave back. I'll kill Abel. Absolutely murder him.

Team Android starts over to the table. *Status: All systems destabilized. Meltdown approaching.*

Bree LaRue cries, *Sim is completely asexual!* Father Mike opens to Chapter 3 of *Put on the Brakes!*: **When you feel "temptation devils" dancing on your shoulder, just imagine a life alienated from God, full of cheap, temporary pleasures that leave you more and more hopeless and empty. Is that what you really want?**

"Are you Brandon?"

I open my eyes.

Say something. Be calm. *Be Sim.*

"I am. Yes."

"I'm Ian. Saw you at the Q&A."

He holds out his hand and gives me a big friendly smile. A real flesh-and-blood boy with kind eyes and a Celtic cross necklace and really, really nice forearms. His presence thrums through me. If I wanted to, I bet we could be kissing in an alley before the next jukebox song is done.

"Mind if I sit down?"

"Yeah..."

I feel my back against a brick wall, my shorts unsnapping.

"Yeah you mind, or yeah you don't?"

"Um..."

Ian blinks twice, waiting. His eyes are gray, almost Sim-silver. The back of my throat goes sour.

"You okay?" says Ian.

"Yeah. Sure. I just—" I feel myself blushing again, which makes me blush more. His weirdo-detector starts pinging, you can tell.

"What's wrong?" he says.

At the bar, Abel raises a bottle and an eyebrow. I want to explode his head, burn his $600 fake python boots and his cheap Cadmus shades. I hate Cadmus. *Hate.*

"Look, I'm really sorry," I blurt. "My boyfriend's twisted."

"Your—him? That Abel guy?"

"Yeah." I aim a glare at the bar.

"He said you weren't together."

"Well, we are, but I don't know why." What am I doing? "He's pretty rotten. He loves seeing other guys flirt with me, and he knows I get embarrassed, but he does it anyway. It like, turns him on."

"Ew."

"I know."

"So he set me up?"

"He set us both up. It's one of his sick little power games."

"Wow. Uh...okay. Sorry." He shoots a dark glance in Abel's direction. Abel gives him a goofy thumbs-up. "'Scuse me."

I'm not proud of myself while Ian's bitching out Abel. I thought it would be more satisfying, but instead it just feels like that time in the sacristy when I blamed Pete Mertz for knocking over the Communion wine. The more Abel protests, all cartoony *wasn't-me* flailing, the more pissed off Ian gets. He finally leaves the bar, slamming the door behind him.

Abel clomps to our table. Tank Top Guy smirks.

I get a whack on the head with the heel of his hand.

"That was mean, Brandon!"

61

"Ow."

"Listen, toolbox: I don't know what head games you and Zander used to play, but I don't do that shit. *C'est compris?*"

"Yeah..." Cartoon stars, little birdies of pain. I deserve them.

"What kind of person are you? Seriously?"

"I don't know."

"I mean, what—you get your heart smashed one time by one loser and you think you get to be Mayor of Doucheville the rest of your life? Because let me tell you something, absolutely no one's going to—oh, *shut up!*"

He yanks his buzzing phone from his pocket. Beer sizzles in my stomach; I'm not used to making people mad. ***Get out of this place. Say three Hail Marys and ten Our Fathers.***

"Oh." Abel's mouth drops open a little. "Oh my."

"What?"

He taps the phone screen. "Nothing."

"Tell me!"

"We got a text. From Bec." He sighs. "Don't freak, okay?"

He turns the screen around.

NEW HELL BELLS POST @CADSIM COMM
OMG FREAKY
HURRY BEFORE THEY DELETE IT

7»

"I GOT A SCREENCAP. Don't worry."

By the time we get to the Cadsim fanjournal on Abel's phone, the Post of Doom's been blipped into oblivion. Bec's prepared, though. When the cab drops us off near our SavMart campsite, she's waiting for us in the doorway of the Sunseeker with her glasses on and her hair in a she-means-business bun.

"It was so dramatic, you guys." She yanks us inside and locks the door. "They all attacked like, the second she posted. It was like a steak in a shark tank."

She points to the laptop. Onscreen is another post by hey_mamacita, featuring a brand-new photo of me and Abel. New as in taken this afternoon, at the Q&A, *without our knowledge.* It's a shot of our backs. We're standing in front of the pull-down screen, watching the fanvids. There's a very, very creepy graphic overlay on the photo: a big circle with a cross inside it.

Like we're peering at ourselves through a gunsight.

HELL BELLS ARE RINGING
THANK YOU CLEVELAND SPY
WE ARE WATCHING YOU BOYS!!
(BFC = coming very VERY soon.)

Under that:

cavegrrl94: MAXIE THIS IS IT. BAN HER NOW.

willabelle: uugggghhhhh this whole thing is SO vile and hideous. I'm actually concerned, you guys. I thought it was all a joke but now I think they're FOR REAL.

mrs.j.cadmus: whatever. i used to hate the hell bells thing but now I'm like screw it, have at 'em

willabelle: Still, guys. I know we're all extra angry after today, but Brandon and Abel are people too.

illumina: THEY ARE NOT PEOPLE THEY ARE HEART-LESS GOONS AND DESERVE ETERNAL FIERY TORMENT.

Another sign. Are you listening yet? says Father Mike.
"They took our picture," says Abel. "Three feet away."
What else will they do?
"This is hardcore. We have organized haters." Abel clasps his hands. "You guys?"
"What."
He sighs dreamily. "I'm so *proud!*"
I stand without knowing where I'm going. Dishes. Perfect. They stack up so fast. I go to the sink and fill it halfway with water, hot as I can stand it, and three pumps of Mom's lemon dish soap. Then I grab a clean sponge and start scrubbing. Hard.
Abel stage-whispers, "What's with him?"
"I don't know," Bec says softly.
"Brandon?"
I don't answer. I plunge a plate in the little basin and Abel's disgusting chili remnants dissolve in the white cloud of suds. He's saying something to Bec. Something I don't want to hear, about time alone with me or whatever. I try to clearly communicate my wishes to her with the side of my head, but our telepathy isn't what it used to be, because she gets up from the table and slips out the door.
Abel comes over. I feel him watching me for a minute, leaning up against the counter.
"You're really freaked out," he says.
Eternal fiery torment.

"Just tired." I start filling the basin again. Hot rinse.

"I'm sure it's just a big joke."

"I'm sure it is."

He reaches over and shuts my water off. He lets his hand brush mine as he pulls it back and I get this stupid lightning-flash impulse to grab it and tell him the whole truth. Pull the plug from the drain. Tell him all about Father Mike. Fake Zander.

"I shouldn't have done that before," he says. "Sent Ian over."

"It's fine." I don't look at him. "I was a jerk too."

"No, you want to know why I did it? Why I care or whatever?"

I stare into the sink, at the suds escaping down the drain. Abel picks up the silver *Castaway Planet* superball he bought from one of the vendors. He starts bouncing and catching in a slow clockwork rhythm: *shthunk, twack, shthunk, twack.*

"Jonathan," he says.

"Who?"

Shthunk, twack.

"My Zander."

I'm not sure I want to hear more, but that never stops Abel, and before I can make up some excuse he's pulled me into his tenth-grade trauma and I'm there with him at this holy roller wedding, exchanging sultry looks with the pretty blond boy at the groom's table. "I knew I was getting in trouble," he says. "Everyone at the wedding had like fourteen kids with the same haircut and a Jesus fish on their car, and they all made this huge creepy deal about how the bride and groom hadn't even kissed yet, like not even one single time. I mean, freako."

Put on the Brakes!, Chapter 5: **Avoid "friends" who would mock the idea of a close relationship with God.**

65

"So anyway, Jonathan gave me a couple super-intense looks across the room and then he left, and I followed him outside and there he was all nervous and shy loosening his tie under a tree, and of course I got a total hard-on for the whole situation, like who wouldn't want to deflower the sweet innocent closeted Christian boy who's been force-fed poison his whole life—like, no offense, Brandon, I know you're cool and you don't believe all that."

My stomach drops. Abel goes on and on about how they snuck around that whole summer, how he was so in love, how every time they kissed or whatever it was like some time-lapse film of flowers bursting open and sunrises sprawling across the sky.

"...And then all of a sudden, he just stopped. Stopped taking my calls, stopped meeting me. Defriended me on Facebook. So I got totally desperate, right, and I sent him this stupid ID bracelet with the date we met engraved on it, and *that* made him call me but instead of being like 'oh, baby, I love you too,' he was like, 'I don't identify myself with your lifestyle anymore.' Your *lifestyle*. All cold and robotic, exactly like that. And he kept saying things like that, like you know he'd been brainwashed, and I started crying and yelling at him and stuff, and finally he told me his mom had read our emails and they had this huge family blowup and they were going to send him to one of those get-right-with-God lobotomy camps unless he turned his life around. So I told him they were a bunch of sick freaks, and he should lie through his teeth and do whatever he had to for now to keep a roof over his head, and he was like—are you ready for this?"

I nod.

"He was like, 'But they're right. God is more important than feeling good.' And I said well, can't you have both?

And big surprise, he was like 'No. I'm sorry. Not like this,' and then bam, he hung up and that was the last time I ever talked to him." He flings the superball across the room; it thwacks the moose pillow and rolls lamely off the couch. Abel rakes a hand through his hair. "So, but the point is—I was absolutely wrecked. I wasted *six endless months* brooding exclusively over this little piece-of-shit cult-member coward, Brandon. Do you believe it? Like, how many amazing people could I have met in six months? My brother had to literally kick my ass to get me over it."

"I'm sorry," I whisper.

"I didn't tell you that so you'd be sorry! The point is, don't be like me, okay? Because..." He sighs. "Because you're pretty much too awesome for that, and I'm one hundred percent sure this Zander tool is not worth it."

He lays this open, expectant look on me, like now I'm supposed to throw my arms around him and spill the contents of my heart and mind. I dump the dishes in the hot rinse basin and turn to the fridge.

There's a ketchup stain by the handle where Abel tossed a French fry at Bec this morning. I scrub with my hands shaking. How much would Abel hate me if he knew what went on inside me all the time, what my brain rejected but my guts still half-believed? It would be the end for sure. No more Screw Your Sensors. No more silly photo shoots with our action figures. No long phone calls at 10 p.m. on Thursdays to pick apart the latest episode. I scrub harder, willing him to stay where he is. If he gets any closer, I feel like he'll know—one look at me, one little touch, and my whole bad history will scrawl itself on my skin.

"What's the matter?" he says.

I keep scrubbing. "I just—I think we should give each other some space this week."

He gasps. "Are you breaking up with me?"

"I'm serious." I thump my head on the fridge, right above the apple magnet holding the Castaway Ball tickets. "Just back off me for now. Okay?"

"Brandon, what is your problem?"

"No problems. Zero problems."

"Are you that mad at me?"

"I'm not mad."

"All I did was try to be your friend and help you out and you're acting like I—"

"Will you *shut up*? For once? Everything's not about you, all right? God!" I yank open the fridge and start rearranging. Juice boxes sorted by size, yogurts lined up straight. "I should be focusing on other stuff right now. College. I shouldn't have said yes to this stupid trip."

"Then why did you?"

"Because you steamrolled me."

"Wha—I did not!"

"You steamroll *everyone!*" I slam the fridge. "All you care about is making people do what you want. It's not even worth disagreeing with you because you just talk and talk until people give in and you think it's because you're so charming but really it's to shut you up." I swoop in for the kill. "The sad thing is, you think you're Cadmus. When actually you're just kind of a dick."

Abel's quiet for a long time, like he's waiting for an *aw, just kidding!* When I don't give him one, he stuffs his hands in his pockets and scuffs at the kitchen mat.

"You know what?" he says. "I'm done. I'm done trying to help you."

"Fantastic."

"Be a bitter loveless loser the rest of your life."

"I will."

"Die alone in the back of a Burger King in one of your

ugly plaid shirts."

"Looking forward to it."

He waits about five more seconds.

"You can go anytime," I say.

He clomps out of the Sunseeker, and the door clangs shut.

He's giving you an out, buddy. God's working through him.

From the window above the sink, I watch him stalk through the parking lot. Bec intercepts him by a green minivan, and he shakes his head and gestures toward me before he strides off in the opposite direction.

I lift the dishes out of the hot rinse. Flecks of hot chili and salsa still cling to the plate Abel microwaved last night, the daisy-patterned one Mom used to use for our after-school graham crackers and Nilla wafers. I grab the sponge and start scrubbing again, and when that doesn't work I throw the sponge in the sink and attack the barnacles of crud with my fingernails, scratching at them hard until the plate is smooth as Sim's skin, and Abel's mess is glugging down the drain.

***

"Don't do it, Sim. Don't you dare!"

Nighttime. While Abel chomps on cinnamon jellybeans and glares at a battered copy of *Stranger in a Strange Land*, I hide in the loft with my phone and watch *Castaway Planet* with Plastic Sim tight in my fist. When I get to Episode 2-17, I yank Nat's old patchouli-scented quilt over my head. I need to be in my own world for this one. Especially this scene. Sim is about to destroy his evolution chip.

"Step back, Captain. I refuse to hurt you." David Darras

is amazing in this scene, so intense that his Georgia accent bleeds through and smudges the R in *hurt*. "Step away, and let me save myself."

I remember the last time I watched this, two weeks before The Talk with my parents. Dad wandered into the living room with his bonsai shears, watched until Cadmus grabbed Sim's face, and gently shook his head and walked back out.

"You made a choice!" Cadmus is yelling now, wind whipping through his spiky hair. "What about your whole 'I-need-to-be-human' deal?"

"No one told me what doubt was like. What fear was like. What it was like to know how much I still don't know. It is extraordinarily difficult, Captain."

Cadmus snorts. "You bet your *ass* it's hard." I roll my eyes. Cadsim shippers love that line. "But look: I'd rather live two minutes as a real person than a hundred years as a robot. Was it really all that perfect before?"

"I was perfect, yes. Perfect by design."

"Someone *else's* design. Someone *else's* idea of perfect." Cadmus grips Sim's shoulders. "Now you get to find out who's really in there!"

"Brandon?"

I jump. Bec's cool fingertips brush my arm.

"Sorry. He's snoring down there," she whispers. She's wearing a black Hello Kitty shirt with the neckband cut off and I smell her vanilla mint toothpaste. "Can I sleep here?"

I shut off *Castaway* and yank my earbuds out. "It's not much quieter."

"That's okay."

I shove over as much as I can, and she squeezes in next to me. We used to do this a lot. First when we were kids, curled up in her pink plastic playhouse with our stuffed-raccoon baby between us, and then when we were older and she'd make up some sleepover-at-Ashley's story to sneak in my window and stay with me. We'd whisper forever about her sister's creepy boyfriend and what superpower we'd want and whether Bob Dylan was amazing (my position) or overrated (hers), and then when the talking was over I'd give her a cheek kiss and fall asleep with my hand on her soft belly, and she thought I wouldn't push for more because I was a gentleman. At least I thought that's what she thought.

Bec's got Plastic Lagarde with her. She's made her a white minidress from a fast-food napkin and a twist-tie; the dress looks weird with Zara Lagarde's buzz-cut and biceps. To the soundtrack of Abel's snores, she hooks Lagarde's arm through Plastic Sim's and walks the action figures up my chest, the world's most improbable wedding march.

"It's cozy up here," she says.

"I have a book light if you want."

She smiles. "I'm not afraid of the dark anymore."

"Right."

Her face is so close I can see the tiny faint freckles on her lips, shiny with a clear coat of white-cherry gloss.

Go ahead. One kiss. Just keep it tame. How do you know you don't like it if you've never tried?

"You can stop waiting, you know," she says.

"For what?"

"For God to strike you down."

"Can I?" I fiddle with Lagarde's tiny machete. "Apparently he's sent assassins."

I force a grin. She doesn't smile back.

"Abel said you had a fight," she says.

"It was nothing."

"You have to talk to him, Brandon. Be honest."

"Like you're honest with your mom?"

"That's different."

"What do you want me to say to him? 'Oh, see, I have this secret tormented inner life where I'm actually exactly the kind of person you hate'?"

"Abel wouldn't hate you."

"Yes he would. Trust me."

Below us on the couch, Abel shifts onto his back in his sleep. His knees flop open and his arm drops behind his head, exposing a slice of white belly.

"How did you get to be an atheist?" I ask her.

She snorts. "That's a weird question."

"I want to know."

"Well, there was this contest to see who could not believe in God the fastest, and I won."

"Okay."

"They gave me a tiara and an Unbeliever of the Month plaque."

"I'm serious." I prop Sim's hands on Lagarde's shoulders. "How did you decide not to believe everything Father Mike says?"

"Like, the stuff about helping the poor and not being assholes to each other?"

"You know which stuff I mean."

She shrugs and handstands Lagarde on my chest. "I don't know. It was easy. I was like, skeptical in the womb."

"But what if you weren't? What if you start out believing it because that's how your brain works, and then you can't completely shut it off?"

"Oh, well, then you're screwed."

"Thanks."

"Kidding." Lagarde tips over. "I guess you'll just have to be braver than me."

"I *am* screwed."

"Oh, stop."

"Why do boys have to exist?"

"You could always date the Phillie Phanatic."

"Oh my God."

"Remember your crush—"

"Yes. Shut it."

"That would be an abomination." She molds Plastic Sim in an evangelical pose, both arms skyward. "An abomination in the eyes of the Lord."

I grin. "Think of the children."

"If everyone married a mascot, we'd all go extinct."

"Marriage is one man and one woman," I huff, "not one man and one phanatic."

She erupts in quiet giggles. So do I, but I'm queasy. Her phone chirps in the pocket of her plaid pajama pants.

"That's your mom," I say.

"Oh, piss off."

"She hears your ungodly—"

"—Eep! No way." She covers her mouth.

"What?"

"It's from that Dave guy. With the Cookie Monster shirt?"

And the stupid hair, I almost say, but I keep my mouth shut. "Why's he texting you?"

"Because I'm awesome? Listen: 'You definitely cool girl. Me going to Atlanta con. Me want to know if me see you there.' That's kind of cute. He even spelled *definitely* right." She starts texting back. "Me see you there. You bring COOKIE."

Status: System disrupted. Remove foreign object to stabilize.

"You don't want to do that, do you?" I say.

"What?"

"Hook up with some guy you met at a convention?"

73

"What should I hold out for?" she teases. "A sham marriage to my best friend?"

I flick her shoulder. "Ideally."

She presses Sim's face to my cheek and makes a smoochy sound. I kiss the top of her head. I try not to, but I picture her in this position with that Lego-haired creep Dave, his lips lingering on her hair and his hands roaming the gentle curves of her body, doing all the stuff my hands would never do. *My Bec.* Not mine anymore. I guess she never was.

She lays Sim and Lagarde on my chest, side by side.

"Everything's going to be okay," she whispers.

"Yep."

Abel snores pornographically, like a prince sleeping off an orgy. Outside on the highway, everyone's going somewhere fast; 18-wheelers and SUVs and slick two-seaters all streak by together in one deep roar of purpose. I press my eyes shut and pretend Bec's shoulder is Sim's, picture his mechanical heart pumping blue in the dark. *You are safe here with me,* he says, and *Shall we watch the skies for falling stars?*, but all I see is Abel's hurt face in the kitchen when I said *shut up*, and all I hear is *Hell Bells. Hell Bells. Hell Bells.*

CastieCon #2
Atlanta, Georgia

8 »

"FELLOW CASTIES." Abel sighs. "A solemn *bonjour* from the parking lot of the Atlanta Superion Inn. Also known as Hell's fiery furnace."

Abel's at the RV desk with the camera on, eating cheese curls that smell like dirty socks and fanning himself with a CastieCon program. I'm folding boxers in the Sunseeker kitchenette and deciding which t-shirts need to be ironed. I refuse to look at him. He didn't even ask if I wanted to do a post, which I guess makes sense because we've barely spoken to each other all week. Whatever. I'm used to showy silent treatments. I have an older sister.

"Since we've been deluged with three whole comments wondering why we haven't posted a vlog entry from the road this week, I figured it was time to sit you down for a heart-to-heart and be honest with you." Abel clears his throat. I turn my back and plug in my iron. "Okay, here's the thing, kids: Daddy and Daddy had a fight. The particulars aren't important; let's just say that Daddy Two was being a raging bitch and Daddy One graciously stepped aside and gave him the *space* he so desperately needed this week."

I slam down the tabletop ironing board. "You're not posting this."

"Did you guys hear something? Like a gnat, maybe?" Abel cups a hand to his ear. "Anyway, Daddy One has personally had an *awesome* week. Cadsim ladies, I so enjoyed that new hurt/comfort fic where Cadmus 'whimpered like a proud wounded cat' and 'dissolved into the comforting clank of Sim's arms.' Also, the road between Cleveland and Atlanta? Let me tell you guys: *Superbly* creepy cemetery in Cincinnati. Amazing drag show in Lexington—Anita Bigwon, you complete me, I'm totally stalking you on Twitter now. Of course, Daddy Two over there spent the entire week sulking in the RV and rewatching Season 1—"

"I'm not listening to you." I wipe sweat off my brow with my forearm. "Just so you know."

Abel rolls his eyes and crunches another cheese curl. "Aaaanyway, kids, just because Daddy and Daddy are fighting doesn't mean we don't love you. We're parked just paces away from the Superion, where we'll be giving you complete coverage of the Tom Shandley Q&A in...t-minus forty-five minutes. Guys: Are you ready to *kneel before Xaarg?*"

"Your phone keeps ringing." I grab it off the desk and hold it up.

"I busted out my black cashmere t-shirt specifically for this occasion, 'cause it's not every day you lift your question paddle before the biggest badass villain on television. Considering he only approves of 'literary fanfic that probes the psychology of Xaarg,' I'm preeeetttty sure he'll be his super duper awesome self and give another fat NO to cave-scene sexitude. We might have to literally worship him then."

I fling the phone at his chest. "Will you answer this already?"

"Jesus, Brandon!" He shuts off the camera, rubbing the spot where I hit him. "What's your malfunction?"

"Nothing wrong with me."

"Normal people don't throw phones."

"Bitter loveless losers do, though."

He checks the screen. "I missed three calls from Kade."

"Tragic."

"You know—"

"Make sure you apologize a million times and ask if he's mad at you until he is."

"I don't do that!"

"It's pathetic."

"At least I have someone."

"Someone with a chicken tattoo."

"It's a *phoenix*."

I give him a smug chuckle, so he thinks I'm stifling a great comeback.

"Screw you." He shakes his head. "Seriously."

Bec bangs in with her laundry bag slung across her shoulder. She looks at me, then at him. I turn back to my Steamium, scrub it across my *Castaway Planet* shirt.

"What's going on?" she says.

Abel's dialing Kade. I shoot a toxic glare at him. "Nothing."

"How long are you two going to do this?"

"I'm not doing anything."

"—Awwww, babe, don't get pissy. I forgot...no, I did!" Abel's saying. "I know, I'm tired too. I was out till two... No! God, not with him. Can you imagine?"

I slam down the Steamium. Bec shakes her head.

"I'm catching a Greyhound home," she says, "if you guys don't stop acting like infants."

"Thought you had fun this week."

She sighs a little, but she smiles. It's been like old times with me and Bec this week—sort of, when she's not texting Dave. A few times she's hung out with Abel, but mostly it's been the two of us chilling like an old married couple, eating cheese fries and chocolate cream pie in diners, fishing at crappy free campgrounds, doing weird touristy things Bec loves, like the Grave of Doctor Pepper in Virginia. I don't really care what Abel's been up to. He goes out at night in whatever town we're in, and he comes back in at two in the morning with souvenirs: a thrift-store snakeskin bomber jacket, a shot glass with a skull and crossbones on it. Sometimes I'm still awake in the loft, fighting off swarms of dark thoughts or combing the Cadsim fanjournal for the next Hell Bells sighting (nothing else, so far). When the door creaks open, I always pretend I'm asleep.

"It was fun," Bec says, "but the two of you are—"

"Talk to him. It's not me."

"It's both of you! I can't stand you guys like this."

Abel lets out a hugely annoying look-how-much-fun-I'm-having laugh. "Nuh-uh! No you didn't. You did not! Oh no, baby, that's not crazy. You want crazy, let me read you something from this FJ...Um, fanjournal? I am *not* a nerd; you're just culturally illiterate..."

"This shirt. For meeting Dave today. What do you think?" Bec waggles a narrow green t-shirt with a deep v-neck.

I swallow hard. "Nice."

"It's not too boob-intensive, is it?"

I'm just about to push out a "No" when Abel breaks in with a couple expletives that would've gotten me three days' detention back in high school. He's staring at his laptop, punching the scroll buttons up and down.

"Babe, I gotta call you back, all right?" he says to Kade. "Something's going down here."

***

I see her fanjournal icon in my head. It pops up in my dreams: the angel statue, the halo of knives.

79

"It's bad, guys," Abel says. "C'mere."

You knew this would happen, says Father Mike.

hey_mamacita is back. This time she's posted a picture I've never seen before. Abel in his *Thundercats* t-shirt, pulling a stern face beside a cinder-block wall.

Under the photo it says:

A MESSAGE OF GRAVE IMPORTANCE.

to miss maxima and the rest of you Cadsim girls: I am officially calling you out. STOP TROLLING US OR ELSE!!! it's one thing not to agree with our manifesto, but CHRIST ON A BIKE it's a whole other bag of crazy to come over and attack us and call us, I quote, "psychotic" and "mentally ill." who are brandon & abel to you, anyway? as far as I recall, you were calling for their heads last year when they ripped apart your fic on Screw Your Sensors every week, so kindly cram it with the mark david chapman references and calling us batshit crazy, especially since you of all people know EXACTLY where we're coming from.

for the record, YES, we will still have a spy (spies plural) at the Atlanta CastieCon today. they're already there, and they are READY FOR ACTION as soon as brandon and abel walk in.

and BFC update = plots are thickening. as we speak. there's still time to join us, IF you dare.

ta-ta.

:-)

We just stand there and blink.

"You guys." Abel taps the screen fast. "That is a personal photo."

"Did you post it anywhere before?" says Bec.

"Facebook, maybe. I don't know."

"Any enemies? Besides the Cadsim shippers?"

"No. I love everyone," Abel shrugs. "Except if they suck. But most people don't—What is he doing?"

I'm already in the back room, unzipping the canvas storage chest under the bed. I find them right away, under a couple flannel shirts and four awful Christmas sweaters from our last Vermont holiday with Aunt Meg. Dad ordered the SAFE-U vests five years ago when someone got shot half a mile from our house during deer season. When we took our Saturday walks in the woods with our binoculars and bag lunches, he wouldn't let me leave without strapping one of these on. *Always best not to take chances,* he'd say.

Abel says to Bec, "What are *those*?"

"How would I know?"

"I thought you knew every inch of this place."

I shrug. "Tell him it's like the vests they wore in Episode 4-23," I tell Bec. "When they're rescuing Dutchie from the tentacle robots? Tell him he should wear one too."

"Did you get that?" Bec asks Abel.

"Uh-huh."

"It's like a costume," I say. "But not so obvious."

"Tell Brandon," says Abel, "that I think he's full of shit, and that those are bulletproof vests, and if he thinks I'm wearing one of those he's one hundred percent demented."

"Tell Abel that they're bulletblocker *panels*, and when your enemies are stalking you and other people are calling them psychotic, it's actually a fairly intelligent

81

idea."

"Tell Paranoid Android he's officially out of his skull, and that no one in the history of fandom has gotten shot over a ship war."

"I bet that's not true."

"And plus there's no way Cadmus would wear one of those."

"Tell him we don't have writers to save our asses."

"Ask Brandon how come he's such a puss all of a sudden."

"Tell Abel to—"

"Shut it!" yells Bec.

I turn around. She's standing in the kitchen nook in a pink bra with red circles, the one that's always hanging damp from her shower rod when I use her bathroom at home.

"Listen, bozos." She tosses her sleep shirt on the counter and starts yanking on her green v-neck. "Do it or don't do it. Fight or don't fight. Love each other or hate each other. Just leave me out of it. Understood?"

I sneak a look at Abel. He crosses his arms.

"Yeah," we mutter.

"You have anything to say to each other?"

"Nope." I shrug.

"Not really," says Abel.

Bec sighs. She shoves Plastic Sim at me. Plastic Cadmus at Abel. Putting on her best Zara Lagarde sneer, she stalks to the door and wrenches it open, flooding the Sunseeker with heat and the sooty gray smell of exhaust. She quotes Lagarde in Episode 2-11, two seconds after I know she's going to:

"Get it together, men. Or *die.*"

9»

CRYSTAL BALLROOM, 10:52 A.M. Eight minutes to the Tom Shandley Q&A. Gold tickets stamped, blue wristbands snapped on. The redheaded girl at the check-in booth gives us a cute gun-finger and says "Have a blast, guys!"

You're taking chances, bud.

I reach in my SAFE-U vest, squeeze Plastic Sim.

"Let's go." Abel shoves rudely at my back. "Seven minutes!"

Inside it's packed. Much more than Cleveland. The booths are swamped and the line for the Shandley Q&A is twice as long as Bree LaRue's, wrapped all the way around the draped table where two of Xaarg's Henchmen are signing a stack of promo shots. We'll have to tromp through an army of strangers to get in line.

I adjust my vest, scan faces. No one looks crazy. But how would I know?

"Help me look for Dave, okay?" Bec says. "He said he'd meet me at the Q&A."

Abel high-fives her. "Woohoo! Get it, baby."

I don't know how they're calm. All I can think of is hey_mamacita. *Plots are thickening. We have spies.* I straighten my back like Sim but it doesn't help; a camera flash pops, a toy laser gun goes *brrrzzapp* and I think this is it, this is how I die, face down on a stretch of paisley carpet by a rack of collectible Christmas balls that say DON'T MESS WITH XAARG.

The doors to the Q&A room slide open. Everyone struggles forward. I shuffle behind Abel, keep my eyes on his dumb yellow rubber watch. I try to look anonymous, which is pretty impossible when the six-foot-two person in front of you has a neon sweatband around his forehead and hair that could signal ships lost at sea.

Abel settles on a space in the center of the crowd. The room feels airless and reeks of floral shampoos and failing deodorants, snack-stand onion rings and popcorn. I'm four inches from the back of some sweaty guy's novelty t-shirt. Cartoon Jesus aims two machine guns straight at my face. The guy's talking to a girl in a candy-red wig with dangly earrings shaped like the Starsetter: *"True, but that's a critical part of Cadmus's backstory. If they retcon it now it'll be a disaster."*

"He's coming he's coming!" I think Abel's talking to me, but then he pokes the stocky lady standing next to him. She's dressed in leather pants and a ripped gray tank top like Zara Lagarde, and homemade replicas of Lagarde's gun and machete are slung across her back. "Oh my God oh my Goddddd how excited are you?"

Lagarde Lady grins. "Totally!"

Bec's waving Dave through the crowd. Hugging him. His hair looks even stupider than before and he's brought her a plastic-wrapped cookie from the snack bar.

Abel rocks on his heels. "I may vomit," he tells Lagarde Lady.

Me too.

The backstage curtains rustle and part and the crowd goes bananas till they see who it is. Just a guy dressed up like one of the Henchmen. Black cloak, ghost-white face, creepy red contact lenses.

He holds a finger to his lips and the room zaps quiet. He reaches in his cloak. Pulls out a wreath of metal brambles with five bright silver bells attached. He shakes the wreath and they cling-clang, the spoon-in-a-teacup sound of the bells I used to ring on the altar at the Consecration. My tongue puckers, bracing for the bitterness of wafers and wine.

The lights cut out.

Bec says, "What the—?" My insides jump.

Giggles.

Nervous whispers.

A voice in the dark: *Um, hellooo?*

The lights flicker on but stay dim. There's a loud wheezy *poof*, like an old-time camera, and a thick cloud of Xaarg's purple smoke engulfs the stage. Red lasers stutter. Xaarg's theme blares: three descending cello notes sawed on a sinister loop. People clap and stomp like it's a monster truck rally and Abel's bouncing up and down, fist-pumping and shouting YEAH WOOO-HOOOO and I look for the nearest exit, just to know it's there.

When the smoke clears, Tom Shandley stands alone onstage, filing his nails with a small silver dagger. He wears his red-and-purple ceremonial robe, a black stole embroidered with gold skulls and swords, and a two-foot-tall red velvet hat.

He cups a hand to one ear.

Cheers. Decibel level: new pope at balcony.

Nothing's left of the Henchman. Just a heap of black robe, a wisp of steam escaping it. Shandley bends down and pinches it between his thumb and forefinger, dangles it like a rotten sardine.

"That's what the little beast gets," Shandley vamps, "for *ringing my bells.*"

Abel hoots and whistles. My vest is unbearable; I un-zip it a centimeter, let out some heat.

Shandley's taking off the hat, smoothing his neat silver hair with a little black comb. He's tanner and thinner than usual and his sharp nose and chin look sharper in person. He loses the robe next, slowly, an ironic strip-tease that more than half the audience seems to appreciate unironically. Pressed gray pants and black *Castaway* shirt underneath.

"Before you ask, let's get a few things out of the way." He plucks the mike off its stand. "I'm a Leo with Scorpio rising, my favorite color is chartreuse, I do all my own stunts, and I will not, I repeat, *not* go to the prom with you." A staff guy hurries onstage with a paper coffee cup; Shandley takes a sip and *aaahs.* "Also, if I were a peanut butter, I'd be smoooooth. Any more questions?"

Everyone giggles.

"No? Damn, easiest five hundred bucks I ever made. Just kidding! Yes, Lady Leatherpants—you first!"

Lagarde Lady wants some dirt on their famous on-set pranks. Shandley trots out a story I've heard before, the one about the fake finale script where Sim malfunctions and kills the entire cast. Abel's grinning like a kid at a circus and laughing at the story like it's new, and I should be too, I should be sharing this with him, but I can't. I keep staring at the Henchman's abandoned robe.

"Do you believe in heaven?" I'd asked my dad once. I was nine, and my goofball teacher Mr. Ratison had just died in a car crash in Maine. I hadn't slept with the light off all week.

"Absolutely." Dad pulled my plaid comforter up to my shoulders and tucked it tight around me like a cocoon. *"There's a lot in life I'm not sure about, but I know there's a God, and I know he's got a place ready for us when it's our time to go. And as long as we're good people, that's where we're going to be someday, with God forever and ever. You can trust in that, Brandon. Okay?"*

He ruffled my hair and shut off my light, thinking he'd comforted me. I lay there stiff and wide-eyed until two a.m., listening to my baseball clock tick. What would you do in heaven if it lasts forever and ever and time never ends? How could quiet eternity not feel like water torture? And heaven was the *better* option. There's no way I'd be good enough to get in, not with all those shivery thoughts about kissing Spider-Man upside-down and...

"Next! Yep, you." Tom Shandley's pointing right at us. "Well, well, Mr. Neon Sweatband. I like it. Very Olivia Newton-John."

Abel's been Summoned by Xaarg.

He steps forward like Cadmus, chin held high, hands on the hips of his tight dark jeans. He's asking our question. I'm sweating through my shirt. I lob the maybe-God a softball: *If you're up there, give me a sign. If Shandley says no, nothing happened in the cave, then Father Mike is wrong. You're okay with this trip. You're okay with me, just the way I am.*

"...so do you think they did anything in the cave, for real?"

Say no, Shandley. Say no.

"Yes, I do. Unfortunately."

Crap.

Abel's shaking his head. "Are you serious?"

"I think that was the implication, yep. Bray hasn't confirmed, so I'm talking out of school. But I wouldn't be shocked."

A cheer shoots up in the corner.

"You sound disappointed," says Abel.

"Well, yeaaah, I don't think that's the smartest move, to be honest. I hope we don't go there next season."

"Yeah! They're like, exactly wrong for each other."

"No, it's just—you know. The sensational aspect of the storyline."

Abel's jaw tenses.

"What do you mean?" he says.

"Oh, I dunno. It just seems so, ya know, *desperate*. Let's have a big gay story to pump things up. Win some awards."

"That's sort of cynical."

"Eh. It would backfire, anyway."

"Why is that?"

"You know why. If it was a glorified sidekick, someone like Dutchie, then sure. Aww. Cute little neutered gay. But make the show's primary hetero heartthrob a sudden secret queer and just watch how many people tune out before sweeps."

"That's not very nice," Dave pipes up. His gross hipster hand is around Bec's waist but I feel too sick to react.

"I'm just being honest," Tom Shandley shrugs. "Bray's got to think of the ratings. If your main character's in a relationship you have to show it, and I don't care how many gay fans *Castaway* has: you can't turn a major network show into *Queer as Folk* and not expect a backlash. We're not that evolved yet. *N'est-ce pas?*"

Abel folds his arms. "*Mais non,*" he says.

"Well, aren't you an optimist."

"You're selling people short."

"Bigots exist, dear."

"They exist but they're not important."

"They have remotes. Remotes equal importance."

"They shouldn't. Leonard Bray shouldn't worry about a bunch of fucking idiots. They're too stupid to be real fans."

I hear people around us pull in a sharp breath, as if Shandley could really incinerate us with his eyes if he felt like it.

"He's the showrunner." Shandley cocks his head. "The show lives and dies on its fans. Even the stupid ones. You're smart enough to know that, aren't you, sweetheart?"

"Yeah, but if he never takes a real chance—"

"The network will be happy. So I hope he doesn't."

"But listen! Don't you think challenging things and making like, a legacy—"

"Aaaaand could we get a new question? 'Kay? I love a debate, but cheez *whiz*, you guys." He rolls his eyes and sips his coffee. "I'm a god, not a politician."

A murmur races through the crowd. Some girl lifts a question paddle and asks a polite, careful question about Shandley's stint with Shakespeare in the Park. For a second I just stare at Abel's profile—the tension in his jaw, the rare *you-have-angered-me* flare in his eyes. He took on Xaarg. Just like Cadmus. I never could have done that. Even when I sat at the table and came out to my own parents I barely looked at them; just traced the parading goose families on Mom's plastic placemats while Nat listened from the kitchen, ready to jump in if I chickened out. I can make excuses, say I only appear timid to the naked eye because I see things the way Sim does and tolerate all points of view, but the truth is that 95% of the time, I'm mostly too terrified to say what I think.

Also, this is really not the point at all, but Abel McNaughton is hot when he's mad.

You're not listening, says Father Mike.

Shhhhh. Not now, please not now.

You got your sign. Shandley said yes.

My eyes drift down to Abel's forearm, Malibu-tanned from resting in the RV's open window. Today's belt buckle: pewter thorns and roses wreathed around the words TRUE LOVE.

Stop looking at him.

What if I don't?

Maybe God will take him away. To make it easy.

I press my eyes shut. Shandley answers the next question, some egghead ramble about Xaarg and the perversion of free will. When I open my eyes again, I'm alone in the crowd. Bec's drifted away from me, whispering to Dave with her hand on his shoulder. And Abel's gone altogether—his spot beside me filled by two teenage girls in sunflower shirts, as if he'd never existed at all.

10»

I SCOUR THE LOGICAL places. The costume stand, the make-shift prop museum, the alcove where *Castaway Planet* blooper reels flicker on a loop. Nothing.

"He's about six-two, black shirt, yellow rubber watch, white hair that goes like *ppfft* all over?" I tell the costume-stand lady. She's filling a display stand with ten-dollar replicas of Sim's mechanical heart—slim pods cased in cheap frosted plastic, blinking out of sync with each other. She nods indulgently, like I'm describing an imaginary friend.

"If I see him," she says, "I'll tell him you want him."

I do a fast sweep. The hotel lobby, the indoor pool. The east end of the ballroom, where a dozen girls bicker in a fanfic workshop. I circle back to the Q&A just as the Shandley mob floods out. Bec's green shirt glints through the crowd. I push through people to get to her.

"Jesus. Where'd you go?" She hooks my arm. I steer us to a calm corner, in front of an artist hand-painting Star-setter nutcrackers.

I grab her shoulders. "Did you see Abel leave?"

"No, I—"

"You didn't?"

"I was...busy."

"Right. Right."

"Why are you so frazzled?"

"We should stick together!"

"I'm sure he's okay."

"How could he disappear?"

"Brandon, I'm sure he just took a walk. He looked really pissed."

Dave bounds up with a wide white smile. "You ready?"

"Meet you out there," Bec says.

"Cool." He touches her arm. "See ya later, man," he says to me. I get a half-salute and he lopes away.

"What was that?" I ask.

"I have a date."

"With him?"

"No, with Shandley. We're going ballroom dancing."

"You're not driving anywhere, right?"

"I don't know, Dad. Why?"

"He could be a serial killer. How would you know?" I can tell I'm being annoying, the kind of annoying where it feels like I haven't showered for days and everyone should just stay away. Bec sticks her hands on her hips.

"Are you mad 'cause Tom Shandley's a dick? I could've told you that."

"I'm not mad."

"People are assholes sometimes. You can't let it get to you."

I sigh. "Please just help me look for Abel?"

"I can't. On account of the aforementioned date." She pokes my stomach. "What, you think those Hell Bells people are holding him hostage?"

"Stop."

"Like, maybe they'll be tightening the thumbscrews, trying to get him to recant his Cadsim hate, and you'll burst in like the conquering hero just as—"

"Quit it!" I shrug off her hand. "I'm serious."

"Will you lighten up?"

"Don't even joke about that!"

"Why?"

"Forget it. Forget it. Just go out. Go meet *Dave*. Have a

really awesome time."

"I will. He's fun."

"Maybe you can share a milkshake and buy some ironic t-shirts together."

"You're being a jerk."

I shrug.

She shoves the camera at me.

"Upload the vid yourself," she says. "When I get back, you better be human again."

She huffs off down the merch aisle, ducking a juggler by the autograph table and a crying girl in a platinum Leandra Nigh wig. I congratulate myself on my freshly acquired talent for pissing off the few real friends I have. Outside the glass doors, Bec meets up with Dave and he drapes his arm around her like I used to in the halls before our first-period Chem class, my hand trying different positions and grips in the hope that just one might feel natural. They disappear past the thick crowd of travelers in the lobby. She doesn't look back. Cold clangs in my chest, and my brain calls up Episode 1-7: *Captain, if I could experience real love for one day, I believe it would be ...*

Men.

Two men at the action-figure booth. Black trench coats, black hats. Their faces are painted Henchmen-white and they've got the red contact lenses and the same cool concentrated stares, like they're unlocking the dark little room in your brain where you stuff all the thoughts that would make your parents blush.

But what I really notice are the t-shirts.

They're hidden at first, just thin slices of white underneath the coats. But then the taller guy moves his arm and I see the intricate image on the shirt. It has to be homemade. There's no official merch with that picture on it, and it looks hand-drawn by someone devoted to detail.

Obsessively, psychotically devoted.

The Hell Bells.

I zip up my vest. *Status: High alert.* I feel every one of the zipper teeth, the sick uphill click-clack of a roller coaster ready to drop you into blackness. Their white faces tilt together. One of them starts to whisper.

They're walking my way.

***

I don't wait. I run for the RV. Through the lobby, down a glass corridor, out the doors and across the hot parking lot. Abel's face looms in front of me as my sneakers smack the pavement. He wouldn't do this. He wouldn't run from them. He'd walk right up to them and say something bold like *What's your deal?* Like Cadmus did to Xaarg in 1-04, like Abel did to Shandley in the Q&A room.

I'm running so hard I can't stop in time. I smack into the side of the Sunseeker. I gasp in a breath, look behind me. Scan the parking lot.

No one. Empty.

I open the door, slowly. It's dark and stifling inside, like a confessional on a summer day.

"Abel...?"

He's not the one who answers.

Come in, Brandon.

I always hated confession. I would make up sins like swearing and shoplifting gum to hide the real ones: masturbating in the shower, impure thoughts about Luke Perry in those ancient *90210*s Bec loves.

Someone important wants to talk to you. Isn't it time you started listening to Him?

I lock the door, latch all the windows, and pull down the blinds. I thump down in the passenger seat and dial my parents. I don't know why. It's not like I can talk to them about this, but I like tapping the familiar pattern of their phone number. They're not home. Of course. Saturday dinner with the Donnellys. Mom's curled her hair and brought her shepherd's pie in a white casserole dish; Dad's wearing a plaid shortsleeved button-down and his thin hair is wet and carefully combed. They're drinking red wine and saying the words "Loyola" and "Communications major" a million times, trying to convince everyone they're still proud of me.

I try Nat next, but who knows where she is. Her cell's turned off and I get her message: *I'll call you back, maybe*, over the anguished background yodels of some girl-punk band I'm not cool enough to listen to. Whatever. I don't want to talk to her anyway. Last time I asked her for advice she lit a cigarette and said "God is like junior high, Brandon. Graduate already." Then she told me she was thinking of moving to Kenya with some greasy philosophy major she'd known for five weeks, and possibly getting an ankh tattooed on her shoulder.

Plastic Sim is still in my vest pocket. I fish him out and spread his arms to the sides; trace a slow T across his body—wrist to wrist, chin to shin. One time when I was eleven or twelve, I was in St. Matt's alone after serving Sunday Mass, and I sat down in the front pew and stared up at Jesus on the cross. Our Jesus was really realistic. You could count his ribs, trace the subtle definition of his muscles, gauge the strength of his legs just by the synthesis of sinew and bone. I tried to pray a decade of the rosary but the prayers never made me feel much; the *thees* and *hallowed bes* were too foreign and too familiar all at once, and God was probably so mad at me he didn't want to hear it anyway. I ended up dreaming of what sex would feel like, to be so close to a man you could feel his bones with your bones. And then a shadow slanted across the pew, and a warm hand clapped the back of my neck.

"Whatcha thinking about, Brandon?"

Father Mike above me, smiling in black with a white square at his neck, boyish in a blue-and-gold St. Matt's windbreaker.

My stomach contorted. I weighed the choices: *Confess the unconfessable. Lie to a priest.*

I did the thing I do best. I ran away.

I ran to the boys' room and gripped the sink like I'm gripping the sink in the Sunseeker now, blasting cold water and dousing my whole head. It feels fantastic and horrible. When I can't take it anymore, I shut the water off and stand there like the world's biggest idiot, my hair dripping puddles on the kitchenette floor.

Outside, in the near distance, gravel crunching under feet.

Here they come.

It's not Abel. I know his footfall, like a trick-or-treater bounding up a walkway. These steps are heavy, joyless. Sinister.

Four clomps. Five. Six. Coming closer.

A pause.

Then a creak, and the Sunseeker shudders.

They're on the steps.

We have an Atlanta spy. Plots are thickening.

Someone sits on the step with a thud and I hear a metallic clink that could be lots of things, none of them good. I see the Hell Bells post in my head, that weird "BFC" thing. Bullets From Crazies? Beat Fags Cheerfully?

My hands scrabble for weapons. Not a mop—stupid. Frying pan—no. I'll go bold. There's no choice.

My heart chugs wildly. I tiptoe close to the door and put my mouth right on the crack. Ragged breathing on the other side. I tighten my throat and set my jaw, shift my feet apart like tough guys in movies who say stuff like this, in exactly this booming rat-a-tat voice:

"I'VE GOT A GUN!"

"Auuugh!"

The scream scares me so much I lose my logic, fling the door wide open. Abel's stumbling away from the Sunseeker, clutching his chest. On the pavement by the steps: his keys and a replica of Cadmus's ray gun, still spinning where he dropped it.

He gulps in a breath. "You scared the shit out of me!"

"I didn't know it was you!"

"Who'd you think I was?"

"I don't know!" The door starts closing on me; I punch it back. "Where *were* you?"

"Out! Walking! Is that allowed?"

"Yeah, I just—"

"Oh my God. My heart."

"I'm sorry..."

"Forget it. Forget it." He snatches his stuff up and clomps into the Sunseeker, squeezing past me in the doorway. I haven't felt this dumb since the Timbrewolves concert when I screwed up the solo on "My Girl." His eyes are all red and I want to ask him about it, but he catches me searching his face and looks away fast. He yanks the fridge open and stares inside for a long minute. Then he slams the door.

"Why is your hair wet?" he sighs.

"Dumb story."

"I'm sure. You want to go somewhere?"

"Where?"

He reaches in his back pocket and pulls out a bright yellow flyer. "Some coffeehouse, they're having a *Castaway* marathon."

"Maybe."

I take the flyer from him and scan it. I wait for Father Mike to weigh in, but there's nothing much in my head right now, just an ache and a dull gray hum.

"So Kade dumped me."

I look up. Abel's wiping his nose with the back of his hand. He doesn't look at me.

"When?"

"Forty-five minutes ago." He pumps some gel into his hand and starts punking his hair up. "On *Twitter.*"

"Oh my God."

"Whatever. At least he DMed me."

"I'm sorry. That's rotten."

Abel shrugs.

"Why'd he—"

"Zzt!" He holds up a hand. "Completely expected. Not a huge deal. No questions, no sympathetic looks. Them's the rules. Okay?"

"I guess, but..."

"You call a cab. I'll pay."

"I saw the spies."

He stops attacking his hair. "...What?"

"The Hell Bells spies. I think I saw them."

"What'd they look like?"

"You know. Menacing."

"Menacing how? Like—" He makes a bucktoothed monster face.

"Not exactly."

"Were they goons?"

"I don't know what a goon looks like."

"You'd know one if you saw one."

"I guess they were."

"Big dudes?"

"Big enough."

"They follow you?"

"For a while."

Abel shakes his head. "Are you *sure*?"

"Pretty sure, yeah."

"Wow." He leans against the fridge and shudders. "Creepy."

"I'm not sure we should go out. Maybe it's too—"

"No. No, I'm calling the cab right now."

"But they could be anywhere."

"I'm not living in fear, Brandon. Screw it. That's so 1952."

"Why 1952?"

"I don't know. Like, Rock Hudson or whatever." He holds up his phone. "Are you coming or not?"

I fiddle with the zipper pull on my vest.

"We should stick together," I say. "Stay in crowds."

He smiles a little.

"Roger that," he Cadmuses.

"We shouldn't sit by a window."

"Heavens no."

"And also—"

"—you should take this off."

He unzips my SAFE-U vest with the tip of one finger, like Cadmus undid Nigh's jacket in the Season 1 finale. Then he crosses his thick arms in front of him and pulls his tight black t-shirt up over his head. *Crap, crap, crap.* My whole body heats up. I've never seen a naked torso that wasn't on a cross, at least not so close up. I don't know where to look. His belly button. Belly button. *Look at the belly button.*

He's holding his shirt out. "This is more you than me."

"I don't need to change."

"Yeah you do."

He grips the front of my shirt and pulls me closer,

makes his voice all low and raspy like Cadmus.

"You'll want to look sexy for Jesus," he says, "in case it's our last night on earth."

11»

NEAR THE MOUTH OF THE crystal spider cave, now definitively sealed by a Xaarg-generated avalanche, Cadmus and Sim huddle together for warmth. Or Cadmus huddles close to Sim, if you want to get technical about it. Sim controls his own body temperature. He turns up his own regulation switch, just behind his right ear, and then dials it back when the heat gets too much.

"Captain, I must apologize for this detour," says Sim. "I have long suspected a malfunction in my compass application."

"Ahhh, don't be sorry." Cadmus shivers. He pats Sim's arm and gives it a squeeze. "It's Xaarg. Either way, we were screwed."

Some girl goes *Boom-chicka-wow-wowww,* and giggles erupt in the Lunar Rose Coffeehouse. That flyer didn't mention this was a Season 4 marathon, or that 80% of their clientele are apparent Cadsim shippers. By the time the cave episode rolls around, I've already endured the full horror of hearing Sim's best lines chanted out loud, like some kind of deluded shipper incantation, by a bunch of girls in costumes and homemade t-shirts that say TEAM CADSIM in blue glitter. Abel and I scrunch down on a battered velvet couch at the back of the room, hoping no one recognizes us from Screw Your Sensors. These girls would eat us for dinner.

I check the door every few minutes. No Hell Bells spies yet. Abel's probably right—who would follow us here?

"This episode blows," whispers Abel. He's sipping a

cinnamon latte and scarfing a second giant snicker-doodle, like he didn't just show me his naked torso less than two hours ago. I still can't look him in the eye. But at least we're not fighting.

"I know," I whisper back. "Terrible."

"That speech Cadmus gives Sim about how his dad missed his graduation?"

"Shameless."

"So out of character."

"Sim's *should-I-have-stayed-human* angst is a two-ton anvil, too."

"Yeah, like, why do we need a *Breakfast Club* scene where they talk it into the ground?"

Onscreen, the arm touch segues into lingering eye contact and the girls go bananas: *Kiss, kiss, kiss!* I shake my head.

"It's fanservice. Pure and simple."

"It's lazy. Snickerdoodle?"

"Just a tiny piece."

Abel breaks a big chunk off for me and drapes his arm across the back of the couch. I move a little bit, just out of habit.

"Oh...I'm not in your *space*, am I?" he grins.

"Shut up."

"You started it," he says.

"Yeah, well, you disappeared on me. Call it even."

"Sorry," he mutters around his cookie.

"Why'd you just leave like that?"

"I dunno. Shandley was such a dicksmack, I couldn't deal. You get in your bubble, you forget what the rest of the world's like."

"I don't think he's a bigot."

"Self-loather?"

"Maybe."

"Ugh. They should die in a fire."

"Why?"

"What do you mean, *why*? Sooner they go extinct, the better. They make us look bad."

"Don't you feel sorry for them, though?"

Abel flicks my ear. "Quit being nice," he says. "You make me feel like a turd."

"Sorry."

He takes another bite and brushes crumbs off his shirt, red with a neon old-school joystick on the front. He leans his head back and lets out a long, showy sigh. "So he hooked up with Arch."

"Who did?"

He makes a *duh* face. "Kade."

"Oh."

"*Arch*. Even his stupid name tries too hard. He's like 27 and he wears these Goth t-shirts from the mall." Abel wipes foam off his upper lip with the back of his hand. "He met my sister once at Antonelli's when my family was out to dinner, like right after she published the book with Mom, and he talked to her like she was a cocker spaniel. And then he was all like 'I really *admire* people with Down syndrome,' like he was in a stupid man-pageant and the world-peace answer already got used up. He asked her for a signed copy of *Susannah Says*. I wanted to kick him in the nuts."

"I'm sorry."

"I really really liked him."

"Arch?"

"*Kade.*"

"I know."

"And he was all like, 'Uh, I'm sorry, were we mono-gamous? I missed the memo.' Like it's my fault he just couldn't wait to fuck someone horrible."

"That sucks."

"Susannah didn't like him. I should've known. My sister can spot a cockpunch from fifty paces."

"Screw him."

"*Screw* him."

"He was too skinny anyway."

"You think?"

"He looked like a stork." I grab another chunk of snickerdoodle. "And that name? *Kade*?"

"Tacky. I know."

"Kade and Abel. Like you're reading Genesis with a cold."

He laughs like *pffffff!* and sprays tiny crumbs. "You been saving that one?"

"Since we left."

"Well played. Hey, can I tell him we're doing it?"

"Huh?"

"He was jealous of you. It would make him nuts."

"Why was he—"

"Ugh, forget it. Forget it! Why bother? I don't care."

Abel knots his arms and sighs at the screen, his knee leaning lightly on mine. I try to refocus on the show. Sim and Cadmus aren't in this scene; it's the subplot with Dr. Lagarde and Dutchie fighting over the rescue mission. Dutchie yells, *Just because you're in charge doesn't mean you're right!* All I hear is *He was jealous of you.*

He was jealous. Of you.

Then I get the shoulder tap.

"'Scuse me...hello? Hi-ii!"

I steel myself and turn around slowly. It's this short girl with thick brown hair, a glee-club smile, and a tinfoil Xaarg hat. She's got on these goofy glasses with pink plastic frames and a white tank top that spells out BELIEVER in little craft-store diamonds. She leans right over me to talk to Abel.

"You're the guy from the Q&A!" she says.

Abel lights up. *"C'est moi."*

"I think it's really cool what you said to Tom Shandley. He was being a creep."

"Aww, thanks!"

"Everyone was talking about it. You're like, convention-famous."

"Really?"

"Yep. Thanks for defending Cadsim."

"Oh no, I wasn't really—"

"Can I get a picture with you?"

"Uh—yeah. Of course!"

This is so dumb, but I figure I'll let Abel have his moment. "Want me to take it?" I ask Pink Glasses.

"Who are you? Are you his boyfriend?"

"We're just friends right now." Right now?

"Oh, you get in too! Here, my friend'll—ANNIE! Take our picture, okay?"

This stringy blonde comes skulking over. She's got on Cleopatra eyeliner and a black tank top with a small silver *Castaway Planet* logo, and she looks vaguely embarrassed that she's required to exist, let alone document the evening. Pink Glasses perches on the edge of the couch and leans into us while Annie snaps photos. Then she grabs the camera back and takes a few more herself, framing the shots and barking orders like a fashion photographer: "Smile for my CastieCon scrap-book!" "Look super-sexy, guys!"

Abel blows kisses and aims a silly grin at the camera. It's good to see him do that, even if he's playing it up. There's something about his face when he smiles, like he's a stained-glass window with sun beaming through. I have to smile too.

105

"Captain...I notice you are still awake."

Onscreen, it's time for the big Cadsim scene. The girls abandon picture-taking; clasp hands and dart off with a squeal. Abel nudges me.

"Pink Glasses and Annie," he whispers. "I kind of ship it."

All the girls find their seats and the room gets so church-quiet you can practically smell holy water. Abel shifts closer—not to touch me or anything, just to draw a clear line between us and them. Warmth glows in the sliver of space between us. We each train our eyes on half the TV screen: his boy on the left and mine on the right, murmuring to each other in the dark.

"I'm so tired of running. Tired of the fight." The girls in front recite it reverently, in perfect sync with Cadmus. *"You know, I'm almost glad I'm stuck here with you. I'm free here. I don't have to hold it together."*

"Perhaps you underestimate yourself, Captain. You are always free."

"Not like this. I only feel this way when you're around. Maybe we should just stay here forever, huh?"

"The notion is highly impractical, though you would be an agreeable companion."

"It's so quiet in here, Sim."

"Yes, Captain."

"Like it could swallow up all your secrets."

"Quite..."

Meaningful look. Another lingering arm touch. Fade to black.

Abel pokes me and I gulp in some air.

For crap's sake: the holy-grail scene of the world's most ridiculous, implausible ship, and I was holding my breath with the rest of the room.

"Wanna go somewhere else?" he says.

I close my eyes and shudder. "Definitely."

***

Across the street from the Superion Inn, within sight of the Sunseeker's parking spot, St. Agnes is having a summer fair in its freshly blacktopped lot. The second he spots the plaster clown head from the cab, Abel wigs out and I know I'm getting dragged over no matter what.

We buy a roll of red tickets from a standard-issue church lady—billowy flowered blouse, little gold cross, glasses dangling from a beaded chain—and roam around the crowded fair. It's pretty much like every other church fair I've been to. The basketball toss has the same sad shredded net, kids shriek in a red and blue bouncy castle and chuck dented ping-pong balls at goldfish bowls, and the snack stands sell sausages and roasted corncobs and cones of hot popcorn in that radioactive yellow. Everything's familiar. Except now I'm here with a boy.

It's weird. No one's giving us a second glance now, but it would be so easy to attract bad attention. All I'd have to do is slip my hand in Abel's and walk around like that, like all the other teenage couples linking arms and holding hands and kissing in line for the dunking booth. I can see the expressions now. Guys who look like my dad, chewing their tongues and hunching their shoulders up. Women who look like my mom, sighing a little and glancing away but thinking so loud I can hear every word.

And they would be right.

"What's up, Tin Man?" Abel pokes me.

"Hm?"

"You all right? Your bolts too tight?"

"I'm fine."

This shivery energy thrums between us. I tell myself

it's sugar and caffeine. Keep my arms folded in front of me.

We try a few rounds at the ring-toss stand and Abel just misses our shot to win a giant stuffed penguin with a half-unraveled scarf. To make up for it, he runs over to a stand and buys me a puff of blue cotton candy. Like we're dating or something. I can't look him in the eye when he hands me the white paper cone, so I glance past the rides and snack stands to where the blond stone wall of the church is, but I can't let my eyes linger there either. It's like looking at a house you don't live in anymore. You wish you could go in again, but strangers live there now and you aren't welcome, and it wouldn't be the same anyway.

"So what were we talking about?" says Abel. "Back in the cab?"

I tug off a small neat piece of cotton candy, the color of Sim's hair. "If they were on Earth. Their jobs."

"Right, right." Abel helps himself to a big bite of fluff; a fleck of it melts on his nose. "Sim would make a perfect priest."

"Nooo. No no no. Absolutely not."

"How come? The self-denial thing would be cake."

"I don't see him like that."

"So what do you see?"

"Cadmus. As a bartender."

"Pardon me."

"Mmm, like some super-cheesy creeper from the seventies. He'd unbutton his shirt and make—you know. What's like, an old drink no one drinks anymore?"

"Harvey Wallbangers."

"You made that up."

"I did not. You need to come to my theme parties."

"No thanks."

"Why not?"

"I don't want to wake up in your bathtub with my eyebrow shaved off."

"That only happened once, and Alex deserved it."

We stop in front of the Tilt-a-Whirl. A light summer breeze unsettles our t-shirts and lifts all the hair on my arms. The cotton candy's left this cute little blue spot on his nose. I can't help myself. I lick the tip of my index finger and rub at it: gently, like he'll crumble if I touch him too hard.

He giggles. "What're you doing, freako?"

"Sorry, it's driving me nuts."

Be careful, says Father Mike.

Abel catches my hand and twirls me around. "Let's get on."

"What?"

"The Tilt-a-Whirl."

"Nah."

"Why?" He cocks his head at me. "You're not scared, are you?"

"No! No, I love rides," I lie. "It's just—I just ate, you know?"

"Oh, come on. Pretend it's the Starsetter. We can write our very own horrible Cadsim fic." He's edging us close to the Tilt-a-Whirl line. "I'm a rogue captain on the run...I steal a starship and kidnap you, the hot navigation android programmed to do the right thing...or *are* you?" Couples step up on the creaky platform, settle into identical half-shell cars. "How should our fic start? We get stuck in an elevator—"

"No no. We meet in your bar," I break in, ducking away from the line. "It's an alternate-universe earthfic."

"Bold choice." Abel follows me, grinning. "Okay. You be Cadmus."

"Noooo."

"Why not? Stretch yourself."

"No way."

"Okay, fine." Abel slips on his Cadmus shades and makes wiping motions above a picnic table. "Hey there, customer. What can I pour you this fine evening?"

"Oh, ah, I am unsure." My ears get hot. Why did I start this? "I am an android, and as such I have no need to imbibe."

"So how come you're at my bar?"

"I cannot say. Perhaps a malfunction in my compass application."

Abel narrows his eyes, like Cadmus does when he's negotiating with Xaarg. "I smell a lie," he says. "You came to get laid, didn't you?"

Two nuns stroll by. My face burns. "Negative," I murmur.

"Aw, why not? Makes you feel like a real boy."

"I am uninterested."

"Uninterested? You smooth like a Ken doll down there?"

"On the contrary. While I have had many, ah, high-quality partners, the simple fact is—"

Flirting can seem like harmless fun**—Chapter 8, *Put on the Brakes!*—**But that person you're teasing is a vessel of the Holy Spirit. Should you really be treating them like a carnival ride?

"Ye-es?" Abel's grinning. Waiting.

I clear my throat, scramble for Sim words.

They're gone.

"I can't do this."

"Why not? You're good."

"No, it's just—you know."

"What?"

I gallop my fingers on the picnic bench. Think. Think. *Lie.* "Um, well, Zander and I used to joke around like this all the time, so—"

"Oh my God!" Abel slams his hand on the picnic table. An abandoned paper boat of French fries tips off the edge, splatters ketchup in the grass. "Will you shut it about Zander already!"

"But it's true."

"I don't care!"

"It's just part of who I am. I can't change it."

"Christ." He shoves both hands in his hair. "You know what, Brandon? You know what? That is IT!"

His hot hand locks around my wrist and before I can open my mouth again he's yanking me through the crowd, past the Tilt-a-Whirl and the candy-striped tents and a bunch of kids playing that balloon-dart game that rattled my nerves as a kid. *Pop pop pop.* My insides crackle. He could do anything with me now, take me anywhere.

We stop behind the funhouse.

He slams me up against it.

I turn my face fast, fix my eyes on the funhouse mural. Creepy clowns, sword-swallowers, Mardi Gras masks.

"Look at me," he hisses.

"Why?"

He grabs my face and turns my head slowly. My eyes press shut.

"Look at me," he says.

I hear my dad: *Never ever stare directly at the sun.*

"Fine, then. Don't. Just listen. Listen to every single word, okay?" He grips my shoulders. "Zander. Is. Gone. G-O-N-E. No more!—I'm serious, Brandon!" He shakes me. "This is total insanity and I want you to repeat after me: I. Am. Damaged." Screams from the funhouse. "Say it!"

I whisper, "I am damaged."

"I am acting like a pathetic irrational loonytunes in direct opposition to my actual awesomeness."

"I'm pathetic," I admit.

"I need to be punched in the face repeatedly and then kissed until my lips hurt."

I open my eyes. Across from the funhouse, a mini-freefall jerks a carful of kids off the ground. They shudder to the top, right under a clown's gruesome red mouth. The car stops a second, just for torture, and then drops them down with a mechanical *whoosh* like when Cadmus stole Sim, the door of his charging dock sighing open in a white breath of steam.

"Go ahead!" Abel prods. "Say it."

"I need to be..."

"Say it! You know it's true."

"Punched..."

"In the face."

"In the face."

"Repeatedly."

"And then—"

He kisses me.

It's not gentle, the way I picture it with Sim. It's rough and hard but in a funny way, like in old movies when their faces desperately smash together and then they break apart and breathe their poetic devotion. Abel's hands are firm and warm around my face. The rest of the fair dissolves; I'm on another planet that's spinning so fast I can feel it. The three silver moons of Castaway Planet dazzle in the hot black sky and his lips are Sim-blue and he smells sweet and dangerous, like liquor and cotton candy.

Status: All systems suspended.

Then it starts again. The thing that happened after Ryan Dervitz, in the Dairy Queen bathroom with my head between my knees. A rush of memories—Mom's eyes welling up when I told her, Dad alone in the backyard staring up at my old treehouse, his hands stuffed in his pockets. And then Father Mike calmly crashing through my consciousness, like some movie hero busting down the door to a burning house. His face fills up the whole screen in my head. It isn't an angry face. He never needs to be angry, not really, because he's so sure he's right.

Stop. Stop. Stop.

I shove Abel away.

"What's wrong?"

"Nothing—just—"

I have to walk. Which way is the hotel parking lot? I don't even know. I just start moving my feet. I dart across the street on a green light; a red car swerves and honks. My eyes flick over a sea of cars and lock onto the Sunseeker's roof in the near distance. I pick up the pace. Abel's big boots clap the blacktop behind me.

"What, you're mad again?"

"No."

"You are!"

"Stop talking, okay?"

"Brandon, look." He swings in front of me. "I just—I was trying to help. I thought I could snap you out of it. Hey!"

He grabs my arm. The Sunseeker's three rows away. His breath warms the side of my face.

"It's not a big deal," he whispers. "Okay?"

It's not such a great exchange, is it? A few moments of pleasure, in exchange for—

"So is this how you act?" I shove his hands away. "Like, the day someone dumps you?"

"What?"

"You know." I have no clue what I'm doing, but it's too late now. "It's kind of gross, that's all."

"What are you talking about?"

"Your 'relationship.'"

"I'm not in one."

"You were this morning."

"I don't live in the past."

"I'll say. You trying to get back at him?"

"No! No. That's not what—"

"I think that's exactly what it is."

"Brandon, I swear—"

"You think you're so much better than he is? I think you just got lucky."

"Lucky?"

Don't say it. Don't say it. "That he cheated first."

"Well, fuck you very much."

"No thanks." I start for the RV again.

"Right. Riiiiiight. Because anyone who touches precious little you has to be completely pure, oblivious to all others, a paragon of—"

"I'm not talking to you."

"Oh, fine. It's fine. I mean, if we did it and you liked it, then you couldn't feel sorry for yourself anymore, and then where would you be?"

He ducks in front of me again, sticks his hands on his hips.

"Get out of my way," I mutter.

"I'm not good enough for you anyway, right? Like, who knows what I'll make of myself? You want a med student with perfect hair and a wine cellar. 'Ooh, look at us! We're pre-engaged! He gave me his promise ring and someday we'll get married and adopt an orphan from Zimbabwe and name him Aiden!'"

"Are you done?"

"Plus what would the rest of the Thumper family think?"

"My parents are not Bible thumpers!"

"They sure had it in for me."

"Right."

"I saw them. The way they looked at me when I met them? Tell me they weren't judging me."

"Maybe you deserve to be judged a little."

He flinches like I've punched him. I want to take it all back, tell him there's a monster snarling in my throat right now and he'll say anything, anything to keep Abel away from me.

He steps close. I feel his breath feather my forehead. He touches his finger to the tip of my chin and tilts my face to his.

"I get it," he says. "I'm a sinner. Is that right?"

"No—"

"You're just like them. Just like your parents. You hate yourself, don't you?" His fingers brush the side of my face, skate the curve of my jawline. "Or do you just hate me?"

"I didn't mean it. I was just—"

"See, I knew something was off. Right? When you said you used to be an altar boy, I was like 'how does he not have issues?'" He claps my shoulders. "Stellar job pretending, young man. *Very* convincing pantomime of sanity. I was fooled."

"Abel."

"Like, I can't even be mad. You know? I just feel sorry for you."

I wriggle away, speed-walk for the Sunseeker.

"Hey!" he calls. "Brandon!"

I walk faster.

"There's no Zander, is there?"

He knows. *He knows.* I confirm it when I stop too short in front of the Sunseeker steps, as if the labyrinth monster from Episode 3-8 just reared up in front of me and peeled its black lips back from eight dripping fangs.

"Oh my God," he says. "It's true."

Sweat prickles my neck. My stomach rethinks the lattes.

"I thought all those stories you told me sounded like bullshit but you know, I was like, ehh, his first love, you always remember it in such glowing terms and all. God, everything makes sense now!"

"Shut up."

"That's why you never had me over. Your stupid graduation party—that wasn't family-only, right? You were just too chickenshit to invite me."

"Abel—"

"What a coward. Unbelievable. You're a virgin, right?"

My fists curl up.

"What is it? Do you like, see Jesus weeping on the cross when some guy tries to kiss you?"

"Stop talking."

"What about when you fap? You're not supposed to do that either, right? Do you have to flagellate yourself? Wear a hairshirt to bed? I bet you confess your—"

My hands crash into his chest and he staggers two steps backwards. This weird strangled sound punches out of him and he tugs down his t-shirt, gasping in a breath.

"What're you *doing*?"

Crazy. He's staring like I'm crazy. My palms smack his shoulders this time.

"Oh God, you're ridiculous!" He catches both my wrists. "You're seriously going to fight me?"

I yank free, answer him with another shove.

"Great." He's laughing. He shoves me back a little. "Do it! Get it all out, baby. Maybe then you'll—"

I don't hear the rest. I run right at him, ramming him

with my whole upper body until his legs give out and we're falling together and when his back hits the pavement it sends a rude jolt through my body: *oh God I'm on top of him what do I do? How do I fight?* I've only seen it on TV. I don't want to punch him, Dad says one punch can kill someone if you know the right spot and I don't but what if I hit it by accident? Abel lets out this nasty snicker then, like I'm some pathetic little kid, and my whole body lights up with rage and I feel my hand shoot out and Abel grabs his face, twisting away from me.

"Owww!" He shouts at the pavement. "Son of a bitch!"

My hand tingles. Blood trickles between his fingers.

"You slapped my *nose*, dipwad!"

"I—"

I made someone bleed.

"Son of a *bitch*!"

He kicks my leg with his heavy boot, hard. I kick him back. He lunges at me and we roll over and over, scratching and pulling, a cartoon cloud of elbows and hands and knees. He won't give in and neither will I so we scuffle like that on the pavement until we hear the Sunseeker door swing open somewhere behind us, and Bec yells:

"Guys. GUYS."

I roll off him. He shoves me once more. I spit out gravel.

"What're you *doing*?" Bec says.

"Nothing," he says.

"Nothing," I say.

We glare at each other.

Bec studies us, shaking her head. She's changed: cutoffs and a red soccer shirt. She sits down on the bottom step and crosses her legs sloooowly, like she's teaching a preschool class how it's done.

"In case you're interested," she says, "I know what that

Hell Bells thing is."

The fight blips out of my head. We scramble over, attack her with *what* and *how*.

"Dave and I did some research after dinner. He was really sweet and concerned, Brandon, so I think you can cross him off the America's Most Wanted list." She takes out her phone, starts navigating. "Membership's closed right now. I had to write to this hey_mamacita woman to join. I convinced her I had inside information on you. My icon's your senior picture, Brandon; do you think that's too on the nose?"

"Bec," I say.

"Yes, Brandon."

"Tell us."

Her eyes flick across the little screen. "What would you like to know?"

"Are they just hating?" says Abel. "Or are they like, actively plotting?"

"Neither, you idiots."

She holds the phone out to face us. I see the Gothic header first—THE CHURCH OF ABANDON—and then a tagline that says *"Because love is like the Hell Bells: it comes when you least expect it."* Between the header and tagline is a doctored screencap from one of our first vlog posts. Abel's hand is on my shoulder and we're gazing at each other, halos bursting saintlike from our heads and a blue heart blinking between us.

"They're shipping you."

12»

BEC POURS US SOME TEA and leaves us alone. We sit at the Sunseeker table with Abel's laptop, twin plumes of steam curling from our Grand Canyon mugs.

There are seventeen members. Sixty-five fics. Dissections of every single one of our vlog posts, starting with the very first one when I joked about the sandstorm CGI in Episode 4-05 and Abel "lovingly" punched my shoulder.

The most recent post is by a_rose_knows. She has a photo of herself as her icon. We recognize her right away from the coffee shop. The tinfoil Xaarg hat, the pink-rimmed glasses.

"A freaking spy," Abel breathes. "Good. Lord."

The post says:

Ahem. Fellow Abandon Shippers:
HELL BELLS IN ATLANTA.
SPOTTED ~AND~ DOCUMENTED IN COFFEEHOUSE!!!!!
Ear-flicking. Whispering. Sharing of snickerdoodles.
FULL-ON LIP-TO-EAR CONTACT.

[clicky here for photographic evidence!!]

"I might *actually* die," says Abel.

"Click it," I tell him.

The photos under the cut aren't the posed ones Annie took. They must've snapped these from across the room with some kind of evil zoom lens that incriminates the innocent. In photo #1 Abel's talking to me with his arm

119

draped across the sofa back, leaning closer than I remember. In #2 he's passing me the snickerdoodle half, and our fingers are brushing each other slightly. Then there's #3, where—*what?*—I'm making a weird cupping gesture with both my hands. The last one contains the most damning piece of evidence: Abel's leaning in and murmuring to me, probably about Kade or the stupid cave scene, and the angle makes it look like his lips are on my ear. Like, *nibbling* it or something. To underscore the significance of this imaginary gesture, a_rose_knows has blown up that part of the picture and circled my pixelated ear in red. This has made all the other usernames dementedly happy.

doomerang: omg you guys. I CAN'T EVEN.

amity crashful: rosey you are a heroic stalker, please have my babies

retro robot: They are flawless. That is all.

sadparadise: MY BRAIN JUST LEGIT EXPLODED

whispering!sage: snickerdoodles. the official cookie of us.

thanks4caring: lol @ brandon's "cupping hands." like, "abel baby, back yo ass up into these"

sadparadise: can you blame him? DAT ASS.

lone detective: Question: Is Brandon, in fact, wearing Abel's shirt?

a_rose_knows: Yes, it looks that way, but I can't confirm 100%. all I can say is, the convo they were having? INTENSE. You could tell.

doomerang: Rosey what were they doing when they

left??

a_rose_knows: They looked close. I mean, Abel held the door for him and kind of put his hand on his back a little. Abel totally smells like cinnamon. Also? Brandon at one point said "we're just friends—RIGHT NOW."

sadparadise: OMG "RIGHT NOW."

retro robot: right now right now right now right nowwwwww <3

thanks4caring: mamacita? where is our fearless leader??

hey_mamacita: JESUS HORATIO CHRIST ON A MOTOR-BIKE WITH A DIME-STORE UKULELE AND A RASPBERRY BERET, CAN YOU BELIEVE THIS UNBEARABLE WONDERFUL MADNESS???? ugh, rosey, you are queen of everything. miraculous pics of our boys; they look so effing precious I could eat them both like tiny perfect gingerbread men. BRB, writing fic all night! CURSE YOU.

"Click off." My mouth is dry. "I can't—"
"Let's read the manifesto."
Abel's face is pink. I've never seen him blush. Through the fingers over his face, I think he might be smiling a little.
"What manifesto?"
"There was a link on the main page—here. Oh. God."
There's a manip. Of course there is. I've seen them all over the Cadsim fanjournal—horrible fakes of Cadmus and Sim kissing, holding hands, cradling adopted alien babies. This one is like, *intergalactically* worse. They've shopped my head onto Sim's body and Abel's head onto Cadmus's, smushed our hands together, and stuck us on top of a wedding cake. ABANDON is scrawled on the side in blue icing.

121

"The hell is 'abandon'?" I say.

Abel smirks. "Our portmanteau."

I lay my head on the desk.

"Better than 'Brabel,' no?"

"Don't talk to me."

"It's just getting good, though."

THE MANIFESTO OF ABANDON
by hey_mamacita

"True Love is kinda like Xaarg's Hell Bells—it comes when you least expect it, and it torments you until you give in!"—Abel McNaughton, from recap of *Castaway Planet*, Episode 4-16

once upon a time there were two boys with a vlog. the cute short one loved an android, and the cute tall one loved a space captain. the boys also loved each other in a completely repressed and thoroughly maddening kind of way, but instead of admitting it and having lots of blazing hot toe-curling bonobo monkey sex, they spent all their time bitching about Cadsim shippers and how the android and the space captain should never ever get together, like, JESUS MARY AND JOSEPH ON A UNICYCLE WITH X-RAY SPEX AND SARAN WRAP, could you boys be any more transparent??

anyway. the logical outcome of this delicious little story should be abundantly obvious to anyone with an internet connection and a basic knowledge of how romantic comedies work, but until abel smartens up and brandon gets over his tragic religious paranoia as detailed in his sister natalie's awesome but defunct blog (screencaps <u>here</u>!), we at the abandon community are fully committed to—*ahem!*—lubing things up. we send good vibes. we catalog Hell Bells (i.e., indicators of true love). we conduct official events such as our BellFic Challenge (BFC), where NC-17 plots thicken biweekly. and we firmly believe that when the scales fall from their eyes and all obstacles are removed, these boys will GET MARRIED IN SOME WINDSWEPT MOUNTAINTOP PARADISE and roses and unicorns will spontaneously generate and glitter will rain from the clouds and God herself will smile a giant rainbow across the heavens and say "ohh, yeah, baby. It. Is. GOOD."

Abel pushes his chair back. Ten seconds click by on the wall clock.

"Holy cow," he says.

I can't talk.

"I don't even remember saying that Hell Bells line," Abel says. "Did you know your sister had a blog?"

I shake my head.

"Go ahead," I say. "Click the link."

"Are you sure?"

My hands make a *whatever* gesture.

He hesitates, but he clicks the screencap link. This page pops up with a blog entry titled *"Okay, so my little bro FINALLY came out..."* I peek at it through my fingers. It's Natalie, no question. Her username is Vashta and she makes halfhearted stabs at concealing identities—"B" for me, "Father X" for Father Mike—but the story's all there. How my mom let the leftover meatloaf sit on the counter and spoil that night. How my dad kept saying *but how can you be sure*, as if it was a diagnosis that needed a second opinion. How I sat on Nat's bed and cried about the sermon

Father Mike had given two weeks earlier, the one where he held up a picture of Jesus, Mary, and Joseph and gently explained the "true definition of family." *Poor little nerdling,* Nat wrote. *I nagged him into this coming-out drama and maybe he wasn't ready. He was a Father X fanboy as a kid and now he's so terrified of his real self I just want to smack him. I think it's his destiny to be fucked up his whole entire life unless he gets serious help.*

I go lie down on the couch. I think of Sim on the Henchmen's operating table, his chest pried open and his cold organs clicking and whirring out of sync. Abel takes another minute with Nat's blog entry, and then he comes over and kneels down beside me.

He's quiet for a minute. Then he reaches out and pats my hand.

I don't know what about that sets me off. It's kind of a neutral gesture, something Sim would do, and maybe that's part of it. Or maybe it's just that it's so unlike Abel, or maybe my nerves are rubbed raw right now and any little touch would have done this, make my sore eyes fill up and spill over.

"It's okay." He squeezes my hand. "Seriously."

I drape my arm over my eyes.

And I tell him everything.

I tell him about Father Mike. I tell him about *Put on the Brakes!,* my three awkward months trying to date Bec, my parents and the sad looks they shoot me when they think I won't notice. I even tell him about the Ryan Dervitz kiss and the Dairy Queen freakout. When I lift my arm off my eyes I see him watching me like I'm some TV show about one-legged orphans with Olympic dreams, and it kind of makes me want to smack him but it feels so good to tell him that I keep going and going until the cut on his lip opens up again, and I remember what happened outside.

He grabs three tissues from the box on the desk. One for his lip, two for me.

"I'm so sorry," I whisper.

"Just forget it."

"What I said—"

"Forget it, Brandon. All that shit in your head—"

"I'm used to it."

"And I'm such an idiot, I kept shoving boys at you."

"Only two."

He glances over his shoulder, as if someone's watching at the window.

"So..." He lowers his voice to a stage whisper. "Do they really tell you all that?"

"All what?"

"Like, you have a 'special calling' to be celibate?"

"Pretty much."

"'Cause if you believe that you should totally talk to my dad's friend Mitch, he's this Unitarian minister or whatever and he's on his third husband so maybe he can help you—"

"I don't believe it. Not anymore." I sigh and stick my hands in my hair. There's no way I can explain this logically. "It's just hard to turn it off."

"Why?"

I pick at the hem of my shorts. "There's still this little part of you that's like 'what if they're right?' What if there is a hell and you're like gambling with eternity just because you want a boyfriend, so you get terrified and think it's not worth it, I'll suck it up and be alone forever, but then on the other hand what if it turns out there is no God or he's up there shaking his head because people keep twisting the Bible around, and you wasted your life being alone and miserable for *nothing*, and then—" I'm babbling like a freak. "Stuff like that. You know."

Abel lifts the tissue off his lip and runs his thumb over the splotch of blood. "That Father Mike guy never...like, *tried* anything with you, did he?"

"No! No. Never. He just has really specific ideas about God."

"You believe in God?"

"I'm...confused."

"That wasn't my question."

"I left my church."

"So? You can believe in God without church. I do."

I blink at him. I would not be more surprised if David Darras pulled up in a white limo with two dozen blue roses and begged me to elope with him. I've consistently shut up about religion around Abel; he talks so much crap about it I just assumed he was like Bec. "You do?"

"I believe in *something*, yeah. I just think the world's too complicated and amazing not to." He's folding the tissue into a lopsided rose. "I mean, I don't believe in a big bearded badass on a cloud throne, but I can buy a loving creative higher power that wants everyone to be happy. Something that roots for us. Like, the anti-Xaarg."

I shake my head. "I have no idea how to think that way."

"Why not?" He lobs the tissue rose at me. "I mean, if no one knows for sure what God's like, then why don't you just believe the people who think he's all rainbows and sunshine and loves you no matter what?"

"Because it's too easy."

His eyebrows steeple.

"Suffering's supposed to be valuable." Abel opens his mouth but I cut him off. "I'm just saying. That's what they teach you. They tell you when you suffer you share in the passion of Jesus and so God doesn't save us from suffering because..." I glance up at him and let out a long sigh. "Forget it."

Abel leans forward, elbows on knees. Probably trying to gauge the depth of my mental disturbance, so he'll know how far to sit from me.

"I totally want to hug you," he says.

"You do?"

"We wouldn't piss off Worst-Case-Scenario-Angry-God if we hugged, right?"

"Nope." I gulp. "Probably—"

His arms are around me before I can finish. He still smells like popcorn and cotton candy and he feels so warm it's like diving under an electric blanket after midnight Mass on Christmas Eve. I try to melt into the hug, the way Cadmus and Sim are always melting into hugs in Cadsim fics, but my nose is running and leaving horrifying wet spots on his army-green t-shirt and I'm positive I smell like sweat—not the clean I've-been-working-out kind but the toxic nervous kind I specialize in. It figures. My first lingering hug from a cute guy, and I'm too screwed up to enjoy it.

"God..." I murmur.

"I know. I'm a great hugger."

I pull back, hold him by the shoulders. "Abel."

"Brandon."

I take a deep breath. "I am so *fucking* ready to be normal."

"Fun normal or boring normal?"

"Fun normal."

"Congratulations. How can I help?"

I just look at him. My lips vibrate from spitting out the f-word. He freezes in the Empathy Position, head cocked and one hand resting on my knee, like an action figure of a perfect boyfriend. I know exactly what I want. To be able to hug him over and over again, to sling my arm around his waist in public, to feel his warm reassuring hand around mine on a regular basis, without any real sex stuff ever getting in the way. I know that's about as realistic as Cadsim fic.

And then a second later, I know how to make it happen.

I sit back down at the desk, in front of the laptop screen with its orderly selection of Brandon/Abel make-out fantasies. Plastic Sim and Plastic Cadmus lie flat on their backs in a scatter of cinnamon jellybeans, like they've both been struck dead from secondhand embarrassment. I stand them back up. Scroll through the fic titles. "Whispers of All Our Tomorrows." "Anatomy of a Saturday." "How to Repair a Mechanical Heart."

"Uh, Brandon...?"

"Hm."

"What are you thinking?"

I tap the wedding cake manip. I blurt it before I lose nerve.

"You want to have some fun," I say, "with the Church of Abandon?"

A complicated smile flits across his face. I get a nervous thrill, like when Cadmus got Sim to jump into the Red River with him to escape the Henchmen. *C'mon, Tin Man,* he'd shouted above the wind, the two of them clutching arms on the cliff like a romance-novel cover. *You haven't lived till you've done something really stupid!*

Not the best philosophy, bud, says Father Mike.

Shut up, I tell him simply, and turn back to Abel.

"What'd you have in mind?" he says.

CastieCon #3
San Antonio, Texas

13»

ABEL AND I SIT SIDE BY SIDE on the concrete edge of our campground pool, dipping our feet in. He is shirtless. Leaning back on both arms, he holds his pale soft stomach taut, trying to forge a six-pack. He grins at the fake hickey on my neck, courtesy of some blue and purple eyeshadow we bought on the road in an Alabama dollar store. I held still while Abel brushed it on, his breath tickling my cheek and smelling of cinnamon. It was safe, and incredibly fun.

The San Antonio sun breathes biblical heat on us. My *Castaway Planet* shirt roasts on my back and the cool clear water sparkles temptation as I swirl my toes through it. I want to jump in, all the way in, but there's something we need to do first.

"You sure about this?" Abel murmurs.

I nod. "Totally."

"You don't want to take your shirt off? They'd flip."

I cringe. "I'm really pale..."

"That's fine. Yeah. You're a man of mystery. I might put my hand on your knee, is that cool?"

"My leg is your leg."

Bec clears her throat. "Can we get this over with?" She's bobbing chest-deep in the water with her camera, shivering a little.

"Sorry," says Abel. "Rebecca, what do you think? Is my hand on his knee too much?"

"Don't pull me into this. I'm just the cameraperson."

Abel nods. "We'll play it by ear. See what happens."

"Fantastic." She rolls her eyes and hits record.

"*Salut,* dear Casties!" Abel says. "My partner and I are coming at you poolside from the, ah, *Longhorn* Campground in San Antonio, where we have been staying in all our carefree, half-nude glory for three days."

"Three lonnnng, *hot* days."

"They have been especially *hot*, haven't they, Bran?"

"Scorching."

"Miss Rebecca, by the way, is looking stunning today in her bangin' new halter bikini."

"It's just a two-piece."

"Whatever. Dave, if you're watching, it was between this one and some striped tankini disaster. You'll thank me when you see her in Long Beach."

I break in, as scripted. "Ahem."

Abel's like, "Ye-es?"

"You have yet to comment on my new swim trunks."

"I think that's best reserved for a..." He leans in, stage-whispers. "*Private* moment, don't you?"

I giggle; I can't help it. "If you say so."

"Aaanyway, guys: Two o'clock today, Q&A with Augie Manners, who for the past four seasons has infused the character of Dutch Jones with a complex blend of angst, dopey hotness, and nine other exotic spices."

"Hmf."

"Yes, dear? What is it?"

I feign a pout. "If you love him so much, why don't you marry him?"

"Mm-mm. Not my type."

"No? Who is your type?"

"I think you know, Brandon." He rests a hand on my knee. A tiny spark dances up my thigh. "I think. You. Know."

***

131

The second Bec snaps the camera shut, Abel grabs my elbow and hauls us both underwater. The blue shock of cold hits me hard—*I'm not ready*—but then I open my eyes and he's making this face that makes me forget, crossing his eyes and puffing out his cheeks. His white hair billows around his face like the manes on Bec's old Rainbow Ponies when we'd take them in her mom's pool. For a long time we stay like that, in a safe underworld where our bodies stay light and dreamy. Five seconds. Ten seconds.

We come up laughing.

"*'Best reserved for a private moment'*?" I splash him.

"Did I go too far?"

"No! It was brilliant."

"Um, so..."

"What?"

Abel bats his eyes. *"Why don't you marry him?"*

"Ugh! I'm a horrible flirter."

"No, no, no. You've gotten loads better since Saturday."

"Really?"

"When you said *scorching?*" He taps his heart, smirking. "I felt it right here."

Bec bobs by on a clear inflatable raft. She looks all patriotic: navy blue bikini, white belly, sunburn on her round freckled shoulders. She peers at us over cat's-eye shades.

"You guys," she tsks, "are mean."

Abel's eyes go wide and innocent. "How are we mean? It's what they want!"

"But it's not real."

"So? They love fiction. Right, Brandon?"

"They do seem to enjoy it."

He swims close to me, his chin skimming the water.

"What's your favorite fic?"

I peel my wet shirt away from my chest and pretend to think. I have a real answer to that question, but I can't get into that with Abel. As far as he knows, the Abandon fic we've been reading for the past five days has been 100% pure comedy, something to giggle over in greasy diners and campgrounds while Plastic Sim and Plastic Cadmus perch on opposite corners of the laptop, watching us blush and bump elbows.

"I like doomerang's stuff. And sadparadise. The *Castaway Planet* crossovers," I lie.

"Yeah? Not a fan, actually."

"How come?"

"They're like, good writers." He makes a *blech* face. "Well-written fanfic is *no* fun whatsoever. I looooove thanks4caring's high-school-angst."

"'The Locker Said FAG?'"

"OMG. The ultimate." We're bobbing in a circle now. *"Brandon's sea-blue eyes exploded into desolate tears."*

I grin. *"He felt his tater tots rise up threateningly in his throat."*

"He raced breathlessly—Breathlessly?"

"I think."

"—down the school hallway and stumbled falteringly into the men's room to call the one and only person who would ever understand him fully:" He strikes a pose. *"Abel!"*

"The next part is best."

"What part?"

"What the men's room smells like."

"Adverbs?"

"No."

"I'm blanking."

"Urine and boys."

"Urine and boys!" He snaps his fingers. "Straight girls

really do their research, no?"

"You don't read the NC-17 ones, do you?"

"Wouldn't you like to know."

"Oh, jeez."

He clasps his heart. *"Abel's piercing green eyes danced impishly as he unbuckled Brandon's—"*

"Stop!"

"His eyes roved hungrily over the smaller boy's body..."

I plug my ears and *la-la-laaa.*

"...and he thought, For such a short boy, he certainly had a long—"

"Oh my God!"

I heave a shelf of water his way and he yelps and pulls me under again. I used to hate when I was a kid and things would get rough at the pool—the big Tortelli boys sneak-attacking in the deep end, yanking us down by our feet like Jaws and holding us under until we kicked and flailed. But with Abel it's different. He lets me push back, only touches my safe parts—my elbow, my shoulder. And way before things get scary, he hooks my wrist gently and pulls us both up to the surface.

We stand there, chest-deep, smiling and shivering. The air is full of happy smells: snack-stand lemonade, soft pretzels, pina colada sunscreen. I almost strip my wet t-shirt off. Right now, right this second, if we were on Castaway Planet and Abel said *hey, let's check out this crystal spider cave*, I think I'd go with him. I'd be scared, but I'd go.

"Abel," I say.

"Yes, my pseudo-darling."

I grin. I'm brave as ten Cadmuses. "Never had so much fun," I say. "With anyone."

He looks down, swirls a finger in the water. *"Pas de quoi,* cutie."

"—Okay, you horndogs." Bec's standing on the lip of

the pool, wiggling into her polka-dot flip-flops. "You want to eat something before the Q&A?"

Abel's face gets kid-on-Christmas bright. "The Double T?"

"I think the lunch special's fried meatloaf."

"Sold." Abel grabs the ladder and hoists himself out of the pool. There's all kinds of dripping and glistening going on. I try not to look. "You in, Bran?"

I think it over. On one hand, it's been great this week; flirting lightly and safely for the cameras, hanging out and playing five thousand games of WordWhap with a cute nonthreatening guy who knows how screwed up I am and still wants to be my friend. On the other, there's something I desperately have to do back at the Sunseeker, and I need to be alone.

"Bring me back some cheese fries," I tell them.

***

I pull down the Sunseeker shades. Lock the door.

Bec gave me the camera before they left, so I take a second to upload our poolside escapade to Screw Your Sensors. While it's loading, my phone goes off. HOME CALLING. I pick it up, all relaxed and friendly. I *wow-mm-hmm* politely through the latest on the new-parish-hall saga and update Dad dutifully on my RV maintenance. Yes, I cleaned the fresh water tank, sanitized the hose.

When I hang up, I go straight to the Church of Abandon.

I know what's going to happen there in the next ten minutes. Someone will link to our new post, and there'll be OMGs and trembling-Spongebob gifs and dissections and debates over every little thing, from the sincerity of Abel's *dear* to the way my eyes lingered on his wet swim trunks. Abel and I will soak it up later, and laugh.

Right now I have a new chapter to read.

It's normal to feel tempted, Father Mike tsks. ***Just distract yourself with other things. Get out in the sunshine and go for a walk...***

My fingers hover over the keyboard. Plastic Sim stares at me, tipped over on Abel's box of Ho-Hos. I straighten his legs and stand him up in my new *Castaway Planet* mug, beside Plastic Cadmus.

Then I find hey_mamacita's latest post and click her name.

Her personal fic journal pops up. I click User Info, just to see her photo again. Nose ring, thick dark dreadlocks, bold Celtic-cross neck tattoo; everything says *I'm brave.* She's standing in front of the neon-green Virgin Mary statue in her overgrown front yard, opening her scruffy leather jacket and showing off what's underneath: a tight tattered t-shirt, its big red sequined heart shooting off tiny light beams like a superhero insignia.

The bio underneath is just one line:

SENT BY GOD HERSELF to make Abandon happen.

I'm not dumb enough to think that's likely. I mean, last year when Aunt Meg met a guy in the Target returns line and Mom said "God made that sweater too small for a reason," I rolled my eyes so hard I think I sprained an optic nerve. If God exists, there's no way he bothers with matchmaking.

It's eerie, though. Right?

I keep asking for signs. And here she is. Someone who prays to a neon Virgin Mary and lives her whole life in all-caps and thinks God and my happiness go together just fine. I don't think she was sent. Not in a literal Biblical-prophet way. But the fact that hey_mamacita a.) exists and b.) found me? It just seems like some power somewhere in the universe is maybe on my side.

I click the fic tab. Right up top I see the little green "NEW CHAPTER!" burst and my heart jogs faster. Most of the other Abandon girls write us into the *Castaway Planet* universe—I'm an android, Abel's a studly ensign—or concoct these high-school melodramas where I get a beatdown from some closeted quarterback and end up in the ER and then Abel brings me a giant teddy bear and we do it in my hospital bed. hey_mamacita is the only one writing her vision of this trip we're on, a crazy, sprawling fourteen-chapter epic called "How to Repair a Mechanical Heart."

I grab a can of BBQ chips from the food bin, pop the top, and read.

Just as their lips were about to finally touch with a lovely trembling sweetness, a pair of headlights sliced across the parking lot and locked on the two boys like a tractor beam. They saw the black Cadillac creep toward them in the dark with sinister sharklike intensity, the blood-red rosary swinging from the rearview and the license plate blaring the grim heavy sledgehammer words Brandon could never forget: I-JUDGE.

The car shuddered to a stop.

"Get in the RV, Brandon," Abel murmured.

Brandon shook his head. "I won't," he replied, raking up all his courage. "This is my fight, too. I know that now."

Out of the shadows clacked the heavy black boots of Father X, his craggy face glowering with malevolence and his silver crucifix clutched in a fist that was ancient and bony but could still crack a sinner's arm in half. His grease-slick hair swung like blades across his face. He crushed his cigarette out on the inside of his palm and his mouth cracked open in a twisted smile that showed his gray and rotting feral teeth and prickled the hairs on Brandon's neck. He LIKED THE PAIN. That much was clear. Brandon thought, God, that must be why he wants us all to hurt.

"So this is where you go to practice your DEPRAVED FORNICATIONS," Father X snarled, pointing the cross at them. His red eyes glowed in the blackness and the cross spat hot electric bolts of silver light. "In the NAME OF HEAVEN, I command you, Brandon Page, to cease this charade of sin and misery! Return at once to the blessed desolation of the chaste and celibate life God created you to lead!"

Brandon, in reply, brandished a dagger. It was a letter opener from the CastieCon souvenir stand, but Father X didn't have to know that. He strode up to Father X like a cowboy at high noon and—

I crack up laughing. I always do when I read her fic, but I mean it as a compliment. The more awesomely campy it is, the better I feel. I grab a sharp-tipped pencil from the Cape May mug on the desk; practice brandishing and pointing it.

"It ends here," Brandon rasped. "All my life I've been your robot. Wind me up and my heart has done your will. Believe this, sacrifice that. Accept that God created you to be alone. Tick tick tick, yes master, I believe. Well, guess what? I'm done. I met someone who fixed my heart. And you can't do anything about it."

He slipped his warm hand into Abel's. The next thing he heard was—

Sirens.

Sirens outside, off to the west, straight in the direction of the Double T. I run to the window, scissor open the blinds with two fingers. I picture Abel on a stretcher. Blood on a white sheet. A crumpled fender, some girl sobbing *God, I never even saw him* while someone's cell shrills over and over, sad and steady and unanswered.

It's mine. My phone. It vibrates across the desk and I catch it just before it goes over. *Father Mike?* The weird thought clutches me. Just for a second. Then I pick up and hear:

"OMG MY VAG IS ON FIRE!"

I giggle. *"What?"*

"Sweet merciful baby Moses, San Antonio is the city of *magical love witchcraft!"* A big knot loosens inside me. I drop back down in the desk chair. I picture Abel reading off his phone in a corner booth while Bec snort-laughs and stirs her iced tea. *"I legit peed myself you guys and my heart went supernova and how do these boys even exist??"*

"I take it they liked our pool video?"

"You haven't *checked*?"

I glance at the screen. "Been busy."

"doomerang already coughed up a flashfic called 'I Think You Know.'"

"Can't wait."

"amity crashful counted how many times we've called each other 'baby' this week—did you know we hit 15 already?"

"Impressive." I lick BBQ dust off my fingers. "We must be in love."

"Then Miss Maxima and a couple of her minions came over from the Cadsim fanjournal to bitch about how disgusting and intrusive real-person shipping is, and they all got banned, it was hilarious...OH! And."

"Ye-es?"

"There's a San Antonio spy now."

"Who?"

"retro robot. I love her! She wrote that one where we're nineteenth-century vampire hunters? She's driving all the way from Tulsa so we *have* to ramp it up at the Augie Manners Q&A."

"Okay."

"I'm warning you now: There might have to be back-rubbing."

"Maybe even a public hug."

He gasps. "I'm shocked, Tin Man. Shocked. What's next?"

"Depraved fornications."

"You know what?"

"What?"

"I like this new Brandon."

I blow crumbs off the keyboard and scroll up to the start of hey_mamacita's chapter, so I can read it all over again.

"Me too," I say.

14»

AUGIE MANNERS PLAYS THE lovable stoner every single time he's onscreen—from *Castaway Planet* to those old burger commercials where his catchphrase was "Dude, can I have your pickle?" When he scuffs onstage for his Q&A there are zero surprises. Surf-shop t-shirt, sleepy smile, dumb fisherman hat hiding raggedy red-blond hair. His cargo pants look slept in and his weird rope sandals are almost certainly made of hemp. If he was in a comic strip, squiggly lines of visible weed fumes would follow him everywhere.

He throws his arms wide open. "Hel-loooooooo San Antonio!"

Cheers and wolf-whistles from the girls. Abel and I shoot we've-got-a-secret looks at each other.

"Wooooo! Yeah! Dutchie is in *la casa,* so let the party commence!" Augie Manners lifts his arms above his head and cracks his knuckles one by one, just like he does on the show. There's a firefly-flash of cameras. "Oh, wow, you guys—seriously, are you *Castaway Planet* fans, for real? I was expecting geeks out the yin-yang but you guys are *hot.* Lorda-mercy!"

He tosses his dirty hat in the crowd and starts in on some story about a Riverwalk bar that has eighty-six kinds of beer, and I have to smile a little. I hated the Dutch Jones character for the first half of Season 1 when he was just crude comic relief, but he got pretty interesting with the OCD and the photographic memory and the talent for peacemaking, which kind of came out of nowhere but somehow made perfect sense.

I can't focus on him for the first five or six questions, though. Because Abel is leaning close to me, whispering *Castaway Planet* lines in my ear so it looks like we've got secrets.

"You ready to take it a teeny bit further?" he murmurs. Some girl just asked Manners about that episode where Xaarg makes Dutchie walk on his hands the whole time. He's eagerly reenacting, his hemp sandals waggling in the air.

"Yeah," I whisper back.

"You sure? No imminent freakouts?"

"All clear."

"You should know the risks ahead of time."

"Of what?"

He sighs. "My sexual charisma."

"Give me the disclaimers."

"Well, side effects may include dry mouth, nausea, dizziness, blood clots, cardiac arrhythmia, dia-bee-tus—"

"Only in people over fifty. I heard."

He narrows his eyes. "Would I wound you like that?"

"You might."

"That's it. I'm going to whisper something highly provocative."

I bump him with my hip. "Go ahead."

"It may reorder your entire universe."

"I'm ready."

He touches his lips to the rim of my ear. "Duuude. Can I have your pickle?"

I snort. I can't help it.

"Shh!" he hisses. "Don't laugh!"

"Don't make me."

"You think retro robot saw?"

"I don't know." I crane my neck.

"Zzt! You'll make her suspicious." He wraps an arm

around my shoulders and murmurs, "Just enjoy my attentions while you can."

"Oh, so this is a privilege?"

"I'll have you know I'm in high demand."

"Right, right." I flick his hair. "Who wouldn't love the cockatoo version of Laurence Olivier?"

He giggles and pulls me closer. I tense automatically, but then I let myself relax, muscle by muscle. It's nice. Really nice.

"Oh by the way, guys and dolls—I brought a present for whoever's got the best question today." Augie Manners holds up this grubby burlap hippie sack with a happy face embroidered on it. "So lemme hear from someone sexy now—yeah! You in the Xaarg shirt."

A chubby guy with a black samurai knot lowers his question paddle. "Yes, in your opinion, are the writers purposefully ratcheting up the tension between Cadmus and Xaarg as a commentary on the futility of prayer in the face of an indifferent god, or is the conflict actually going somewhere?"

I don't hear the answer. Abel's hand has slowly migrated down my back and now it's in this scary normal teenage-boyfriend place, fingertips tucked in my back pocket. He leaves it there for one more question and then two more, adding little whispers in my ear about retro robot and great photo ops while the stubborn enemy part of my brain tries to talk my body into freaking out.

My hands stay dry. I slip one into the slim back pocket of his dark jeans.

Brandon, who are you? Father Mike, but faded now. *I don't recognize you, bud.*

hey_mamacita answers for me: *I'm your worst nightmare, Brandon said, waving the dagger like an outlaw. I am a VIGILANTE OF LOVE.*

Father Mike tries to say something else, but I paper right over his face with hey_mamacita's silly Father X— the craggy sunken cheeks, the feral teeth. A fun villain, the kind that's good for cheap scares and cheaper Halloween costumes, powerless once the book is closed or the TV's switched off.

He keeps quiet.

A giddy laugh throbs in the back of my throat. It's like Episode 2-14, the scene where Sim first got his evolution chip. His skin went transparent; all his nerve endings crackled with white-hot sparks and his silver eyes sizzled into tropical blue and he threw his head back and let out a full-body wail I used to think was all about pain, but now I know better.

I curl an arm around Abel's waist.

"Let me ask the question."

My voice doesn't sound like mine. He startles.

"What?

"The question. I'll ask Manners."

"You want to?"

"I do."

Abel whistles. "Look at you, all bold and brazen."

I grab the question paddle and wave it around. Augie Manners calls on me right away. He locks eyes with me when I ask the question about the cave episode, and I'm not even nervous—it's as easy as a vocal warmup with the Timbrewolves, the lip trills and scales I can do in my sleep.

"Ooh, Cadmus and Sim." Augie Manners rubs his hands together. "The bazillion dollar question. Right?"

Girly cheers clash with some baritone *boos*. Abel gazes at the side of my face and smooths a wisp of hair off my forehead. I catch an eyeroll from Bec. She looks away fast, goes back to her camera.

"I think," says Manners, "that humble ole me is going to kick that question to the lovely and *very* intuitive ladies here in the audience. Should I?"

"Cheater," Abel grouses, but he's grinning.

More cheers; an *awwwww yeah* that was probably louder than the shouter intended. Augie Manners steps up to the lip of the stage and hunches down, hands on thighs.

"A'ight, ready? Ladies who think Cadmus and Sim *didn't* do the ol' *coitus androidicus* in the crystal spider cave, lemme hear you put your hands together."

A sprinkle of claps and a low frat-boy howl.

"Uh-huh. Uh-huh. Now if you think they totally boned, make some noise!"

Full-on eardrum assault.

"Whoa nellie!" Augie Manners shouts, trying to quiet the crowd a little. "I guess that's a yes, guys!"

"Guess so," I say.

"Sounds clear to me," says Abel.

"How 'bout you two guys? What do you think?"

We glance at each other. He set us up perfectly.

"We're...actually not sure yet," Abel fibs.

"Yeah. We're, uh, trying to keep an open mind, right?"

"Absolutely. Cause you know, sometimes you *think* you feel one way—"

"—and then something changes and you realize you might have been totally and completely wrong."

We indulge in some moony eye contact. I hope retro robot's filming; they'll go nuts for this. I see Bec out of the corner of my eye, shaking her head like a mom watching her kids gorge on blueberries despite warnings of tummy-aches and purple fingers.

"That is so true, you guys," Augie Manners says. "So true. Awesome! Okay, any other questions for me before I hit the Alamo?"

Abel pinches me. "Did you see that?" he hisses.

"What?"

"His eyes, like, *lingered* on you!"

"They did not."

"Did too."

I pinch him back. "Maybe it's my *quiet yet forceful magnetism.*"

"Is that from a fic?"

"Yep."

"Whose?"

"No one's. Forget it." It's weird. I can't even say her name.

Onstage, Augie Manners shouts "Know what? You all win!" He opens up his hippie sack and flings a huge handful of *Castaway Planet* trading cards into the crowd, and then another and another till chaos breaks out, everyone squealing and shoving while the silver-backed cards snow down. Abel and I dive right in, trying to get our hands on the good ones: Sim in his charging dock, Cadmus brave and bloody in the Starsetter wreckage.

"Brandon!"

"What?"

He dangles a card from the cave scene.

"Oh God!"

He mimics the Meaningful Look in the photo and makes a wet kissy noise. I flick a card at him sideways. He flicks one back. It nicks my ear. I put up my fists and he yelps and takes off and this is what it feels like to chase a boy, no fear or shame or anything, just the two of us gasping and laughing like kids as we zigzag the ballroom and skid around chairs and run right into the shiny gold badge and foreboding beige shirt of Johnny Law.

Johnny Law is what my dad calls cops, or anyone in a

vageuely coplike uniform. He's probably the only person who uses the term with hushed respect and not irony: *Slow around this bend; Johnny Law hides out there. If I ever get a call from Johnny Law saying you've been drinking...*

"You two," says the security guard. "Hold up."

My stomach knots. Johnny Laws make me nervous, even when I haven't done anything wrong, and even when they're frog-eyed and freckled with a friendly broom of orange bristles right below the nose.

"He started it," Abel says. "He's a terrible influence."

I smack him. "Sorry, sir," I say. "We'll stop running. I guess we got—"

"No no no. That's not it."

"Oh."

"It's Mr. Manners. He'd like to see you backstage." Johnny Law lets out a tiny sigh and loosens his stiff brown tie. "It's, uh. Urgent."

***

The corridor smells like chlorine and coleslaw. We follow Johnny Law past the glassed-in pool and seven or eight closed doors. The change in his pocket jing-jangs like cowboy spurs.

Abel's going *omigod omigod.*

"I know," I whisper.

"My heart's going supernova."

"What do you think he wants?"

"You."

"Really?"

"Maybe."

"He's got a girlfriend."

"He could be bi."

"This is crazy."

147

"Eh. Maybe he's just a fan."

"Of us?"

"We have fans!"

"What, so he sits around in his trailer watching fan vlogs?"

"Maybe he's bored."

"Maybe he ships Abandon."

He shoves my shoulder. I crack up.

"Guys—guys." Johnny Law makes a *simmer* motion. "He asked that the room be kept quiet, okay?"

"Yeah. No problem." Behind his back, Abel gives me an exaggerated shrug, eyes wide and laughing.

The door we go through has a VIP sign taped to it, but the meeting room inside doesn't look too special. There's a bunch of long tables and folding chairs with convention equipment scattered around—stacks of crinkled programs, empty boxes with bubblewrap crumpled beside them. Johnny Law marches us up to a partition of flimsy black curtains. One of the curtains has a paper sign pinned to it: ACTORS LOUNGE. QUIET PLEASE!!

I hold my breath as he nudges the curtain aside. Augie Manners is right there, right in front of me, so close I could take three steps and touch his arm. It's so weird. Usually he's covered with grease from trying to patch up the Starsetter, or he's roasting a sand rat over the crew's campfire, his fingers caked with dirt and blood. Now he's nibbling from a tray of rolled-up deli meats, wearing noise-canceling headphones and reading some book called *Still Life with Woodpecker*.

"Heyyyyy, guys," he says. "Come on into *mi casa* here."

The guard's like, "Should I stay?"

"Naw, they're cool. Right?"

"Definitely," says Abel.

Johnny Law looks us up and down like he expects to

148

see us in a lineup later, but he leaves. When he's out of sight, Abel immediately dorks out:

"Mr. Manners I just want to say we're such huge fans of the show, like since episode one, and I know we have this vlog and we kind of make fun of things a little but for real, just being able to be here and meet you is amazing and we—"

"Awesome, yeah, that's sweet, man." He's looking at me. He steps closer and rests his hand on my upper arm. *Dutch Jones,* I tell myself. *His hand. My arm.*

"Lemme ask you something, okay?"

"Sure."

"It's gonna seem..." He shakes his head. " ...*totally* out of the blue."

"Okay."

"Can I have your shirt?"

"My—"

"Yeah, not the blue button-down thing, that's like J.C. Penney or some shit, right?"

"I don't know..."

"This t-shirt." He opens up my button-down and ogles the tee underneath.

"Ohhhh, yeah. Oh, baby. Ka. Ching."

My starstruck-ness starts to fade; he smells like old socks and this is really pretty goofy. The shirt he's Salivating over is a baggy old Bob Dylan concert tee, and it's not very sexy. The image on front is a foursquare grid— three of the squares hold cartoon outlines of faces, and then the fourth one is filled in with Dylan. There's a rip near the neckline and it's been washed about five thousand times, so I can't imagine what he wants with it.

Manners cracks open a beer. "My mom, right, is this huuuuuge Dylan fan, like she's got a Scottie dog named Zimmy and she makes these giant replicas of his album covers with bottle caps and everything—Beer?"

"No thanks."

He takes a big swig. "—and so this one time in college I took one of her t-shirts, like *that exact shirt*, and I left it at the beach like an effing moron and oh my God you'd think I murdered her dog 'cause she never let me forget it. This is authentic, right?"

"Yeah."

"From the '88 tour or whatever?"

"I guess."

"Where'd you get it? It's super-rare. I've looked *seriously* everywhere!"

"I don't know. My sister got it for my birthday."

"Birthday. Exactly. Mom's birthday's in two days." He claps his hands and rubs them together. "So how much you want for the shirt? Two hundred?"

I glance from Abel to Manners. The character I am in "How to Repair a Mechanical Heart" clicks to life. *Brandon realized that the man looming before him was just a person, not a god. He felt a white streak of power surge through him. He could say anything. Do anything he wanted.*

"It's pretty sentimental, sir." I shrug. "I don't know."

"Two-fifty. And my shirt, here—" He starts peeling off the surf-shop tee, unveiling his pale freckled chest. "You can sell it to some fan or whatever. My sweat's all over it."

I glance at Abel. Vibrating, sucking his lips in.

"Well, that's a generous offer," I say. "But—"

"Your sister would freak, Brandon," Abel tsks. "You know how Natalie gets."

"Mm. You know she just had another breakdown, right?"

"Did she? No! I'm so sorry." He shakes his head. "I

150

thought she'd gotten so much better since the staple gun incident."

Augie Manners gets this shifty, desperate look on his face. "Okay. Okay okay oh-*kay*." He peers outside the curtain, and then he goes, "THREE-fifty, plus my shirt, plus my official Series 1 action figure, still in the box, which I will autograph RIGHT NOW, plus this—" He digs deep in his army-green rucksack and pulls out a wrinkled envelope with a coffee ring and a smudged *Happy Birthday!* on the front. He leans close to me and talks through his teeth. "Keep this on your person and if anyone asks, I didn't give it to you. Okay?"

"Yeah. Sure." I peek inside. Six thin homemade cigarettes rolled in blue paper.

"They're Spaceman Straws. You drink in some serious wisdom with these."

"Huh?"

"You heard me. I'm not responsible for what happens if you decide to partake." He claps me on the shoulder like a grandpa, stuffs the envelope in my shorts pocket. My eyes trace the Big Dipper in his chest freckles. "Just make sure you're someplace safe. *Comprende?*"

***

I don't plan to exit the Actors' Lounge naked from the waist up. It just sort of happens. When we pass Johnny Law he barely lifts an eyebrow, which kind of makes me wonder what kind of deranged stuff a hotel security guard sees on a daily basis. I button my shorts pocket over the joints.

Abel's dying. He's absolutely losing his mind, bouncing all over the corridor like a sheepdog on uppers.

"Ohmygodohmygod," he says. *"Augie Manners gave*

us—"

"Shhhhhh! Don't broadcast."

"Brandon. *Brandon.* Tell me you're going to do it!"

"Smoke?"

"Walk back through CastieCon shirtless."

"Well," I spin the Augie Manners shirt on one finger. "retro robot's probably still hanging around, right?"

"Undoubtedly, sir."

"So let's give her a show."

He skids to one knee and grabs my hand.

"Brandon Gregory Page," he says.

"Yeah."

"Will you have my fictional space-babies?"

"What will the neighbors think?"

"Do we care?"

Brandon planted himself behind the wheel and gunned the engine, says hey_mamacita. *He knew the torments of his past might trail them all the way west, but for now they shrunk in the rearview and he surrendered every last care.*

I grab his hand and run.

15»

SAN ANTONIO.
SHIRTLESS. HAND. HOLDING.
OMG DEAD.
(photos inside!!)

amity crashful: ABANDON IS REAL OMG OMG I'M STROKING OUT

doomerang: *ovaries exploding*

whispering!sage: baking celebratory snickerdoodles!

sorcha doo: retro robot how are u still alive

retro robot: haha I don't know! I saw them run right in front of me holding hands and I was like OMG I just wrote porn about you an hour ago...sooo surreal

a_rose_knows: Can we call it official yet??!?!?! obvs something going on

sadparadise: idk idk it seemed like just a joke. or a dare maybe. brandon's way too neurotic to do that on his own.

doomerang: Still, you guys. SHIRTLESS. HAND. HOLDING.

retro robot: They are legit doing it. That is all.

lone detective: They may be getting closer but I don't think it's a done deal yet. And I hate to be Debbie Downer but Disturbing Thought: ***could*** it be fanservice?

thanks4caring: omg. what if Miss queen bitch Maxima spilled about us???

whispering!sage: nope. no way. she'd never ever mention us to them. she's uber creeped out by real-person shipping.

sorcha doo: if they get together global warming will stop and wars will end and kevin will love me again.

amity crashful: hey_mamacita are you here?? we neeeeeeeed you.

hey_mamacita: OMG SOBBING AND SHAKING AND VOMITING RAINBOWS. LIKE WHAT IS THIS LIFE EVEN.

amity crashful: your last fic made me cry like a bb

hey_mamacita: LISTEN: it's not fic anymore. okay? It is PROPHECY. i mean SHIT ON A SHINGLE, SON it is SO CLOSE to happening and I don't give a porcupine's bumhole what maxie & her minions at Cadsim think. anyone can see how far they've come. look at brandon's body language in Photo 1: looser, more open. examine abel's eyes in Photo 4: they have that silvery sparkle now when brandon looks at him. THINGS. HAVE. EVOLVED.

amity crashful: omg I worship you. Never stop saying words.

hey_mamacita: I won't!! EVER. not until they're together for 10000000% sure. SWEET FANCY MOSES IN A HULA SKIRT, BOYS, just freaking do it already! We are...

"...Dying over here!" Abel rakes his hands across his chest and slowly teasingly trails them downward, his second Spaceman Straw dangling from his lips. I cough out smoke and we laugh laugh laugh and our laughing sounds huge as if there are a hundred of us in the Sunseeker, communing with the Abandon shippers and huffing in some serious wisdom.

154

"How are u still alive?" I ask Abel and he giggles.

"IDK, IDK." He flops down on the pinecone rug. "I saw you shirtless and OMG, dead! Vomiting rainbows!"

"Ooh, turn over, turn over."

"Like this?"

"Yeah..."

"Why?"

I shake my head and whistle. "DAT ASS."

We explode again and it hurts this time, like the laughing is turning me inside out. Bec is perched up in the loft with her ankles crossed and my Phillies shirt on and she watches us like a wise old owl in a children's story who hoots about danger to kids who won't listen. She stopped after a couple puffs. I probably should've too but oh well.

"Father Mike would be *so* disappointed," she tsks. *"Your bodies are temples, guys..."*

She says his name and my memory strains; he's a book I read once in first grade and can only remember part of a picture, a snippet of a sentence. Snippet. Is that a real word? I lean my head back and swivel in the desk chair and feel like I'm falling but gently, like a million dandelion seeds after someone puffs them free.

"Oh babe—look look!" Abel pokes my ankle with the head of Plastic Sim. I'm in his red SEX BOMB shirt and it smells like his soap and sweat. "They're already making a meme from your shirtless picture."

"Beautiful."

"Abandon shippers are so much more awesome than Cadsim shippers."

"We have very smart fans." The ceiling is the most amazing shade of white.

"They love us, so they must be smart. OH! Oh, we should tell them how smart and awesome they are!"

"Shhhhhhh!" I sit up fast. The room whirs. "No no no

no..."

"They wouldn't know it was us. Bec joined with a sockpuppet—hey Rebecca? What's our username, doll?"

Bec sighs. "brandonrox."

"Perfecto." Abel takes another drag and grins around a channel of smoke. He cracks his knuckles and starts typing and he's so so fast, like I bet he's the world's very fastest hunt and pecker, and he reads out loud while he types.

"Dear Abandon shippers: you are the greatest! I'm friends with Bec and have met Brandon many times and you're totally right, he is a neurotic mess..."

"Hey!"

"But hopefully soon he will see the error of his ways and let Abel get in his pants... Is that right? Is that even English?"

"So to speak." I get down on the floor and crawl over to him.

"Are these words supposed to be moving?"

"I don't think so."

"Ugh. No more Spacemen."

Bec turns over in the loft and switches my book light on and it glows like the pale third moon of Castaway Planet. Abel stabs out the Spaceman Straw and replaces it with a red lollipop from the bag of junk food we got at the 7-11. I unwrap my second cupcake and take a huge messy bite and oh God, I've never tasted anything so good. We bought so much incredible food. In the lobby at CastieCon we sold the signed action figure and the sweaty Augie Manners shirt to some trembling superfan who kissed us both on the lips and gave us a trading card of Cadmus and Sim on the mountaintop, so at this moment we are also five hundred dollars richer in addition to being high as the sun.

Abel refreshes the page.

amity crashful: OMG do you still talk to them??

lone detective: Are you for real?

retro robot: *HEART. ATTACK. IMMINENT.* Do they know about us?

sorcha doo: if they don't are u going to tell them? pleeeeaaaasssssse don't!!

hey_mamacita: SHHHHH BACK OFF. LET THE MAN OR LADY SPEAK.

"Our fans. Are so. Amazing." Abel flexes his fingers over the keyboard.
   "Don't be mean to them."
   "Are you kidding? They'll *love* this."

They don't know. And I won't tell. I'm sort of a shipper myself, to be honest.

sorcha doo: lol what do u know about Brandon. can u give us more details

whispering!sage: yes please. insider details. we will venerate you forever and bake you snickerdoodles. from scratch.

lone detective: IF you're legit. Ha.

Oh, I'm legit. Let's see...

Abel looks me up and down.

Brandon's eyes, close up, are the deep and mysterious blue of an ocean at midnight. His hair smells intoxicating, like freshly mown grass and dryer sheets. He is a man of exquisite intelligence and sensitivity, as evidenced by his music collection which is crammed with Dylan and Jeff Buckley and Elliott Smith and a buttload of other dead or half-dead singer-songwriter types. He irons his shorts, he reads vintage Ray Bradbury, and he likes plates with compartments because he can't stand when food touches other food, which could be annoying but is actually kind of adorable.

Plus...he secretly thinks Cadmus is H-O-T-T.

He taps *post comment* and cringes. "Don't kill me!"

I don't care about the Cadmus thing though, the room is spinning and why why why did he type *adorable,* like, you wouldn't type that about someone unless you thought it on some level, right?

"Does my hair really smell like grass?"

"And Bounce. I wouldn't lie about something so important."

He aims a sparkly shivery grin at me. I lean over him and refresh the page.

hey_mamacita: I choose to believe you, mysterious stranger.

sorcha doo: me too me too me toooo omg 5 million goosebumps rte now

lone detective: Sounds a little too breathless for me, tbh.

thanks4caring: what about Abel? Do you know him too?? DETAILS.

I drag the laptop up on my knee.

"What're you doing?"

"Shh." I'm already typing.

His shoulders bunch and he fakes a shudder. "Should I be scared?"

I narrow my eyes. "Terrified."

I don't know Abel as much as I know Brandon. However, I can tell you that he smells like cinnamon soap, he has beautiful greenish eyes like old bottles you find on the beach, and when he makes Mac-in-a-Minit it comes out extra cheesy. He gets excited about everything remotely cool or interesting, even a dumb belt buckle with a rooster on it, and he makes you excited about it too. He's a great hugger and a compulsive matchmaker and he loves karaoke even though he can't sing and he's sweet and patient with his friends, even when they're hopelessly screwed up. And reportedly Brandon thinks he looks amazing in his new snakeskin bomber jacket, even though he kind of made fun of it at first.

ALSO, here's a scoop for those of you attending the Castaway Ball in Long Beach. THEY'RE GOING. Together. I heard Abel bought the tix before the trip even started.

"Wowww."

Abel's chin is on my shoulder and his finger is tracing my words in the comment box and the room is seriously tilting, his warm breath prickling my neck and setting off tiny electric shocks all through my arms and legs. My knee is touching the wreckage of a WordWhap game from earlier; the tiles are all jumbled now except for Abel's winning word: R-A-P-T-U-R-E.

I tap *post comment.*

The community goes ballistic.

amity crashful: I am smiling so hard I literally cannot

feel my face now

sorcha doo: i squeed so loud my mom came running she thought i was dying lol

hey_mamacita: HOLY MOTHER OF PEARL EVERYONE PAINT YOURSELF A TECHNICOLOR PICTURE OF THE GLORIOSITY THAT AWAITS AT THE CASTAWAY BALL. IT IS JUST EXACTLY WHAT I PLANNED FOR THEM. i'm not even kidding you guys. chapter 18 of "how to repair a mechanical heart," verbatim from my outline: *Brandon and Abel attend the ball together at the Long Beach con. By now Brandon has fully connected with his inner Cadmus and Abel has embraced his inner Sim, so they show up dressed as each other's ultimate fantasy. Hot Abandon action on the dance floor ensues.*

retro robot: OMG mamacita that is eerie. I love you so much.

sorcha doo: mamacitaaa u give me life.

hey_mamacita: THIS HAS TO HAPPEN. WE WILL WRITE IT INTO BEING.

We can't stop giggling. I shove the laptop off me and Abel takes its place, he twists around and drops his head in my lap and laughs through his fingers and wow his head is heavy and beautiful, like some sort of ancient stone that glows inside and holds all the secrets of the universe. He clasps Plastic Sim to his chest. I pluck Plastic Cadmus from my neckband. I walk him down my arm, hop him lightly over Abel's smooth forehead, nose, chin, throat. I tap his clavicle with Cadmus' tiny boot.

"Hey. Tin Man."

Abel closes his eyes and grins. "Yes, Captain." He gets the Sim voice just right: smooth and clipped, like a sexy

GPS.

"Got a proposition for ya."

"I shall look forward to receiving it."

I draw a slow circle around Plastic Sim with the head of Plastic Cadmus, skimming the center of Abel's chest. I pretend it's my finger there, tracing and retracing a ring around his heart.

"We should do it," I murmur.

Abel's eyes fly open wide and I see Bec sit up in the loft.

"No. No no, not that." I pat his hair. It's so soft, like fresh cotton candy. "I mean we should give the fans what they really want. At the nerd prom."

"I should deflower you under the disco ball?"

"Nooo...But what about a kiss?"

He lifts his head off my lap.

"For serious?"

"Why not? We're the creators."

"Like, full-on—"

"Full-on fanfic fantasy. We'll dress like Sim and Cadmus. Plan the whole thing out this week. Their heads will *explode*."

"What about you?"

"What about me?"

"I mean..." He picks at the pinecone rug, biting back a smile. "Can you handle that?"

I quote hey_mamacita's new chapter. *"I'm ready for anything."*

"Brandon?" Bec's shimmying down from the loft. "Can I see you a second?"

"What's up?"

"Outside. It's about Dave."

"Sure..."

She hurries me outside to the kiddie playground two

161

RVs over and it's so so beautiful, it's like a snapshot of every summer we RVed together as kids, the same creaky swings and dented slide and monkey bars curved in a rainbow arch. You can almost taste the juice boxes and smooshed PBJs. She sits me down on the rusted merry-go-round and claps her hands on my shoulders.

"Remember that time—"

"—we exploded marshmallows in your mom's microwave? *Yes.*"

She sighs. "Remember two years ago, when Nick Fazzolari wanted to take me to Burning Man and when I told you about it you just did *this* with your eyebrows and then the next day I backed out?"

"Yeahhh..."

She gives me the eyebrows.

"Aw, what?"

"I'm ready for anything?"

I tamp down a laugh. "So?"

"This is quite the turnaround."

"Yeah, well, it happens." I stretch out on the merry-go-round platform. "Sudden conversion. Road to Damascus. Bam!"

"Uh-huh." She climbs up next to me. "Tell me you know what you're doing."

"It's all fake. Relax."

"Fake."

"Yes."

"A hundred percent fake."

"Yes." I think about Abel's head in my lap. "...Eighty-five percent."

"Brandon!"

"What?"

"Just—proceed with caution."

"It's Abel."

"Hence my concern."

"He's awesome."

"Yeah, but—"

"I thought you *wanted* me to find someone. You were like, 'you can't stay fucked up forever'—"

"I know! I do. I want you to. Just..."

She sighs and leans her head back on the metal bar, like she used to during our late-night campground games of Truth or Dare.

"Just be careful," she says. "Don't lose yourself in this too fast."

"Whatever. Old Brandon was nothing but...tin and bones." I crack up at my own stupid joke. "Who cares about him?"

"I do," she says softly.

I feel a distant twinge because I've made her sad for some reason I can't grasp but really I just want her to worship the stars with me which are bigger and brighter than I've ever seen. I lift my finger to the sky and play connect the dots. "Becky," I say, because I haven't called her Becky in forever, and I love her and her hair is so pretty in the lavender light of the bug zappers.

"Yes, Brandon."

"Father Mike was right."

She lifts her head. "Huh?"

"God works in very, very mysterious ways."

"Oh boy."

"*Every world, even this one, has its unexpected mercies.*"

"Easter sermon?"

"Episode 1-16."

"Okay, weirdo." She kisses me on the forehead. "Clearly you're hopeless tonight."

She swings herself off the merry-go-round and gives it a shove before she scuffs away. I always forget how strong she is. The platform spins and rattles and the stars whirl into streaks and if hey_mamacita were writing this she'd say it was like the crash of the starship in the *Castaway Planet* pilot, the last thing they saw before they all clasped hands and said their brave goodbyes, and then woke up bloody and alive on a whole new planet.

I picture hey_mamacita crosslegged on the platform beside me, the red heart on her ragged t-shirt flickering like a hundred tiny votives. Her dreadlocks are streaked with gray and she smells like clean dirt and salt water and her knife halo glints, ready to defend me. She rests her rough hands on mine like a different kind of mother, the kind who roller-derbies and lives in an electric blue cottage and writes campy redemptive porn about you, and she leans close and whispers in my ear:

Don't worry, she says. *Even God ships Abandon.*

I wait for Father Mike, for a random earthquake to hit or an airplane part to fall from the sky and crush me but nothing happens, nothing nothing nothing and I feel pure liquid freedom shoot through all my veins at once.

It's set.

Six days. First kiss. A fake kiss, but whatever. It's a start.

SWEET BABY MOSES ON A MOTORBIKE, says hey_mamacita.

And I'm like, *What have I done?*

hey_mamacita: THE CASTAWAY BALL CREED. a communal prayer by the church of abandon.

sorcha doo: omg lol

hey_mamacita: O MY FELLOW DISCIPLES

i call on you now, as our blessed boys

tango straight to the edge of their incandescent fate

FOR THE LOVE OF ST. IGNATIUS LET US GIVE DESTINY A RUTHLESS FREAKING TURBOCHARGE

sorcha doo: let us hold nightly abandon prayer circles lol

a_rose_knows: Let us create a new Abandon playlist: 1. "Strange Powers" ~ Magnetic Fields 2. "Heartbeat Song" ~ Futureheads ...

retro robot: Let us assail the universe all week long with the hottest dancefic our giant intellects can produce.

whispering!sage: we shall make them make out on the dance floor like whoa

amity crashful: omg to "such great heights." that song is everything they choose to be.

hey_mamacita: YEA, VERILY I SAY UNTO YOU, they shall dress up like sim and cadmus and give each other overpowering hotpants as they do each other's makeup and sensuously button each other's buttons.

sorcha doo: **dead**

retro robot: May our words take wing and lead them ever closer to each other as their wheels roll closer and closer to Long Beach. May they lock eyes over Ramen noodles in the RV and waltz in a Laundromat as their clothes entangle in the dryer.

hey_mamacita: we ask this in the name of the Captain, the Android, and the Holy Spirit of One True Love.

amity crashful: amen!!!

retro robot: Amen.

hey_mamacita: AMEN.

CastieCon #4
Long Beach, California

16»

"FELLOW FANS AND devoted followers," Abel says to the camera, "welcome to Room 809 of the Long Beach Monarch Inn. Where right now, right in front of your very eyes, Brandon and I will perform an act of unprecedented intimacy."

"I found the mascara," I say.

"Perfect. Sit down, love. So tonight, obviously: the Castaway Ball. Which will change our lives forever, since the ballroom stage eight floors below us is now prepped and ready for two very very special guests—Sim and Cadmus themselves, David Darras and Ed Ransome. Bran...you okay?"

I'm fanning myself. "Whew. Just feeling faint."

"You and every Cadsim shipper in this freakin'-damn hotel. So anyway, a sad and little-known fact about me and my friend here is that both of us missed our respective proms: Brandon tells me he was huddled miserably in his room, listening to Season 2 commentary tracks and nursing a pint of Cherry Garcia, while I on the other side of town was swearing oaths of eternal devotion in the blacklit basement of my ex-boyfriend, who in retrospect was so not worth it. So tonight we both get a do-over. And to make our evening an extra-large slice of teen-geek heaven, we've decided to give each other a little gift."

"Yep. So stay tuned, to this space..."

"...because in less than a half-hour we'll post again, and you'll see exactly what happens when two ordinary queer boys from central PA become each other's..." He swoops close to the camera. "...*ultimate* fantasy."

I say, "You first, Tin Man."

He says, "It will be my honor. Captain."

***

This is how you turn a boy into an android.

First, on the long road from San Antonio to Long Beach, you read a half-dozen fics about this exact moment: when you're in your hotel room and the Castaway Ball is a half-hour away and you're standing in front of his black leather swivel chair, a confusion of dollar-store makeup pots and brushes spread out on the table. You act out details from the best stories. The way you dip the largest brush in the silvery powder and smooth it across his cheeks, and then lean in just a little to blow stray flecks off his nose. The way you gloss the comb with Amp-U Electric Blue gel, just enough to streak his white hair Sim-blue. You're so gentle with the comb, it makes him think of when he was five and his mom would detangle his wet head while she told him his favorite bedtime story.

Then it's your turn.

He's faster with the hairspray and makeup brushes, just like the fics predicted. He makes your face a screenshot of Cadmus from the season finale's last scene: bloodied and triumphant, right before he collapses from the crystal spider bite. Red lipstick blends with brown mascara for authentic blood spatters; he tousles and softspikes your hair to perfection and mists it with a spray that smells like apples. Then he swoops in close to draw the spider bite on your neck with an eyebrow pencil, like he does in this week's installment of "How to Repair a Mechanical Heart," except in the fic he's also shirtless and his pecs are *like a love poem engraved on his torso.* Your heart whirs faster anyway.

Time to get dressed.

You both turn your backs, though you've spent the whole week fine-tuning these details together while you drove and cleaned the RV water tank and cooked franks and beans over an Arizona campfire. How many strategic rips to make in your tight black Cadmus t-shirt (four), how to make a Sim collar for his shirt (a strip from a white plastic butter tub and two silver buttons), how to flip his six-dollar Goodwill wingtips from black to white (five coats of spray paint and a Hail Mary). You draw a breath and put on Cadmus. You shrug on Abel's snake-skin jacket and buckle on the big fake-leather replica boots he bought at the Cleveland con, hoping he can't hear the rustle of the newspaper you had to stuff in the toes. You listen to him curse his floppy collar and hum a Goldfrapp song while he yanks on his pants, and you think there's no way he'll transform his huge undeniable self into the trim elegant machine who makes your blood buzz in your veins.

Then he turns you around, and wow.

It's perfect. The slicked blue hair. The shiny shoes. The fitted white pants and slim jacket he paid too much for at that fancy mall in Tucson. All of it = perfect.

He. Is. Sim.

And I'm in trouble.

Abel looks at my boots—his boots—and scratches the back of his neck. "You, uh, look great," he murmurs.

"You too."

"Nah."

"No, I mean, the costume is—" *Flawless. Revelatory.* "Actually not too bad."

"Just put on my corsage," he says. "Okay?"

He reaches in his pocket and pulls out a small pod of white frosted plastic. He flips a tiny switch on the side, and a cool blue light glows off and on inside it.

I brush my fingers across the plastic. "You bought a mechanical heart?"

"At the Cleveland con. I was going to give it to you, but..."

This is better.

He hesitates a second, and then he quickly undoes a few of his shirt buttons. Now he's staring past me, at the framed ocean painting on the wall behind us.

"Just hook it to the undershirt." He blinks fast. "Actually, it's tricky. If you can't get it I can..."

"I got it." I catch the little metal hooks into Abel's shirt and button him back up, which is the exact opposite of what I want to do with those buttons right now and oh God why did I suggest this?

Stupid Augie Manners and his stupid Spaceman Straws.

We can't go through with this. We can't fake-kiss on the dance floor tonight like we planned all week. He'll feel me *melt into his embrace* and *hungrily devour his lips* like in fic, and when we break apart under the swirls of disco starlight he'll know it's not fic for me, not anymore. And everything will be ruined. He'll tilt his Sim head with lighthearted pity and I'll get one of those sweet and mortifying speeches about how *someday, I'll find a guy who really appreciates me* and how I'm *such a great friend, let's just keep it that way...*

He's already gearing up for it. I can tell. He can't even look me in the eye.

"Brandon?"

Bec's voice, muffled behind our door. Her room is down the hall. I lunge for the doorknob, relieved for something neutral to do. Abel retreats to the bathroom and turns the water on, full blast.

Bec is dressed in a way my parents would fully approve of (on this trip, anyway): hair twisted up, siren-seductive in the slinky black '70s number she picked up on Wednesday at a vintage shop in Phoenix. "This says *I dance with gay boys, and possibly try to convert them*," Abel had grinned, holding the dress up to her chest as I admired his profile in the shop's dim Tiffany lamplight. He picked great: I've never seen her look so comfortable in a dress. It's nothing like that night at my house, when she stopped by post-prom in that stiff pink thing her mom had bought her and we ate Ben & Jerry's and bitched about boys until two a.m.

"Wow." She appraises my Cadmus transformation. The *wow* sounds complex.

"Look, I don't need a lecture because nothing's going to—"

"I don't lecture. Since when do I lecture?"

"Never. But I know you think—"

"I'm the sidekick." She fiddles with a pin in her hair. "Doesn't matter what I think."

"You're not."

"It's okay. I just came to give you something." She pulls me out in the hall with her and digs in her black sequined bag. Her eyelids are brushed with silvery shadow. I'm thinking a mini Sim bobblehead from the souvenir stand, or a funny haiku like the ones we used to make up together during study hall.

Instead, she pulls out a little foil packet.

"What's this?" I back up.

"It's a lubricated, extra-large, glow-in-the-dark—"

"I know what it is."

"Just in case."

"No. There's no way."

She slips the condom in my jacket pocket and gives it a pat.

"If your heart gets broken tonight," she says, "I'm just down the hall."

"Won't you be...busy?"

"Oh no. As I found out today in the autograph line for the Henchmen, Dave is saving himself for marriage."

"Really?"

She points a gun-finger at her head and *blams*. "I'm finally hundreds of miles from Mom and it's like she picked him out."

"Sorry."

"He's still adorable. Ugh!"

Our talk is all wry and surfacey and I kind of want to grab her by the shoulders, dare her to tell me what she thinks will happen tonight if I go through with the plan and kiss Abel on the dance floor.

But I don't want her answer. Not really.

Dave comes loping around the corner. He's got on a fashionably small brown suit and a *Where the Wild Things Are* t-shirt, and he's crunching on cheddar popcorn. Bec elbows him playfully and grabs a handful. They look good together, friendly and fun and equal. Not like her parents; they'd make you tense, like a grizzly bear glowering at a crow that won't stop cawing. I like Dave better now that I know he won't be having sex with Bec tonight while I brood alone in the hotel room we splurged on, Abel snoring obliviously one bed over.

"Great costume, man," Dave says. "You look intense."

"Wait till you see Abel," Bec tells him. She lands a soft punch on my shoulder. "Go get him."

17»

AS SOON AS THE FOUR OF US hit the lobby, we hear the Castaway Ball: thudding electro-pop, the din of half-drunk fans. I swallow hard, adjust my Cadmus shades. It's like in the movies when someone's about to be hanged in the square, and he hears the drums and the bloodthirsty crowd in the distance.

Forward march.

Abel jabs me with an elbow. "Ready for *muchas smooches*?" he snarks.

"Don't sound so excited."

"We're going to make it a quick kiss, right? Leave the fans wanting more?"

"Sure." I nod fast. "Right." *What does that mean?*

"How many Abandon spies here tonight?"

"Um, three. At least." A couple girls in Henchman robes giggle past us. "whispering!sage, amity crashful... hey_mamacita."

"Aw. Your favorite."

She could be in there already. She could be right on the other side of the ballroom door. I try to message her telepathically. *Please please send me good vibes. Help tonight not be a total spacewreck.*

My phone goes off. HOME CALLING. Not now. I wait till it stops and then I text back: ALL'S WELL WILL CALL TOMORROW LOVE U.

Abel slips our silver tickets to a girl in a red-and-black striped suit and red Henchman contacts. She geeks out over our costumes, winds on our glow-in-the-dark wristbands, and passes us the question paddle Abel prepaid

174

for and our VIP goodie bags.

Then the double doors swing open.

I'm like...*swept away.* It sounds like fluttery fanfic but there's no other way to describe it. Entering the ball is like crashing on a planet where no one cares how you dress or how you dance or who you love. Everywhere you look there's a beautiful weirdo: the guy gyrating on stilts in a homemade Xaarg cape, the chubby tattooed girl twirling in a skirt made of glow-sticks, the pale androgynous couple in matching Lagarde black leather. Beyond a cluster of small tables with glowing centerpieces shaped like Xaarg's hat, there are even two girls dressed like Cadmus and Sim, holding hands on the edge of the dance floor.

Bec and Dave run off together, disappear into the churn of dancers. I just stand there in the doorway with Abel and grin like an idiot, the disco ball scattering stars on my face and the music pounding me a new heartbeat. I scan the crowd for hey_mamacita, for the sunflower she said she'd pin in her dreadlocks.

"The night that changed everything..." Abel says.

I look over at him, hopefully, but then I see he's ripped his goodie bag open and is holding an oversized trading card, reading the caption under a picture of the smashed-up Starsetter.

"What's in your bag?" he says.

I tear it open, not caring, still glancing around for dreads and a sunflower. A sheet of *Castaway Planet* logo stickers, a few jumbo trading cards, a silver favor bag of cinnamon jellybeans, and a reminder to purchase our pre-autographed Darras/Ransome photos from the booth to our immediate left.

"Thirty bucks? What a rook." He's already fishing in his wallet. "One David Darras," he yells to the booth guy.

"Really?" I poke him.

"It's for you, dimwit."

"You don't have to—"

He waves me off, grabs his change and the rolled-up photo. "Here, babe. Your hero."

"What about your hero?"

"Eh. Got him in my head."

I slide off the rubber band and unroll the photo. Darras is in his Sim costume, perfect as always, but the smile is stiff and cheesy and the signature's so sloppy I can only read the Ds. It's weird; a few weeks ago I would've held the photo up to the light to trace the whorls of his fingerprints, would've nearly passed out just knowing that David Darras was backstage and I was going to lay eyes on him in person within five minutes.

I blink at the photo. I don't feel too much, just a little twinge. It's only special now because Abel bought it for me.

"Thanks," I tell him.

He looks away. "S'okay."

Brandon gathered all his courage like dry tinder sticks and, with a sharp hopeful intake of breath, boldly lit the match.

"You...want to dance?"

"Umm." He fiddles with the collar on his Sim shirt. "Maybe we should wait."

I droop inside. "Why?"

"I don't know. I think maybe—"

"THE MOMENT HAS ARRIVED."

The music cuts off. The blue and purple lights stop pulsing. On the ballroom stage, a single spotlight pops on, and a slick-haired announcer in a tux jacket and logo t-shirt steps into place. Everyone flips into cutthroat mode, squeezing and elbowing toward the stage for prime Q&A

real estate.

"Wanna get close?" Abel nudges me.

Yes. Yes.

I shrug carefully. "Let's stay here."

"Really?"

"We've got a question paddle. They'll see us."

"Don't you want to see them?"

I'd rather see you. God, I need a better line.

hey_mamacita, where are you?

"And NOW, Castie boys and girls," the announcer's saying, "it's my honor and pleasure to introduce the men of the hour—the best of friends and the oddest of *couples*—" He winks, and then waits for the shipper squees to die down. "Let's give a huuuuuuuuge Castie welcome to the Captain and the Android, ED Ransome and DA-vid DAR-rasssssss!"

Ransome and Darras trot out from behind the black curtain. Matching tuxes. *Holding hands.* When they hear how loud everyone's cheering they play it up, raise their clasped hands high like a wishbone and stand there smiling while the whistles and hoots wash over them.

Abel tilts his head. "Ed Ransome's shorter than I thought."

I nod. And Darras is an alien without his pale Sim makeup. Tanned and blond and floppy-haired, with a soap-star smile and a loose, preening walk.

Maybe too loose.

"Your boy's had a few," whispers Abel.

"Okay, ohhhhhhh-kay, settle down." Darras grins, waving his arms like a Muppet. "We know. We're awesome."

"Well, *you're* awesome," Ransome pouts. "I only aspire to awesomeness."

"He sells himself short, guys. All the time. Kinda tragic, don't you think?"

177

They pingpong some more. *I am in the presence of David Darras,* I remind myself, but it doesn't take. I bump my hand against Abel's a couple times, accidentally-on-purpose, hoping he'll get all lust-crazed from gazing at Ed Ransome's rugged face and spiky hair and slide his warm fingers through mine. He just stares straight ahead at the stage, this weird unreadable look on his face.

"Soooo we know you guys have your questions ready," says Darras. "But how's about we start with the big question that's been on *evvvveryone's* mind since the finale."

Ed Ransome nods. "Right. 'Is Cadmus dead?'"

"No no no, dear. Did we do it in the cave?"

Shrieks and catcalls from the Cadsim shippers peppering the crowd. A few boos sneak in, but barely; everyone's too drunk and giddy for ship wars.

"Ohhh, trust me, superfans and slashers," Darras says, eyeing up Ransome head to foot. "Ed and I discuss this *nonstop.*"

"It's true. We do," Ransome deadpans.

"He calls me at three in the morning, people, and asks if I want to 'practice some kissing scenes'...you know, just in case."

"He can't get enough of me."

"For realsies."

"David."

"Yes, Ed?"

"Don't say *for realsies.*"

Darras shrugs. "So, anyway. Regarding Sim and Cadmus. Here's what I think: there was plenty of buildup this season, their friendship's been unfolding in a distinctly ambiguous direction since Day 1, and when two actors bring such undeniable personal chemistry to the table, it'd be a crime against nature to waste it."

My head throbs. *Yes. Yes. Say more.*

"Sooo, as a hopeless romantic and the former treasurer of my high school GSA, I'm gonna say yes! Cave love: it totally happened!"

Two Cadsim girls in front of us lose their minds. Darras and Ransome lean closer and mouth some smiley mystery words to each other. Ransome puts a hand up, waits for the crowd to quiet.

"Welllllll, *I* happen to be a realist," says Ransome, twisting the gold band on his thick tanned hand. "So since there's no hard canon evidence yet, I'm going to poop everyone's party and say no—"

Booing. Darras waves them quiet.

"HOWEVER, however," Darras says. "Let's clarify. You would not have been able to resist me, my dear."

Ransome claps a hand to his chest. "Oh, well, that's a given. Who could?"

A girl in the audience shouts something out. Darras cups his ear.

"What's that? Yeah, you. Girl in the lovely dress with— ohh. Ed, is that an iron-on of *us*?"

"I believe it is."

I crane my neck to see where he's pointing. A stick-figure redhead twirls, shows off a blue t-shirt dress with a Cadsim-kiss manip on it.

"That is...oh, that is really quite special," Darras says.

Abel mutters, "Miss Maxima minion."

"Sweetie, you had a question?"

"Yes! Yes." The girl scootches over to one of the mikes in the audience. "So would you guys—maybe show us what the kiss *would've* looked like? If it actually happened?"

A low expectant *ooooooooohhh* travels the room. Abel freezes. He goes vacant, like Sim does when he's plugged into his charging dock.

Darras puts on this innocent look and starts pacing the stage, swerving a little. "That's...something you guys would be interested in, huh? I don't know..."

Someone whips out the kind of whistle you use to hail a cab three lanes over. That sets the other girls off. More whistles, rowdy YEAHHHs. Darras and Ransome side-eye each other.

"Hmm." Darras strokes his chin. "A real live Cadsim kiss—that's what you guys call it, right? Cadsim?"

The girls in front of us are getting frantic now. I feel it. What they want is so close they're afraid to trust it, afraid it's a tease or a joke. Abel's pale Sim face is three shades paler.

"Okay, but we want to know you realllllllly want it, right, Ed?"

"Nah, they don't look like they want it."

"They really don't."

"Maybe they should show us."

I don't know who starts the chant. But it picks up fast: *"Cad-sim, Cad-sim..."*

"Eh, I don't know, Ed. What do you think?"

"They're pretty quiet, actually."

They layer on claps and stomps, rattle the fake-wood squares of the dance floor. There can't be this many Cadsim shippers here; it's drunk girls up for anything, fans who want a good story to tell, people who think it's just fun to shout:

"CAD-sim! CAD-sim!"

"Uh-oh," says Darras. "They're getting hot and bothered."

"Sounds like it."

"Better break out your Chap-Stick, buddy."

"CAD-SIM! CAD-SIM! CADDD-SIMMM!"

Darras scans the room, taking it all in: the women in

costumes and shimmery prom gowns, ignoring their dates to plead with him.

Then he grabs Ed Ransome, dips him to one side, and gives the fandom the first and only official Cadsim kiss.

People must be screaming, because my eardrums hurt. And the flashing lights, I guess those are two hundred cameras catching history, snatching proof. This is how they did it. This is how they made it look real, even though the kiss was in shadow and no one actually saw their lips lock together. How Ransome's arms flailed around at first, and then settled around Darras's shoulders. How they gasped and flushed when they came up for air; made a big show of smoothing their shirts, fixing their matching bowties.

"I gotta call my wife," says Ransome.

"I'll explain everything," says Darras.

They crack up, high-five. I lean my head back, let the disco ball paint me with spatters of light like Dad's St. Christopher medal spinning from the Sunseeker rearview. I have to go through with this now. They made it look easy. For five seconds I'll get to see how it feels, a perfect easy kiss with someone you trust completely. And afterwards I can smooth my shirt and clear my throat, pretend it was all a big joke. I can even borrow his words: *I gotta call my wife.*

I pop a Tic-Tac. Darras and Ransome are plugging ahead with the Q&A, but I don't hear a word. My head's ballooning with possibilities. Which way to tilt my head, where to put my hands.

Abel pokes me in the back.

"I gotta go," he says. "Sorry."

***

I keep pace beside him. Back through the ballroom doors, into the sallow chlorine-smelling hall, through the too-bright lobby with its throngs of late rumpled travelers.

If I keep up with him, I can tell myself he's not walking away from me.

"You can stay," he mutters. "Stay at the ball, Bran. Have fun."

"What about you?"

"I don't feel good."

"Since when?"

"I dunno." We squeeze through a herd of business-people who gape at our costumes. "It just hit me. I guess maybe the sashimi..."

"Abel."

"My dad says never to eat in hotel restaurants—this one time he had a bad shrimp cocktail at this medical conference in Florida and he—"

"Stop." We're at the elevators. Abel jabs the up button. "What's going on?"

He looks at the floor. I wait for it: *I can't kiss you, even as a joke. You're too neurotic. Too short. Too not-my-type-so-what-were-you-thinking-you-idiot.*

"I don't want to do that," Abel says. "What they just did in there."

"Okay." I nod fast. "It's okay."

He holds the elevator door open. We step in.

"I know I said I would," he says, "but—I mean, it's just gross."

I flinch. "It's fine, okay? I get it."

"Yeah. Right."

He punches the button.

Three floors ping by.

"It's so fucking easy for you," Abel blurts. "This whole thing..."

"What?"

"Nothing." He turns his back on me. "Forget it."

In bad elevator fics, Cadmus is always hitting the EMERGENCY STOP to pick a fight with Sim, which of course always turns into *their heated bodies hungering in unison* two paragraphs later.

I spot the red button. My hand shoots out.

We grind to a stop.

"What are you doing?" Abel's voice spikes up an octave.

Crap. I didn't think it would work.

"You seriously stopped the elevator?"

Brandon drew in a deep, calming breath. I can do this, he assured himself.

"I want to know what you mean," I tell him. "Why is this easy for me?"

"Brandon—!"

I step in front of the button. "We're not going until you tell me."

"Fine." He backs into a corner, as far from me as possible. "You went from one fake relationship to another, and it's not fun anymore, and now we need to stop. Okay?"

"I thought you liked this."

"I do. I *did*," he says to his white Sim shoes. "But like, you get to play Cute Plastic Boyfriends with me for the camera, and it's sweet and fun and safe for you and then you get to turn it off and walk away." I open my mouth but he holds up a hand. "And I mean, look: it's my fault. Okay? I was the idiot. Because I said yes to this fake-flirting thing like it was a game and I shouldn't have said yes because I knew this would happen, I knew I was getting this diabolical crush at just the wrong time and I'd be in over my head but I couldn't say no to you and now it's gotten too weird and too dangerous and I have to end it because one thing I really really cannot do is have you break my heart, because then we probably couldn't be friends. And I want to stay friends. No matter what. Don't you?"

I blink at him. My Abel-to-English decoder spits out the results.

Holy Saint Peter on a hoverboard.

Hot chills wash over me. I take a step closer.

"What do you mean," I say, "break your heart?"

He closes his eyes. The mechanical heart blinks slow and steady.

"Don't make me say it," he whispers.

The rough draft of tonight's story was set in my head this morning, but now it's rewriting itself into something ten times better. It makes a weird kind of sense. It's not going to happen in some expected place like the dance floor, while "Such Great Heights" tweedles in the background and the disco ball bathes us in generic starshine. It's going to happen in a stopped elevator, like the worst, hackiest Cadsim fic on the Internet, only now it's for real and it's going to be amazing, just like if hey_mamacita had stayed up all night to get every detail just right.

I kiss him.

Brandon's blood sizzled as his lips met Abel's: his body sang an anthem of strength and softness, of celebration un-shackled from fear. I'M KISSING A BOY, he silently shouted. They conjugated the verb with rapture and wonder and cinnamon-flavored bliss. Kiss, kissing, kissed. And kissed again.

We break apart, the scent of cinnamon jelly beans tickling my nose.

"You don't have to," he mutters.

"Abel—"

"You just think you like me," he says to the floor. "That's all this is."

"That's all it ever is."

"You think you do, because you told me all those private things and we like, bonded, and maybe you think you owe me..." His eyes are filling up. "Or maybe—"

"*Abel.*"

He looks up. "What?"

"I think I love you," I tell him.

It slips out soft and quiet, and so easily I think maybe I didn't say it out loud. But then I see his face, and I know I did. He tilts my face in his warm hands and kisses me back, and it's like one of those perfect TV kisses they save for May sweeps, the ones the previews tease you about all season until you swear it won't happen, and then when it does the forums blow up and the fans add eighteen exclamation points to everything and swear they'll never ask God for anything else for as long as they live.

Abel rests his forehead on mine.

"That is most welcome news, Captain."

I don't call him *Tin Man*. I exhale, for the first time in five minutes.

I hit the elevator release, and we're on our way.

18»

SIM WASHES OFF HIM FAST, like the cheap makeup Bec and I bought for past Halloweens to magic ourselves into little suburban vampires. I watch his hair and face reclaim themselves, the blue hair gel and silver greasepaint streaking the white shower tiles and swirling down the drain.

"Bran," he murmurs.

"Mm."

"Can I open my eyes now?"

I take a deep breath. *It's okay.*

"Yes."

I feel good when I say it, but when his eyelids actually open I back up a step, clutch the washcloth against me. The hotel shower stall feels smaller, stifling. Am I too hairy? Not hairy enough? Did he imagine I was cut like a marble statue underneath my big t-shirts? Why didn't I do crunches this week at the campground after he fell asleep?

His eyes trace the droplets branching down my chest.

They stop at my waistband.

"Brandon. Cutie."

"Yeah."

"You're still wearing your boxers."

"I am."

"Is there something you need to tell me?"

"No."

"Are you *actually* a Ken doll?"

"Nope."

"Is your dad a secret superhero and you have a bionic penis and you make up this big religious-paranoia back story because it shoots laser beams and has the strength of a bulldozer?"

"Yes."

"I knew it."

"I've never done this." I watch water whirl down the drain between my feet.

"Showered in boxers?"

"Been naked...*with* someone."

"Well, obviously. However, when you said *let's take a shower*, I naively assumed—"

"I know I know!" I draw my arms across my bare chest. "I'm sorry. I felt great and then...It's new. You know?"

"Look, if you want to wait more—"

"I don't."

"But maybe you're too—"

"No! No, listen." I shove my wet hair off my forehead. *I can't screw this up. I won't let bad thoughts in. I won't.* "It's just, when I think about...sex or whatever, it's kind of like on TV."

"Vanilla and hetero?"

"No, like, there's some kissing I guess, and then it fades out."

He gets this stupefied look. "That's all you picture?"

"Kind of."

"*Ever?*"

"Mostly."

"Even your dirty robot dreams?"

"Especially those."

"Oh-kay. Wow." He weighs the full pathetic horror of my PG-13 dream-life. "So is that...all you want, or is there—"

"No no. I want more." My eyes wander down past his waist and *oh my God I saw it crap crap don't freak out it's normal it's beautiful it's*

"Eyes up here for now." He tips up my chin and kisses me lightly. "Let's not frighten you further, darling."

"I'm not."

"You are, but it's fine. We can work with this."

"Okay." I'm starting to shake. A good shaking. I think.

"So what do you think you'd like?"

"I don't know." I squeeze my eyes shut.

"Don't freak. I won't judge."

"I know. But it's like, I don't even have the words."

He pauses. Long pause. Then I hear the shower door creak open, and I feel him slip away.

I twist the water off and scramble out of the stall. He's pulling on a white bathrobe, raking his hands through his wet hair with purpose. *I'm losing him.* For crap's sake. I can't even take a half-naked shower with someone with-out—

"Come on, Bran." He throws me the other robe.

"What are we doing?"

He peers at me over his shoulder and grins.

"Imitating art."

***

I follow him into the bedroom. He flops onto the first bed and grabs the open laptop.

"Um..."

"So you know this happens in every fandom, right?" he says. "Especially real-person shipping?"

"What?"

"Here, sit here." He pulls me down next to him and kisses my cheek. "There's always that fic where they *find* all the fic their fans wrote about them, and they pretend to be all shocked and horrified at first, and then they read it together—"

"In some fancy hotel room."

"With cute matchy-matchy bathrobes. And then they get drunk on cheap champagne, and as *their inhibitions melt away* they end up—"

"—acting out their favorite scenes," I sigh.

"Exactly."

"Oh my God."

He hits his bookmark tab and scrolls down to the bottom. "I think this one was kind of hot. The one where we do it in the bowling alley—"

"Abel!"

"It's *useful*, Bran. Trust me! This way you just point to the stuff you want to try—oh. Except that."

"What?" I hide my eyes.

"Right, I bookmarked this fic to laugh at it. Sorry." He giggles. "This **sorcha doo** person needs an anatomy lesson. Did you read this one?"

"I skim the sex scenes." I uncover one eye, see the word *slick*, and re-cover fast.

"Yeah, in *that* position, your first time, in a bathroom stall? I think *dizzying heights of ecstasy* are out."

I cringe. "I figured."

"And honestly—I hope you're not disappointed when I say this."

"What?"

"I don't think I can unbutton your shirt with my teeth."

"That's okay."

"Here, this one's pretty good, though." He clicks on **retro robot**'s "You Can Drive My RV" and scrolls down. "The part that starts *Abel's back hit the wall with a thud?* Definite possibilities. Just look."

"Yeah, I can't."

He leans over and nips one of the fingers that cover my eyes. I grin. He nips another one, and another one, until I smack him away and coax my eyes back on the screen.

I make myself read the words this time, instead of skipping to a safe part. The first few lines are like medieval torture, but then the shock wears off and it's pretty okay, not much different from the Cadsim fanfic I used to sneak. It's creative. Ridiculous. Funny. Sort of hot, if I ignore the fact that they're straight-girl masturbatory fantasies about us. We spend the next half hour taking our time with it: laughing at the bad scenes, poring over the good ones. I go through my backlog of embarrassing sex questions, all of which Abel answers with casual directness, like a wet and sexy stranger giving directions to the post office.

"Okay." Abel stretches and cracks his knuckles. "So definitely that bit from the steampunk AU except minus the brass goggles and mechanical claw, and then we mix in some 'Three Little Words.' And—what else?"

I scroll down shyly to "How to Repair a Mechanical Heart."

"Chapter 18," I say. "I'd like to start here."

"Is this the one where we conjugate the verbs?"

"Yeah. But the scene right after."

He skims it. "Nice. A little overheated, but whatever. Okay. We'll keep these up for inspiration, but we'll improvise too. Plan subject to modification at any time, depending on our mood and your comfort level. Sound good, Captain?"

I nod fast. "Yep."

He tosses the condom on the nightstand. "When and if, okay? Don't look at it; it's like a little foil packet of intimidation."

He reaches across me and snaps off the lamp, so the only light left in the room is a gleaming rectangle of laptop screen. He pushes that off to the side. Cold prickles tick across my neck. All my elevator bravado whooshes away.

No more jokes.

We're doing this. For real.

Oh God.

"So first," he murmurs. "I'm supposed to *tenderly reveal your sculpted chest, as if unwrapping a gift.*" He kisses me, whispers in cinnamon against my lips. "Lie back for this, okay?"

Okay. I sink into the cool white pillow. I can do this. Obey commands. I glance at hey_mamacita's words on the laptop, blurred and unreadable from here. He tugs at the tie on my bathrobe and slides the terrycloth off my skin: chest first, then the rest of me. He unpeels my boxers, still damp from the shower, in one fluid move. Like I needed a reminder he's done this before. Many times. And there's no way I won't disappoint him.

"How's that?" His fingers trail down my chest and up again, lingering on—*God I hate the word "nipple" so much, I can't even.* "Good?"

I swallow the rock in my throat. "Good."

"I can't see your eyes. Are you freaking?"

Status: Naked. On bed. With boy. Systems overheating. Sudden doubts multiplying. Meltdown imminent.

"No," I lie.

"Now, that scene you like has you taking the reins pretty early on, remember? I mean, if you're too nervous we could change that, but I have total faith in you." He's shrugging off his own robe, tossing it on the floor. It's too dim to see much but I shut my eyes anyway. "What do you think?"

My throat creates some affirmative syllable.

He drops down on the pillow beside me and sweeps me on top of him. I go taut with the warm shock of skin to skin, the huge undeniable fact of his hardness insisting itself next to mine. I think I have to pee. I wish I could brush my teeth again. What if I do everything all wrong? What if I die of happiness and then go right to hell? A vague panicked **stop stop stop** wheels through my head and I'm gripped with the worst fear of all: what if I run away?

"Your scene." Abel brushes damp hair off my forehead. "You take over."

"I don't know what—"

"Yes you do." He pecks two kisses inside my hand and presses it to his heart. I feel its warm steady knock against my palm. "You do, sweetheart. *Relax.*"

The word sends a thunder of calm rolling through me. My fingers twitch to life. hey_mamacita whispers in the sultry, cocksure voice I imagine for her: *With bold nimble hands he bolted Abel's wrists to the smooth white sheets and braved the distance between their lips. It was shorter than he'd imagined. Because now he was free.*

I let her words fill my head, guiding my first moves.

And then, in the pale glow of the laptop, I start to write my own.

19»

WE LAY TOGETHER in the wrecked white bed, sprawled side by side like action figures someone just got done playing with. Except I'd never mistake myself for plastic, not now. It's like Sim said in Episode 2-15, after he first got the chip: *I was never fully aware of my body before. Now every part of me is alive. Electrified. Am I wrong to feel joyful, Captain? Is it foolish not to fear pain yet?*

I feel Abel still awake, fiddling with the sheets beside me. We're on the same page, I guess, trying to sidestep morning-after awkwardness by not sleeping at all. I wish he'd talk first. I don't know how to break the seal. I have some sincerely stupid questions—like, I'm not sure what we did tonight actually counted as losing my virginity—but that's kind of a question for Dan Savage and not really sexy afterglow talk, which I still have no clue about even after a hundred Cadsim and Abandon fics and really all I want to do is pull a guitar out of thin air and serenade him with "Here, There, and Everywhere," like I do in Chapter 18 of "How to Repair a Mechanical Heart."

Abel taps my cheek. "Hey...?"

I turn my head, smile. "Hey."

His eyes flick down to the space between us. I look down and see what he's done.

Plastic Sim and Plastic Cadmus: tucked snugly under the sheet together. *Spooning.*

I crack up laughing.

"So?" Abel says.

"So."

He cringes cutely. "How...was it?"

193

I would write horrible fanfic. The mechanics blur; the last thing we did blasted my mind inside-out and left me clear and calm and goofy-dreamy.

"Great," I tell him.

"Well...*mostly* great. Right?"

I hide my face in the pillow. "Sorry I couldn't do everything. I just—"

"No no! Oh God, that's not what I meant." He knocks on the back of my head. "I meant that one part where I freaked you out. I just didn't know you hated feet so much."

"Neither did I."

"That's what's so fun, though. Figuring all that stuff out." He walks his fingers under the covers. "On the other hand, I discovered your inner thigh is especially—"

"Ooh! Stop."

"What? It's cool. Next time I'll bring some feathers and we can—"

I kiss him to shut him up. We are both imperfect in so many ways right now—his hair sticking up like angry-rooster hackles, the fuzzy morning taste in my mouth—but I don't care. We smile when we break apart.

"So be honest: what's going on in your head right now?" He crooks Plastic Cadmus's arm tighter around Sim. "Good stuff? Bad stuff?"

"Good. All good."

He cocks his head.

"I mean it." I lean over the action figures and kiss him again. And again.

"Okay, 'cause if you're going to cry or drop to your knees and pray or whatever, do it now so I can—"

"Did he do that?"

"Who?"

I roll my eyes. "Him. Jonathan."

194

Abel picks at his thumbnail. "There was definite weird-ness. Yeah."

"Well, *I* am completely fine."

"Really? Hundred percent?" He reaches over and hooks my pinky with his. "I'll also accept ninety-five. Or ninety..."

I consider my answer. Bad thoughts still creep around in my subconscious; I'm not dumb enough to think one night with Abel's blasted them away. But for now I'm too happy to let them get close. I've got a force field around me made of Abel's kisses and hey_mamacita's evangelical ranting and the steady blue thrum of my mechanical heart.

Thank you, I venture. *Thank you thank you thank you.* I send it out to the universe, to Abel's *loving creative higher power that wants everyone to be happy.* Right now that seems so incredibly possible.

"Okay, you're pausing way too long," says Abel.

"Well. I do have *one* confession," I tell him.

"Sure. Sure, get it out." He unhooks our pinkies and shifts under the sheet, bracing for full-on Catholic-boy freakout.

"It's about Cadmus and Sim."

"Oh!"

"I might sort of...ahhhhhh..." *Say it. Get it over with.* "...thinkit'salittlebithotnow. Just a little!"

I bite my knuckle, awaiting judgment.

Abel lets out a deep relieved laugh. He pulls a pillow over his face and crosses his arms over it.

"You too?" I tug the pillow.

"Uggggghhhh," he moans.

"Since when?"

"Dunno. I guess since the coffee shop marathon?" He shoves the pillow away and props himself up on one el-bow. "The stupid cave scene felt different. I like, watched you watching it. Watching him. And I started..." He sighs.

"*Feeling* things?"

"To my horror. Yes."

"There were twinges?"

"Definite twinges. Oh my God, Brandon." He shakes his head at our spooning action figures. "Are we turning into...*Cadsim shippers*?"

"It's possible."

"What about the dumb bet?"

I shrug. "Call it off."

"Just like that?" He does a low whistle. "Miss Maxima would—"

"Who cares?" I twist Plastic Sim's waist and tweak his legs so he can cuddle Cadmus with maximum efficiency. "Why waste time feuding with the Cadsim girls? I'd much rather hang in the Church of Abandon."

Abel studies me. A grin sneaks across his face.

"*What,*" I say.

"What? Nothing."

"You're plotting."

"Is it that obvious?"

I shove at him with my foot. He rolls off the bed and goes for his big black bag, humming that Blondie song about hearts of glass. I pull on my boxers from last night.

"Don't look," he says. "Close your eyes."

I hear the contents of the bag shift and clink; he's got enough souvenirs and truck-stop junk and retro shirts in there to fill a Goodwill. A plastic *pop*: a marker uncapping? I wait till I feel light cotton whap my face, and then I pull it off and unfold it.

A white v-neck undershirt, ABANDON Sharpied across it. He's got one to match.

"What are these for?"

"We're making a vlog post."

"Here?"

"Yes sir."

"What for?"

He whispers in my ear, even though no one else is in the room.

"Oh no. No no. We can't."

"It'll be *epic*."

"They'll die."

He slips the shirt over my head and kisses my nose.

"In a good way," he says. "Trust me."

***

He turns the camera on.

"G'morning, Casties. It is now...five a.m., Pacific time, and Brandon and I can't sleep. We have a very important announcement that will be of great interest to quite a few..."

He keeps talking. I barely hear a word; I'm just watching his lips move, mystified that I kissed them and can do it again whenever I want.

"...so first of all, to Miss Maxie and the rest of the Cadsim girls: We'd like to call a truce with you. It deeply, deeply pains us to admit this, especially since we've seen better writers in the *7th Heaven* archive on fanfic.net, but whatever: Cadsim is *kiiiind* of hot. Okay? We said it. So I guess we're all playing on the same team now. Miss Max, we know you're going to be at the next con in Salt Lake City, so we'd like to invite *you* to ask the cave scene question at the Della Wolfe-Williams Q&A, presuming you still want to know the answer. And in the interest of burying the hatchet, we'd like to invite you to lunch with us after."

He elbows me.

"Definitely," I say.

"Long as you don't expect us to rec your fanfic or anything. Which brings us to our second purpose—right, Brandon?"

"Uh...I guess."

"Don't chicken out. Look right into the camera and say hi to the Church of Abandon—oh, right, ladies. We know about you. We have for a few weeks, and we'd like to inform you that you're living every real-person-shipper's dream: your fanfic *totally* brought us together last night."

He's spreading it on so thick. I pull the sheet over my head.

"It's true!" Abel pokes me. "As of 9:48 this evening, Brandon and I are officially Doing It. Ladies, our love lives were ready to stall out, but you inspired us to unprecedented heights of passion with all your wackadoodle sex melodramas and extraneous adjectives." He yanks the sheet off me and he looks so adorable with his mussy sex hair that I have to laugh. "Bran. What do you say to our freako fairy godmothers out there?

I shut my eyes. "Thanks guys."

Abel tugs off his ABANDON shirt. "We're going back to bed now."

He switches off the camera and tackles me, laughing, and I can't believe we said that and did that and there's no way in hell we're posting it on Screw Your Sensors. But then he leaves a trail of soft electric kisses down my chest and slips my boxers down again, and by the time he's done I wouldn't care if Xaarg himself poofed into the room and challenged us to a life-or-death game of Word-Whap.

I lay there sweaty under the sheet, trying to catch my breath. Abel crawls over to the laptop and uploads the vid. He rubs his hands together and grins, which is supposed to be cute but gives me a sinister chill.

Twenty minutes later, while we're molding Plastic Cadmus and Plastic Sim into X-rated positions and crafting an impromptu photo essay, we get a direct message from our former enemy at the Cadsim fanjournal:

Miss Maxima: laughing so hard I legit peed a little. YES. I will meet up with you lovebirds for lunch in Salt Lake. I'll even buy. See you then, boys.

You have *no idea* how much I'm looking forward to it.

CastieCon #5
Salt Lake City, Utah

20»

I WANT TO MAKE A SWEATER out of this week and wrap myself up in it until it falls apart.

If someone made an Abandon fanvid of the road between Long Beach and Salt Lake City, collaging our good times to a chirpy pop-country song, this is what it would be like:

Scene 1: Vegas. We score last-minute tickets to a cheesy jukebox musical with all 80s pop songs. Abel holds my hand and hums along as guys twirl in neon tanks and acid-washed jeans. We make out shamelessly at the end of the big "Don't Stop Believin'" number and I pretend we're in a movie and all the clapping is for us.

Scene 2: Afternoon hike in Fishlake National Forest. I impress Abel with my arcane Boy Scout tree expertise and he makes a ring for me from a twist of sneezeweed stems. We dorkily reenact the cave scene with Plastic Sim, Plastic Cadmus, and an improvised shanty of slate rocks.

Scene 3: A kiss in the rain. A good montage has to have one. On a campground picnic table, wearing stick-on mustaches from a truck stop.

Scene 4: Bill & Ray's RV Repairs. Dad found these guys online and prearranged a complete checkup, "just to be safe." While they're inspecting the brakes and fixing the busted windshield wiper, Abel and I go around back to watch a rose-and-orange sunset sprawl above Pleasant Grove, Utah, the kind of happy train-set town with rodeos and Heritage Festivals every five minutes. I sit on a rusted riding mower with my guitar and strum his favorite Madonna song ("Like a Prayer"), and I swear these two birds soar over poetically at that very second, settling together in the scrubby grass to feast on a discarded Honey Bun.

It's Friday now, one day from CastieCon #5. The Sunseeker's whipping down I-15; we'll be at our campground near Salt Lake within a few hours. Bec drives with her hair in pigtails and the Futureheads on the speakers; Abel and I sit crosslegged on the bed in the tiny back room. We're wearing matching white baseball caps that say I GOT LUCKY IN VEGAS in glitter, and beside us on two paper plates are remnants of the world's unhealthiest lunch: leftover truck stop biscuits and gravy, plus a fried-egg-and-cheese scramble with onions and tomatoes from a roadside stand near Victorville. There's tomato juice on my *Castaway Planet* shirt and Utah dirt under my fingernails. I've never been happier in my entire life.

He takes a deep breath. "Should we do it?"

"Now?"

"It's been so long."

"Three days."

"Okay. You first."

"No, together."

"On three. One, two..."

We whip out our phones. The no-media rule Abel thought up was great in terms of first-boyfriend-bonding, but it's Day 3 already and our fingers have been itching since Vegas. 72 hours without email or texting, not to mention the Cadsim fanjournal, the Church of Abandon, or the newsfeed at the main *Castaway* site, is kind of like seeing how long you can go without peeing or using the letter A.

"Susannah's in Tucson with my mom," Abel reports. "Just did her twentieth book signing. She tweets 'i miss u, have fun u should kiss brandon.'"

"Aw. Tell her you are, right now." I lean over and give him a peck. "Okay, new rumor: Sim might have an evil clone next season? *Whaaat?*"

"Not true. Darras debunked it last night, apparently."

"When?"

"Twitter party."

"Thank God...Oh, damn. Got a college orientation email."

"Begone. We're not thinking about that." Abel waves it away. "Ahhh, retro robot. How I've missed you..."

Great. Four emails from my parents. I click one.

Hi Sweetie,

We haven't heard from you since Sun. nite—tried calling you twice today but your phone was off. PLEASE make sure you call us tonite!! You know how we worry. Are you and Becky having fun? Hope you're really getting a chance to enjoy your alone time together, you 2 are so good for each other. Dad says to tell you, you can take her out for a special dinner anywhere you want. It would be our treat.

Be very safe! Remember, we love you.

Mom (and Dad)

P.S. Helped Fr. Mike with the ice cream social yesterday – he says a big hello.

I reply *Sorry! All's well, having fun!* and delete their email fast. Not going to bother me.

"You're missing some quality flailing over here," says Abel.

"Yeah?"

Remember, we love you. What was that? The sneakiest guilt trip ever.

"What's wrong?" Abel says.

"Just—annoying emails."

"Well, the night after our little afterglow video went up, there was an all-night party post that hit thirty-six pages by morning."

I grin. "We are legendary."

"The bards sing of us. whispering!sage wrote a series of haiku about how their community brought us together."

"Wow!"

"Then a_rose_knows tried to make the #abandonship hashtag happen in our honor."

"That's awesome."

"Several reports of heads exploding, lady parts combusting...doomerang theorizes that she's actually dead and this is her heavenly reward...lone detective pops in her cynical head to say we're clearly playing them like a fiddle and laughing our asses off."

"Mm. I don't care for her."

"Me neither. You will also be pleased to know that due to our hookup, sorcha doo melted into a pink puddle of happiness and is now typing with her disembodied eyeballs."

"This pleases me."

"It's so great, Bran. Everyone capslocked the whole entire night and they posted gifs of fireworks and Kermit the Frog flailing, and—Oh."

Abel's whole face changes. His eyebrows push together and he cocks his head. "Huh."

"What?"

"Nothing, just..." He hands me the phone, tries to keep

it light. "Their fearless leader appears to be M.I.A."

retro robot: Um, so...I hate to stop flailing for even a second, but WHERE IS OUR MAMACITA?? Has anyone heard from her?

whispering!sage: omg literally not a thing. like I said, she was supposed to meet up with us at the ball but she never showed.

sorcha doo: u guys. that's weird. really.

a_rose_knows: I know. BIZARRE. Packs of rabid wolves couldn't keep her from this place after official Abandon hookup. It is known.

amity crashful: I'm worried, people. I gotta admit.

A little chill flashes down my back. The biscuits and gravy sink in my stomach.
"You don't think..." Abel clutches my arm. "...her head *literally* exploded, do you?"
I tap the second page of comments. I scan it, scrolling fast with my thumb.
"Two hot boys are being sought for manslaughter in connection with the cranial detonation of one hey_mamacita," Abel says into a salt-shaker microphone. "The boys should be considered armed, dangerous, and extremely—"
"Oh God. Look at this."

retro robot: Guys. Guys. Look. HER JOURNAL'S GONE.

amity crashful: no.

sorcha doo: ok I'm seriously freaked now. WTF??? :-(

lone detective: It's true. She pulled all her Abandon fic down. Every single story. It's like she never existed.

amity crashful: omg you guys. WHAT THE ACTUAL FUCK is going on?

lone detective: She abandoned Abandon. Heh.

I find her last post, from right before the Castaway Ball, and try to click through to her personal journal. I get a blue screen with an error message.

This journal has been deleted and purged.

She's vanished. Every single chapter of "How to Repair a Mechanical Heart": gone with the rest of her.

"O lamentations," Abel sighs, hand to forehead. "hey_ mamacita doesn't love us anymore."

I try to swallow. "Guess not."

"Maybe Miss Max ordered a hit on her."

"Heh."

"Whatever shall we do without her literary genius to write us into being?" he snorts.

I hand his phone back and wipe the sweat off my palms, playing it off like I'm scratching my knees. I can't let him see I care. Not this much. "Hope she's okay." I shrug.

"Are you kidding? She's probably passed out from happiness somewhere." Abel flops on his back and hangs his tongue out the side of his mouth. "I mean, what else is she going to do? We're together now. Mission accomplished."

Or maybe...

"What if something bad happened?"

"Pssh. Like what?"

"What if we embarrassed her when we told them we knew about them, and she got in her car all upset, and then—"

It would be your fault.

"Yeahhh, okay." Abel smirks. "And what if she stayed in her house five minutes longer to watch our post, and then when she got to Starbucks the guy in front of her took the last scone so she had a bran muffin instead and choked to death on a raisin?"

"I'm serious."

"I know. That's your whole problem." He kisses me on the cheek and yanks my Vegas cap over my eyes. "I'm sure your little fic friend is fine."

"Why would she stand them up, though?"

"*I* don't know." He swings his legs off the bed. "She probably got bored. Maybe she found some repressed *Star Trek* vloggers who are even hotter than us and—ow! *Dammit.*"

He rubs his heel.

"What?"

He shakes his head, grabs something off the floor.

"Ugh, these things are so cheap. Can't believe I paid ten bucks for one. Think fast!"

He throws it to me. It's the mechanical heart from the Castaway Ball, a wide jagged crack exposing its insides.

"Do us both a huge favor, okay?" Abel says.

I flip the switch. The blue heart-light stutters, then winks out.

"Don't get superstitious."

21»

I'M SHUT IN A BATHROOM STALL at the Royal Court Inn &
Conference Center in Salt Lake City, rubbing Plastic Sim's
head for luck.

Q&A with Della Wolfe-Williams. Fifteen minutes away.
Since we woke up this morning, I've checked the Church
of Abandon four times from my phone, trying to do it in
secret places like these. I thumb through the few new
posts.

Still no sign of hey_mamacita.

And this is on page 1.

thanks4caring: you guys plz don't flame me but now
that b&a are together for real I'm like a little bit over
them...I think I just shipped them cause I thought it would
never happen but now that it did I actually think they
make kind of a bad couple...like there's no way it's actually going to last w/ them...probly mamacita thought so
too lol

I just stand there with my back up against the door,
reading and rereading that post and the eight others that
"surprisingly, sort of agree" with her. I've seen this kind
of thing before in fandom. Shippers slowly jumping ship,
communities unraveling once their leaders disappear.

I shove it out of my mind. *None of this matters. It's fiction. You have a boyfriend, for real.*

My phone shrieks at me. HOME CALLING.

I stuff it in my pocket and bang out of the stall.

"I'm so freaking nervous," Bec says. "I'll babble like an idiot. I know it."

The three of us huddle by the stage in the cold Q&A room, ticking off the seconds till Della Wolfe-Williams. Bec's Zara Lagarde action figure peeps out of her shirt pocket. She's debating whether to wait in the autograph line after the Q&A, but I'm only half listening. The crowd is almost too calm. I glance back at the closed doors. Pull my sweatshirt tight around me. I feel like I'm waiting for something besides Della: a random gunman, a fire breaking out in the corner.

"She's just a person," says Abel. "Honestly? When I saw Ed Ransome in person my crush kinda eased up a tiny bit. Right Bran?"

He elbows me.

"Right. Yeah. Mine too, a little."

"Yeah, well, you had *other* stuff going on that night." She holds Plastic Lagarde up to her cheek and bats her eyes. "Will you all wait in line with me? Please please please?"

"Sure—oh. We can't, babe." Abel knocks the heel of his hand against his head. "We've got that stupid-ass lunch with Miss Maxima."

I forgot all about that. *"Ugh."*

"Brandon, tell me what possessed us to call a truce with her again? Was it really just postcoital bliss?"

"'Fraid it was."

"Aw. You *guys*," Bec saps, messing up my hair. She still thinks we're moving too fast, I can tell, but she's been nice enough to act totally happy for us this week. I relax a little. I swing my arm around her waist and give her a squeeze.

"Oh farts, there she is." Abel pokes me. "The one and only."

He points. My eyes connect his finger to a girl on the far side of the room, shouldering her way through the crowd. Miss Maxima looks just like she does in her profile picture on the Cadsim comm. Like one of those women they used to warn sailors about when my great-great uncles were in the war: fake mole, leopard pillbox hat, tight red dress with big black buttons, five-alarm lipstick on a sideways smirk. She's dragging along a short doughy kid with a paler, plainer version of her face; the girl's got on a cartoon vampire t-shirt and she looks like she wants to disappear. I would too if Maxima was my big sister.

Hello boys, Miss Maxima mouths, her red lips enlarging each syllable. She sends us a dainty finger-wave.

"Gross," says Abel.

"Completely," I say.

"She's so amazing," says Bec.

We both whip around.

"Not Miss M." Bec eyerolls. "Della Wolfe-Williams. Did you know she's a first-degree black belt in tai chi?" She pets the bio in the CastieCon program. "She has two Siberian huskies and on the weekends she goes mountain biking and makes salsa verde from scratch." She blushes. "Sorry."

"Dear fangirl," Abel says, "have you no idea who you're talking to?"

"Do you think she'd take a picture with Plastic Lagarde?"

"Dunno. She seems deadly serious. You should grease her up with some sweet talk about the feminist subtexts of the swamp-monster episode. Or tell her you write fic where Lagarde saves the world with her magic vagina." He winds his arms around me from behind. "What do you think, Bran?"

I hear the words but they breeze right through me. I'm thinking of "How to Repair a Mechanical Heart," blipped out of existence with the rest of hey_mamacita, the copy I salvaged filed sad and unfinished in a private folder on my laptop.

"Sure," I mutter, but no one hears.

Della Wolfe-Williams is coming.

You see her legs first, the thigh-high black warrior boots with skull-shaped buckles and impossible heels. Leather pants, studded belt, brown tank top two shades darker than her skin. Her buzzcut's grown out into short little spikes that look soft and hard at the same time. No makeup except a sharp perfect outline around each eye.

"I want to be her when I grow up," Bec whispers.

"So do I," whispers Abel.

Della's sweeping the lip of the stage, letting her fingers brush fans' outstretched hands. Her face is this cool haughty mask and I wonder if she's smiling inside, parodying herself just a little. She used words like *obdurate* and *paradigm* in her last Popwatch interview, so probably not.

She grabs the mike like a weapon.

"Greetings, fellow travelers."

Some cheers and *yeahs* and a piercing whistle. Bec clutches Plastic Lagarde and looks like she's about to pee or faint. Della raises her hands, tamps down the praise.

"I certainly hope everyone's ready for an intelligent discussion, because as we all know..." She leans in, her lush lips brushing the mike. "I *don't* suffer fools."

The cheers amp up. Abel swings an arm around me and I flinch a little. I hope he didn't notice.

"Well, you all look fairly tolerable, so let's dig right in. Shall we?" Della frowns at the mike and adjusts it. "Tons to discuss and debate this season, right? Some *very* rich visual metaphor, a few controversial arcs and plot twists, shifting character dynamics with deep implications that could reverberate next season and beyond. Someone kick us off with a good smart topic!"

"Did Sim and Cadmus hook up in the spider cave?"

Everyone turns like she's farted in church. Miss Maxima is standing with one ridiculous hand on her ridiculous hip, the fingers of her other hand poised for an imaginary cigarette. Della Wolfe-Williams blinks at her and tilts a little, possibly picturing Maxima's head stuffed and mounted above her fireplace.

"And who might you be?"

"Melissa Arnott. I go by Miss Maxima?" Her fake-smoky voice is about what you'd expect from a theater major with a DVR full of *Castaway Planet* and Bette Davis films. "I moderate one of the most highly regarded fan-journal communities for *Castaway Planet* fans. You might have heard of the Cadsim Connection?"

"I have not."

"Our fan fiction is very widely respected in the *Castaway Planet* fandom, and—"

"Oh, good grief."

"What?"

"Nothing, nothing. Romanticism poisoning the fan experience—trust me, I'm an old-school X-Phile; I know how it goes." She sighs. "I'm sorry. You were saying. People apparently think Cadmus and Sim—" She makes a face and grinds her index fingers together.

"Yes! Well, we're *hoping*..."

"No. Sorry, but no," says Della Wolfe-Williams. "Why do people think this pairing is a good idea? I find it really baffling, if I'm being honest."

Someone yells *boooo!* I sneak a look at Abel. He makes

a halfhearted *herp derp* face.

Miss Maxima's motormouthing: "...would actually make total sense for their characters, if you think about it, and also I heard the plan is to get them together during sweeps next season."

"People actually think that?" Della Wolfe-Williams twists her mouth up.

"Many do, yes," Maxima says. "In fact, two of the biggest believers are right there in front of the stage. In the Blondie shirt? And the baseball cap?"

Abel facepalms.

"These two young men?" says Della.

"Yep. Isn't that right, boys?"

"Ah," I say, "no, we—"

"Oh, don't be modest! They're relatively new converts but they've already written the most *incredible* fanfic." Maxima smirks. "It's just so lyrical and romantic. Emotionally, they build a rock-solid case for the Cadmus-Sim pairing; I mean, you should read it sometime. There's this flashfic set in the spider cave that's almost like a sonnet, and—"

"Uh-huh, uh-huh. Well listen, you two little Shakespeares." Della Wolfe-Williams clicks closer to us. "I studied queer lit in college so I'm nothing if not an ally, but I'll eat my boot if an actual relationship happens. It would be the *worst* storyline disaster since the giant-sandworm episode in Season 2."

Giggles in the crowd. Some grumbles. Bec's holding the camera on Della, but her eyes keep straying to me.

"People. Look." Della holds up a hand. "Clearly I don't know what's brewing in Lenny Bray's cranium; none of us do, but you're asking me, and I say it's not possible on any level. It stretches every reasonable test of credibility, character-wise."

Miss Maxima folds her arms and flicks her dark bangs. "Why is that?"

"Ahh, let's see. Well, for starters..." She looks right at us. "Cadmus: classic narcissistic personality, obsessed with his hair, obnoxious hero complex, etc. And the sad fact is, even if Cadmus changed tomorrow, Sim couldn't. He isn't capable of real love."

The crowd murmurs. Abel slings me a sidelong glance.

"Well, plenty of people think that's a cruel assessment of Sim's character," says Maxima. "My writers—"

"Oh, is that what they think? That if you don't believe in character assassination, you're just a big meanie?" Della shakes her head. "It is a neutral *fact*. Stop romanticizing him, people! He's not going to change, because he can't. Chip or no chip, he's a *machine*. It's crystal-clear from Episode 1: He was built to follow orders, not fall in love."

"Ouch," whispers Abel.

Ouch, says my stomach.

"Besides, isn't that the fun of slash fiction? It plays off subtext," says Della Wolfe-Williams. "If they really got together, guys—wouldn't that ruin everything?"

***

"We try to make peace with Maxie, and she publicly humiliates us!" Abel's pacing in the CastieCon exhibit hall, right next to a display of coffee mugs with the Hell Bells etched in silver. "That's just—that's *not cool*."

I blink at the rows of mugs: green, orange, stop-sign red. *He's not going to change, because he can't.* I don't believe that about myself, not anymore. So why can't I stop replaying it?

"Ugh, here she comes. Look blasé." Abel hooks his thumbs in his pockets and studies the ceiling, whistling off-key. Miss Maxima zigzags through the crowd. Her pill-box hat bobs in a sea of shaggy hair and baseball caps, and her big round face radiates smug.

"Hello, young lovers!" she sings.

"Hey." I stare at her lip. I think the mole is drawn on.

"Sorry it took so long to *wend* my way over; I was having a fascinating talk with Ty Savarese—you know him? Big name fan, co-moderates the forum?"

"Why'd you tell the whole room we write Cadsim fic?" Abel sticks his hands on his hips.

"Oh! Well, I was just having fun. I didn't think you'd mind, with your little *conversion* and all."

"We still have standards."

"Pardon me? Two of our Cadsim writers are Iron Quill winners, so you can drop the snobbery anytime." She takes out a vintage snap-case with some old-timey domi-natrix on it and selects a long brown cigarette. "Now, don't you worry about Della and her *no*s; she overthinks everything. Lenny Bray's opinion matters most—make sure you pin him down in Baltimore. Obviously he won't give spoilers for next season, but I'll bet he'll drop some solid Cadsim hints. See how much you can get him to spill." She passes Abel an antique silver lighter. "I bet you're charming when you want to be."

"Excessively." Abel flips the top of the lighter and holds a steady flame to her cigarette.

"So our lunch. I was thinking the hotel café, just to make it easy?"

I glance at Abel. "I think...we might take a raincheck."

"Yeah. We're tired."

"You do look pale. Especially you, Brandon. But sorry, you can't back out now." She beams a sweet, nasty smile at us. "I've invited a very special guest."

22»

MISS MAXIMA MARCHES US to the Illuminations Café & Grill to the right of the hotel lobby, where she makes us buy her a fruit and yogurt parfait, an egg salad sandwich, and a gourmet iced coffee the size of a Big Gulp. The whole time we're waiting in line she's edgy: looking around, checking her Betty Boop watch. When we settle at a table, she doesn't even unwrap the sandwich. She just takes tense little sips from the coffee cup until she spots someone a few tables away, hiding behind a menu.

"Excuse me," she sighs.

She clacks over in her leopard heels and yoinks the menu. It's the kid with her face, from the Q&A. Maxima's a few yards away now, but her theater voice travels.

"Chelle, what do you think you're doing?"

The kid mutters something to the paper placemat.

"Family drah-maaah," Abel says. He chomps his Spicy Santa Fe wrap.

"What's she up to?"

"Lord knows. Should we make a break for it?"

"She'll get us back if we do."

"Oh, *Brandon*—"

I smack his arm and point. Maxima's hissing at the girl now: "You *better*, and right now, or I swear I will tell Mom what you and Daphne—"

"You're such a *hosebeast*, Missy!"

"Maybe." She spits out something else; it sounds like *But I'm right.*

Then she grabs the girl by the wrist and drags her over.

"Abel. Brandon. May I introduce my sister, Michelle."

"Hey, Michelle." Abel wipes a glob of salsa off his hand and sticks it out. She just whispers "hey," her knuckles blanching on the chair back. She's probably twelve or thirteen, but already she looks like the kind of person who shuffles through life expecting the worst. Her brown hair is cut in a messy bob and her lips are thin and grim and she has cute freckles that look like they landed on the wrong face.

"Let's get comfortable, shall we?"

Miss Maxima sits and starts daintily loosening her sandwich from the plastic wrap. The girl drops into the chair next to hers and knots her arms. She's wearing a giant ring with a bug trapped in amber. She shoots Maxima a filthy look, the same one I gave Nat the time she told her hot friend Mark that I wet the bed until I was nine.

"It's egg salad, Chelle," says Maxima.

"Uh-huh."

"Remember the time you put a worm in my egg salad and I couldn't eat it again for three whole years?"

"No."

Maxima takes a big deliberate bite. She chews slowly, looking back and forth between Michelle and us. I wonder if this is some kind of twisted summer homework assignment for her college improv class. She'll assign us characters next: Abel the rowdy drunk, me the rookie cop.

She swigs her coffee monstrosity and folds her hands on the table.

"So the thing about my little sister is, she's always playing a big joke on me," Maxima says. "See, she absolutely cannot let me have anything nice without messing it up—been like that since we were kids, right Chelle? Remember my Fairy of the Forest Barbie?" The girl glares at her lap. Her cheeks are on fire. "Anyway, this is how it is. Her stuff was always broken and dirty because she never took care of it, and my stuff was always nice because I did, and she never could handle it, so now she takes every opportunity to mock and undermine everything I stand for. Prime example: When I ran for senior class president, Michelle had to run for freshman rep too, and with this *stupid* Free Goldfish for All platform." She narrows her eyes. "I guess it was a short leap from there to here."

"Shut up, Missy," Michelle mutters.

"Unfortunately, what she didn't seem to *get*," says Miss Maxima, "was that creating a fake fan shrine to her sister's arch-rivals just might have larger repercussions than pissing me off."

Under the table, Abel's nails bite the back of my hand.

"I think you owe them an explanation, Chelle." Maxima leans back. "Excuse me: hey_mamacita."

Abel's hand grips mine harder. I yank it away. This doesn't make sense. None of it does. It's a joke, a mean trick. She got this kid to play-act and later she'll slip her a fifty while they snicker about our ashen faces, and when we get back to the RV the real hey_mamacita will have posted. *So so sorry Abandonites, family emergency. I'm BACK! Here's the next chapter.*

"Don't you have anything to say to them?" Maxima swirls her yogurt around. "I mean, you and your minions pretty much used these two pathetic souls like paper dolls and now look at them. They think they're in love. See, this is why my FJ hates real-person-shipping; the fourth wall could crumble anytime, and then you've got a huge embarrassing mess on your—"

"Sorry," Michelle whispers.

"That's all?" says Maxima.

Michelle's eyes flick up at us, just for a second.

219

My breath catches in my throat.

Then she shoves her chair back, throws her balled napkin at Maxima, and rushes for the exit.

"Close your mouths, you two. You'll catch flies." Miss Maxima licks yogurt off her spoon. "I've done you a service. You deserve to know the truth. Especially since you devoted so much of your valuable time to critiquing our fic this year." She taps the spoon against her lip. "What did you say about mine again?—Oh, right: *Hacky and derivative...*"

She's saying more, but I'm not listening. I'm pushing my chair back, stumbling through the maze of tables after Michelle Arnott.

*   *   *

She's good at disappearing.

I check the gift shop, the pool, the corridors—everywhere I might hide if I had to run away. Nothing. Then I start checking stupid places. The men's room. The slim space between the wall and the vending machine. The more places I check, the longer I can put off the full truth seeping in. *hey_mamacita. Not real. Never was.*

A joke.

I step up on the little wooden bridge that arches over the huge clear koi pond in the lobby. The blue and gray tiles on the floor of the pond are littered with pennies, dimes, quarters; my father would say *That's a lot of money to throw away on wishes.* I'm jittering my fingers on the wooden railing, watching a pure gold koi get jostled by his big spotted pondmates, when a small dark silhouette ripples beside me. I hear the crunch of a plastic snack bag, catch a glimpse of an amber ring.

Now that she's here, I think about running. But I don't.

"Gummy bear?" she says.

I whisper, "How old are you?"

"Guess."

"You look twelve."

"I'm seventeen. But thanks. That never gets old."

I shake my head. I can't look at her. "Your profile picture..."

"Some random artist. I was in Baltimore last year and she let me take photos at Artscape. Gorgeous, right? I hate dreads and neck tats in general but on her...?" The bag crinkles and she says her next line with her mouth full. "If you're going to be fake, at least be a badass, right?"

My tongue goes numb. I want to sit but my legs won't move.

"You're not going to sue me, are you?" she says. "I don't think that's legal."

"Why would you do this?"

"You want me to like, explore my psychology?"

"Yeah. Please."

"What am I, a Bond villain?" She drops a gummy bear into the pond and watches it sink to the bottom. "I don't know, Brandon. It started out like, just making fun of Missy and her whole stupid shipping thing in the most ridiculous elaborate way, and then actual people started joining the community—like, who knew you had fans for real?"

"Thanks."

"And so they like worshipped my fic and they started calling me their fearless leader and no one's ever done that before because Missy always butts her way to the front of everything. It was like crack. Just *having fans*, you know?—Yeah, you do. So I just kept going bigger and bigger and deeper and deeper with it and—you know where this is going, right? Standard drunk-on-my-own power narrative?"

I glance at her. "I guess."

"I feel like crap. I totally told whispering!sage I'd meet her at the Long Beach con. Like, why did I do that? You lie enough and all of a sudden it's like lying is the language you speak and your first language starts to disappear." Her eyes get bright and hungry. "God. That's good. I wish I still wrote fic."

She tries a smile. I can't.

"Look, I said I was sorry." She sighs. "What do you want? Money? I'm completely broke."

"No...no."

"Seriously—you can't be surprised. Not really. People pretend all the time. You live online, pretty much everyone's a character." She points an eyebrow. "Even you. Right?"

"That's different."

"Why? Because shit got real and you're all *in love* now?"

"Italics not necessary."

"Oh, Brandon." She crunches up the gummy bear bag. "Don't take this the wrong way, but as the Internet's foremost expert on you, I think you need some therapy."

"Really."

"I mean, whatever: you guys are pretty hot together. I'll admit. I wouldn't have kept writing that silly fic if you weren't, you know...*compelling* in some way. But taking your past into consideration?" She makes a dismissive *tch* sound. "I don't think you're ready for a relationship."

I feel six inches high. "That's...mean."

"No it's not. Look, I freaked when I saw your schmoopy post that night. It was a total what-have-I-done, Frankenstein's-monster moment. I had no clue it would go this far."

"Yeah, well, we would've—"

"Hooked up anyway? Maybe, maybe not. It's a bad idea regardless. I'm a screwed-up Catholic too, you know? I sympathize. I mean, Missy's too full of herself to have hangups but I'm a total chickenshit in real life, to the point where I'm too chickenshit to even deal with being chickenshit, which means I'll never get anything figured out." She pops a handful of gummy bears. "I'll probably be a virgin till I die. I think I might be a lesbian. Or maybe I'm bi, I don't know. I don't have any answers."

"Oh."

"Like, all that stuff I spouted in my fic, how God didn't make us to suffer? *Pfft.* How would I know? Maybe he's like Xaarg and he uses us for his sick amusement, you know? Maybe he thinks it's hilarious that I'm attracted to people, but then I sort of feel like throwing up when they touch me, and I'll probably end up dying alone in a studio apartment with a Chihuahua eating my face off."

I study the railing. "You won't."

"Don't be so sure. Honestly, I don't think people ever get un-screwed-up. I think it's just, how well can you pretend to be someone else, and how long."

Two businessmen in suits clomp across the bridge. The koi startle and scatter. Abel appears across the lobby, scanning with the bewildered concentration of someone trying to find someone.

My time with her is almost up.

"So, ah," I draw in a breath that makes my throat ache. "Guess you weren't really sent by God?"

I try to keep my voice light and jokey, but it splinters on the word *God*. She flicks one last gummy bear off the railing and stares down into the clear trembling water.

"You've thrown a lot of pennies in ponds," she says. "Haven't you."

23»

I DON'T WANT ABEL to find me. Not yet. I duck down a corridor, slip into a quiet stairwell.

I don't think people ever get un-screwed-up.

My heart pummels so hard I expect to hear an echo.

I don't think you're ready for a relationship.

I lean over the railing. My head swarms. I wish I was good at dismissing people. I could be like Nat: What a bitch. Screw her. Who does she think she is?

I don't have any answers.

My phone goes off. I jump. HOME CALLING.

I sink down on the steps and pick it up, not thinking it through. All I'm thinking is yes, please, I need home.

"Thank *God*," Mom says. "Brandon, we were worried!"

"You haven't called for days," Dad snaps. "We just get one email, four words long—"

I feel like crying. "I'm sorry."

"You could've been kidnapped. Maybe someone was impersonating you. How would we know?"

"Did you really think—"

"Oh, it doesn't matter! The point is, you made your mother lose sleep."

"You've just been having fun with Becky, right, Brandon?" Mom says. "That's all."

I drop my head on the concrete step behind me. "Yeah," I get out. "It's been really great."

"That's so wonderful. See, Greg?"

"Did you take her out for that dinner?" Dad harrumphs.

"No, but I will." I close my eyes. "Maybe tonight. I think

224

tonight we will."

"Okay. All right," Dad says. I sense the anger funneling out of him and for now that's enough, making him okay with me again. "I told you, I'll pay for it."

"Sure."

"Wherever you two want to go."

"I appreciate it. Thanks." *I'm a total chickenshit in real life.*

"Brandon?" says Mom.

"Yep."

"Are you all right, sweetie? You sound—far away."

"I am far away."

"I know this is such a...confusing time for you, but—"

You have no idea. "I'm great, Mom. Don't worry, okay?" She sounds so sad. "I'll be home before you know it."

"Maybe you'll come to the St. Matt's Funfair on the Fourth?"

"...Sure." No. *No.*

"You're a good kid, Brandon," Dad says.

I'm not stupid. I hear how he says it: like a command, not a compliment. But his words work on me, independent of the tone, and I want it all back again. I want to be the good kid. I want to be the kid who never made them worry, the one who was safe in his bed while Nat was off at Rocky Horror throwing toast and making out with A.J. Brody. I want to believe what they believe, to feel Mom's smiling eyes on me while I strum "Be Not Afraid" at the Folk Mass, to ask Dad for advice when he stops by my room to say goodnight. Except now my problem is *I'm afraid I'm going to break my boyfriend's heart.* And even if I got brave enough to ask, I don't think he'd sit down on my bed and ruffle my hair. He'd just turn off the light and walk away.

24»

OUR CLOTHES TUMBLE TOGETHER in a dented old dryer at the Compass Creek Campground laundry room. Abel and I sit on molded plastic seats the color of pea soup and watch. I spot my *Castaway Planet* shirt and keep my eyes on that, watching it get tossed and battered and tossed again.

Nothing's changed.

I tell myself that, over and over. Nothing's changed. I'm here in a laundry room doing a quick load of darks with my boyfriend, and then we're going to take a walk in the woods and play WordWhap with Bec and have late-night cherry Pop-Tarts in bed like we've done every night since Long Beach. I tell myself that, and then Michelle Arnott's face pops up and I start breathing faster, bracing myself for all the other bad things to come back. It's like that scene in the cave when Cadmus lit a match and the crystal spiders all started crawling out of secret dark places, hissing closer and closer.

I joggle Plastic Sim in my hand, lose myself in the machine's warm mechanical hum. I want to disappear into Sim again. I want the simple ease of clean robot fantasies that fade out with kissing and don't come with a crapload of complications.

"Brandon," Abel says. "You sneaky bitch."

"What?"

"You're having a relapse."

"Huh?"

"It all makes sense!" He waggles a finger at me like I'm a Scooby-Doo villain. "You were like a billion miles away at the go-kart track."

"Sorry."

"And I made you my world-famous kitchen-sink nachos and you completely failed to rhapsodize."

"World-famous?"

"Well. Susannah likes them."

I force a shrug. "Too spicy."

"Surprise surprise."

Five seats over, some grizzly guy in camo pants is chomping a chalupa and waiting for his afghan to dry. He gave us this *look* when we walked in. I think back to three or four years ago, when Dad's remote stopped at *Project Runway* for five seconds. "What they do is their business," he'd grumbled. "But why are they all so *loud* about it?"

"I'm okay," I lie. "No relapse."

"Want to talk about it?"

"No."

"What'd what's-her-face say to you at the hotel? Just tell me."

"I don't want to." I slouch down in my seat. "I just want to forget her."

He cracks into a two-pack of snack cakes. "It's *almost* kind of funny. If you think about it. Cupcake?"

"No."

"It doesn't change anything."

"Right! I know."

"Like, have you ever seen *Dumbo*?"

"Uh...yeah. Ages ago."

"Remember when he thought he could fly because he was holding the magic feather, and then one day he loses the feather and—what happens?"

"He panics."

"You would remember that. He flies anyway, dumbass."

"Right. The gritty realism of Disney."

"Don't be cynical. It's ugly on you." He pokes my belly button. I poke him back and then he's tickling my ribs, swooping in to nibble a kiss on my neck.

"Abel—" I murmur.

"What?"

"That guy's giving us looks."

"So? He's probably jealous."

"He looks like a gun nut or something."

"Oh, they're all secretly closeted. Haven't you heard?" He studies the guy's profile and leans close to me, dropping his voice to a husky whisper. "Twenty years may have passed, but still he longs for Joe, his truck-driving partner with the sexy sideburns and the shapely—"

I smack him. "Sto-op."

"He still remembers that fateful night...hauling a truck-load of tennis balls through Tuscaloosa..."

"Oh my God."

"The tape deck was playing—help me, Bran."

I roll my eyes. "Journey's Greatest Hits."

"Brilliant." He grins and slides a hand up my thigh. I feel my muscles loosen a little. "Joe's face in the silvery moonlight had never looked so enticing...they sang 'Lovin', Touchin', Squeezin' together, their voices entwining in unexpected harmony."

"They pulled over at a rest stop."

"Yes. *Hot*." He nests his chin on my shoulder. "For twenty stolen minutes, under the stars in a dense patch of forest, they—"

"Twenty minutes?"

"No?"

I'm grinning now. "You're, ah, selling their passion short."

"You're right. For shame." He nips my ear. "For forty-five stolen minutes, they unlocked the secrets of each

228

other...their cares melting away as they whispered—"

"Take it somewhere else."

I jump. Camo Pants is right in front of us. He's chewing on a toothpick and standing like the football players at school did before a big game: fists on waist, legs planted far apart. I go cold.

Abel smiles, still in fic-land. "Sorry. Did you say something?"

"Yep. I said, take it somewhere else."

Abel flutters his lashes. "Like where?"

"Anywhere I don't have to see it."

Shut up. Please shut up, I message Abel, thinking of the call to my parents: *"I'm so sorry. Your son was shot to death in a campground laundry room."* But the guy's done for now. He clomps off to the soda machine, shooting a glare over his shoulder.

Abel snorts and swallows a giggle. I let out the breath I'd been holding.

"What a goon." Abel elbows me.

"Uh-huh."

"Hey."

"What."

"I want to take you on a date," he says. "Like a cheesy old-school restaurant date."

My heart's still hammering. "When?"

"When we're back on the road, like in Nebraska or Iowa. Some weirdo small town where we'll never ever be again. We'll find someplace good." He hooks his fingers through mine. "Say yes."

"Okay..."

"How come you always do that?" He grins.

"Do what?"

"Squeeze my hand twice? It's cute."

"Oh..." Camo Pants bangs out of the laundry room, the

229

rusty bells slapping the glass door. "It's dumb."

"There's a story? Tell me!"

I keep my eyes on the door. He'll come back any minute with a rifle, the same battered .223 Remington he just used to shoot up coyotes in the Utah backwoods. "Mom used to do that when I was a kid," I tell Abel. "Sort of a tradition. She said it was like—" Footsteps scuffle, metal rattles outside.

"Like what?"

It's just an old lady with a shopping cart. "...It was our secret code for 'I love you.' That way we could say it any time, even when we couldn't talk. Like in the middle of church or whatever."

"That's intensely sweet."

"Yeah."

"A good kind of secret."

You can't keep secrets from God, guys. He knows everything.

"Bran?"

He sees everything.

"You okay? What's wrong?"

I stab my nails into my palm. The Father Mike stuff won't come back.

I won't let it.

"You've got cream on your cheek," I tell him.

"Geez. Don't scare me like that." He wipes it off and forces a laugh. "It's like you were past-tense Brandon for a minute."

I get up and start raking our warm dry clothes out of the dented machine, just to shield my face from his field of vision. I don't want Abel to know that maybe there is no past-tense Brandon after all. Only present imperfect. And if I'm not extra-careful now, he's going to ruin everything.

***

CHURCH OF ABANDON ROLL CALL!!

retro robot: helloooooo? who's still here? anyone? **tumbleweeds**

amity crashful: I am!

sorcha doo: me.

whispering!sage: me too but tbh, at this point I'm just kinda killing time until the Castaway Planet premiere. I mean after the hey_mamacita thing...

a_rose_knows: I know, and plus abandon fic is redundant now. like why am I writing you sex scenes when you're doing it for real as I type?

sorcha doo: except rosey your scenes are probably better lol

amity crashful: I have to admit they were 100000x sexier when they were tragic and unrequited. ugh! WTF is wrong with me? this is why all my relationships are doomed.

lone detective: Well, not to worry. IF they're actually together, they'll be broken up soon. Not that any of you will care by then.

sorcha doo: detective will you shut it! why are you still around??

lone detective: Oh, for the most entertaining part of fandom. Fiddling while Rome burns.

25»

"Our first date." Abel clutches my hand in the Tuscan-tiled waiting cove, bouncing on the heels of his dirty white wingtips. "This is so fun!"

God wouldn't call this a date.

The Olive Grotto in Layton, Nebraska is the kind of place where teenagers go for fancy pre-prom dinners, where men take their wives to celebrate anniversaries and surprise them with heart-shaped gold necklaces they saw on TV. It is not the kind of place where two teenage boys walk into the lobby holding hands, unless it's Halloween and one of them is snickering in unconvincing drag.

The hostess has a snappy blond ponytail and quick, efficient hands. She snatches two menus from the pocket on the side of her podium and says "'Kay. You can follow me." She takes off fast, like she's trying to lose us or something. Abel's nodding to the waiters and humming that old song about *your personal Jesus* but I'm taking it all in, and I see how people are looking at his neon polo shirt and skinny white tie and I notice where she seats us. In the corner, with three empty tables between us and everyone else.

I open the menu and start flipping pages.

"What's with the face?" Abel says.

"The hostess," I lie. "Just...reminds me of someone."

"I know, right? She's such a type. Overgrown pageant kid." He cups a hand to his mouth. "Ten to one her parents aren't entirely convinced the earth is round."

"Heh."

"Oh good *gravy* Brandon will you look at that giant fake wine bottle?" He points to a decorative bottle-vase on the opposite wall with two orange poppies stuck inside. "We *must* have it!"

"Uh-huh."

"We can take it to college. We'll share custody."

"You can't take the decorations, dummy."

"Oh yeah?" He takes out a five-dollar bill and brandishes it, doing a sleazy eyebrow-wiggle. "My friend *Mr. Lincoln* says otherwise."

I snort a little. He cracks up. Loud.

"I'm so glad you wanted to come here." Abel reaches out and grabs both my hands. My eyes dart around.

"It'll be fun," I say lamely.

"Yes! *Thank* you. I hate when people are snobby about the Olive Grotto. My dad has this one surgeon friend, he's like the world's foremost expert on being a douche-nozzle, and he's always like 'the Olive Grotto is the Spam of Tuscan cuisine' and I'm like dude, cram it, 'cause sometimes you want to stuff your damn self with chicken parm bruschetta, you know?"

I nod. I wish he'd talk quieter. "The breadsticks are good too."

"They are godlike."

You know what isn't Godlike?

"What would Cadmus order here?" I blurt.

"Ooh! Excellent question." He scans the menu. "I think he's a straight-up lasagna guy. Maybe some short ribs."

"Mm."

"And for Sim...he'd go clean and simple, if he ate at all. Some grilled lemon chicken...?"

Across the room, a gray-haired guy with jowls and a bald-eagle t-shirt is staring at us. He turns away when he sees me looking. Whispers to his wife.

233

"All right." Abel slaps the menu shut. "What's wrong?"

Be honest. Tell him this is a mistake.

"I'm having a..." I hate this a lot. "You know."

"A baby?" His eyes go tender in a cartoony way. "Aww, *honey*. It's just like that mpreg where Cadmus tells Sim he's expecting twins and—"

I wave away the joke. "A relapse. You were right."

"Oh." I see panic cross his face. "Oh. God. Is it because I sang 'Personal Jesus'?"

"No. No."

"It was the dollar store, wasn't it?"

"Huh?"

"Back there, back there! When I made Spongebob eat the nun figurine?"

"No. It wasn't that—"

"God, I'm an idiot! I knew I should've—"

"It's not your fault, okay? Relax."

He sits up straight, nodding fast. "Okay. Okay, then. I don't want this to turn bad. What can I do?"

"I—nothing, really. Nothing."

He blinks at me. "Please don't break up with me at the Olive Grotto."

"I'm not breaking up with you!"

"Well, I have to do something. I'm your boyfriend, right?"

The way he says that is so sweet I feel like crying. What can I tell him that doesn't sound deeply insane? *Well, things just haven't been the same since I found out hey_mamacita is a screwed-up kid instead of a divinely inspired matchmaking warrior.*

Abel folds his hands. "So—I guess, talk to me."

"I don't know where to start."

"Tell me exactly what happens. Do you hear that Father Mike's voice in your head or something?"

"I don't actually *hear* it." I shoot him a dark look. "I'm not crazy."

"No, I didn't mean..." He sighs. "Shit. Sorry. I'm just trying to understand."

"I know." I reach across the table, stroke his arm. "It's more like I remember things he said before. Or I imagine what he *would* say, if he saw me."

"But you said you don't believe that stuff anymore, right? Like, it's a sin or whatever."

"My brain doesn't. No."

"But your heart...?"

"No, my heart pretty much approves, too." I give him a faint smile and squeeze his hand.

"So what's the problem, then?"

"It's hard to explain."

"Try."

"You'll think it's weird."

"What, like, did you see Jesus in your pancakes this morning?"

"Okay."

"Did an angel appear to you in the iHop bathroom?"

"See..."

"*Repennnt! Mortify your flesssssh! Order the Smoke-house Combooooo!*"

"You're getting all judgy."

"*I'm* getting judgy? I don't judge anyone!"

"You get judgy about religion."

"So? I think I'm entitled."

"So it's complicated for me."

"Uh-huh. Okay." He twists his mouth and tilts back in his chair. "So here's what I don't get. You met with Father Mike that one time, and he gave you that stupid *Step On the Brakes* book and quoted the Bible at you, right?"

"Yeah."

"So why didn't you fight him?"

"What, like..." I make a fist, mime a punch.

"No, goofass. Why didn't you argue with him? Tell him you didn't believe God was really like that? And don't say you were scared, because I know you have balls. I've seen them. In action."

I shrug, blushing. "I don't know. It's like, how do you argue with Leviticus?"

"I do. So do tons of people, right? Aren't there gay theology people? Those churches with rainbow flags and shit?"

"Yeahhh, but..." I rub at a water splotch with my thumb. "He'd just tell me they were wrong."

"Which would be his opinion."

"Right, but—"

"And why is his opinion more valid than yours?"

He's hiding a trap in a stupid question. I roll my eyes. *Pass.*

"I'll tell you why." He points at me with his fork. "Because you've been conned into thinking anything that makes you too happy is some kind of sin."

"Oh, okay." I kick at the table leg. "I guess I'm stupid, then."

"No! Not at all. That's just what organized religion does, Bran. I've seen it before."

Mom serving stew at Our Daily Bread. Candlelit "O Holy Night" at Christmas Eve Mass. "That's not all it is."

"Well, that seems to be the key feature."

"You just know about the bad parts. You've never seen the good stuff."

"Oh, well, *pardon me,* Mr. Sudden Random Piety." He's shredding a napkin. Angry eyebrows. "You tell me one good thing about it, then. Tell me what's so awesome, huh? The guilt and shame? The weird rituals? The no-condom rule? The priests who—"

"Stop! That's cheap."

"Facts are cheap?"

"People do great things because of religion, too."

"Uh-huh. Like Bec can't do charity work because she's an atheist?"

"I'm not saying—"

"In fact, it means more because they're not just doing it to get to heaven. Next!"

"Well," I squirm. "The sacraments, I guess...and like, the sense of community."

"Aha. Okay. Sure." He taps his chin and squints. "Whispering your sins in a little closet...eating a flat tasteless cookie once a week—"

"All right." It's stuff I think myself, but when he says it I hate him for it.

"—The sublime joys of singing hymns with folks who think you're earmarked for eternal doom. Now it makes sense."

"You're just being shitty now."

"I'm trying to understand—"

"Well, you never will!" I shoot back. People glance over. "You never will, because you didn't grow up in it."

"Yeah, thank fuck for that." He mashes the napkin shreds into a ball. "My parents weren't sadists."

My mind tangles up with sweet memories. Mom adjusting my pipe-cleaner whiskers on the tiger costume she stayed up all night sewing. Dad narrating backyard batting practice: *Number 44, Brandon Page, steps up to the plate in the bottom of the ninth...*

"Don't talk about my parents," I say, evenly.

Abel blushes.

"I'm sorry. I am." He picks at the spotless tablecloth. "I'm sorry, Brandon, I just—I've been burned by this. Like, seriously."

"I know."

"We'll talk later. I'll play nice."

"Kay."

"I want to have a good dinner. Okay? Can we do that?"

I nod.

"Sure. We can."

***

We can't.

The lasagna tastes like a tire and he stabs at his lobster tortellini the whole time and the conversation starts and stalls. On the cab ride back to the campground, you can feel a fight brewing thick in the air, like that time Dad spilled Mom's embarrassing aerobics-class story at her high school reunion and the whole ride home was a tense tick-down to her explosion.

Bec's curled up on the vinyl couch, watching TV with her phone at her ear.

"Heyyyy, kids," she sings. "How *was* it?"

"Perfect." Abel keeps his back to her, grabs a carton of milk from the fridge and takes a few glugs. I force a smile. It's dark; she can't tell.

"I'm watching an old *X-Files* with Dave." She points to her phone. "Wanna join? It's the one with the killer cockroaches."

"Nah, I'm tired." Abel slams the fridge. He sears me with a look. "Let's go to bed, Brandon."

Bec grins. "I'm turning this up, then." She cranks the volume.

Abel shuts the bedroom door behind us. He strips off his tie.

"What are you doing?"

"What's it look like?"

238

"Shouldn't we like—talk more?"

"I don't dwell on bad things. I just make them better." He tips his chin at me. "C'mere."

I look at the floor. He steps close. His hand hooks the back of my neck and he pulls my mouth to his before I can even take a breath. After a second he senses I'm suffocating; his lips soften and migrate to more innocent places.

It's cruel to you both. Keeping this going.

He drops cute desperate kisses on my nose, my eyelids, my cheeks.

Pull away now. You know you're going to.

"Abel."

"What?"

I toy with a button on his polo shirt. "I just...Maybe we should—"

"She can't hear us. She's in Daveland."

"No, like—" I duck the kiss he's about to plant on my neck. "Maybe we should hold off. Just for a while."

A light snaps off inside him. I watch hurt morph into disgust on his face, like he's just caught me sacrificing kittens in the bathroom.

"Damn," he says.

"Not forever! You know? I just think maybe we did this too fast."

He shakes his head and shoves my hands away. "You said you were *fine* with it, Brandon. I asked you like, every step of the way, and—"

"I know. I know."

"How could you let this ruin things?"

"It's not a choice. It's *in* me. I can't just make it go away."

He wraps his white tie around and around his hand. "So—what? We're just *friends* now?"

239

"No...no."

"Should I like, get written permission to touch you, or—"

"Stop. Abel."

"What? I want to know! What happens now?"

"I don't know!" My arms make this desperate wriggly gesture that's completely offensive, like I'm trying to slough off something gross. "Can we just—hold off on the physical stuff? For now? And then I can work through things, and maybe later..."

"I can't believe this," he says softly. "I can't believe you're breaking up with me."

"I'm not."

"Well, clearly you don't want me to touch you anymore, so that's kind of what happens, darling. By default."

He huddles on the edge of the bed with his back to me. I try to find something smart to say, some bull's-eye quip that'll turn this whole conversation around.

I hear a little sniffle.

Oh. *Crap.*

"Abel—"

"It's okay. It's fine. You can't help this, I know. It's just the way you are." He's speaking slowly and carefully, like he's reading off cue cards. "I mean, it's my fault, really. I've been through this before. I'm so stupid, I just jump in with both feet every time..."

I kneel in front of him. "I like that about you."

"I wanted it to be true. I liked you for so long." He scrubs tears away with his fist and tries to smile, which makes me feel worse. "You just didn't seem interested and it was all Fake Zander and whatever, and I was with that dumbass Kade and then—"

"It was true." I correct myself: "It *is*."

I touch his arm. He reaches out for me, but he pulls me

close too hard and fast and I feel all my muscles go stiff.

He lets go of me. Stands up.

His face erases all emotion, like Sim's face when he's in the charging dock. Then it hardens.

He pulls his big black bag out from under the bed and tosses it on the comforter.

"What are you doing?"

"I'm leaving, Bran." He says it with a simple ease that hurts much worse than bitterness.

"How—?"

"There are these magic things called buses."

I close my eyes. This isn't happening.

"I can't do this again." He shrugs. "Sorry. I can't get all moony and ID-bracelet-y over you, and then get a call from you at two in the morning after some college retreat made you have a backwards epiphany and now you think you're in love with some cute little Polly Pocket who can't wait to pop out your cute Catholic babies. And don't try to tell me that's not extremely likely, because guys like you are a fucking minefield, and I was dumb to pretend I didn't know it."

"Abel..."

"Be logical!" He's shoving clothes in his bag. "What happens if I stay? More awkwardness. More fights. We break up and we can't even be friends anymore because we let things get ugly, and then I end up crying for days and calling up my exes and eating Nutella right out of the jar." He throws his bag on the bed and yanks at the zipper. "So we make a clean break now, and this way I get to keep my dignity, right, and you get lots of time or space or whatever the *hell* you need to figure things out, or not figure things out, whatever works for you. Sound good?"

He grabs the bag. I know exactly what I need now. I need a Speech that Changes Everything. Like Cadmus's quotable "Today, We Survive" speech in the pilot, or the tearful speech Abel gives me in whispering!sage's "One Day More," where we make up in a hospital bed before I lapse into a coma. I catch myself thinking *What would hey_mamacita write?*

Beware of false prophets, Brandon.

Just let him—

"No. Don't go." It's all I can get out. *"Please."*

"Put up a fight, then," he says. "Convince me. Tell me exactly how it won't end horribly."

All the words I've ever learned scuttle out of my head. If I had more time I could call them back, arrange them in just the right order. But I know without looking him in the eye that I've already paused too long, and he's not going to wait.

He hoists the bag over his shoulder.

"Have fun at the Baltimore con," he says. "Tell Lenny Bray I said hi."

***

He's gone.

He can't be, though.

He left Plastic Cadmus behind, face down on the Whitetail Wildlife bedspread.

He left his Sim shirt from the ball dangling damp from the doorknob and the spicy-sweet smell of his cinnamon soap hanging in the air.

He left me standing by the bed with his last kiss still fresh on my cheek and a hundred better things to say.

So I wait, because I know he's coming back. I stand right here in the spot where he left me, rocking gently on my heels. I'll be patient. He went for a long walk to clear his head, took a detour to a diner to sulk at a cup of black coffee, and when he's done making me sorry, making me want him back so much that nothing else matters, the Sunseeker door will creak open again and there he'll be.

I wait.

And wait.

Knock knock on the bedroom door; it slits open.

"Brandon?"

Bec.

26»

HER DAD LEFT WHEN we were twelve. I knew he was going to leave, just like she probably knew Abel was going to leave sooner or later, but we both know the unspoken rule about comforting someone. You pretend you had no clue what was coming, no privileged outsider's view. I sat on her yellow bedspread that day with a stiff arm around her and my head bowed like people do at funerals, letting her know I was sharing her sadness. "You don't have to stay," she sniffled, but she knew I would. That's what we do.

"Do you want to go home?"

"I don't know."

She's running with me. We're running to nowhere, down the wooded path that winds away from our campground.

"Do you want to go after him?"

"No."

"Are you sure? We could find the bus station."

The fic writes itself: I track him down at the crowded station, shout his name over the very last call for his bus. He makes me work for forgiveness when I catch up to him, but only for a minute. We fall into each other's arms and the make-up kiss goes on and on, and all the travelers set down their suitcases to clap for the triumph of love.

I stagger to a stop by a giant cottonwood and close my eyes.

"No," I tell her. "What's the point?"

She watches me carefully.

"Okay, well. I'm up for anything," she says. "Just tell me what you want to do."

She waits in the near-dark. She's wearing sneakers with her pajama pants and the sleeves of her black t-shirt are rolled up to her shoulders, like she's ready for a fight. I think of Sim. Standing outside Lagarde's hut with a knife pointed to his right temple, where the evolution chip was installed. *Take it out,* he'd begged Lagarde. *How do people live like this?*

When she refused, he'd picked up a thick long branch, like this one, and beat it against a tree until it shattered into splinters.

Like this.

Bec watches. She doesn't try to stop me. She just lets me pummel the poor old tree like a Boy Scout gone savage, smashing one branch after another until I'm out of branches and out of breath and I give up the fight, collapsing limp against the ancient bark.

I hear a distant trill. My phone.

"That's him," Bec says.

She sounds so firm and hopeful that I believe it too. I yank the phone out of my pocket and answer fast, in the dark. If I'd checked the screen first, I would've seen the warning.

HOME CALLING.

"Brandon?"

Damn.

"Uh. Hey!" I force a smile into my voice. "Everything's great. Can I call you back?"

"No, actually," Dad says.

"Brandon," says Mom, in the same tone she used when I was twelve and she found the *Tiger Beat* stash in my closet. "Is there something you'd like to tell us?"

27»

"I WOULD LIKE TO KNOW," my father says, "why your mother had to find out in an email from *Mary Beth Heffler* that you were driving across the country with a boy we clearly do not trust."

"What?"

"Facebook doesn't lie, Brandon. Mary Beth's daughter posted on Bec's wall. Something about...you have it, Kathy."

"'*Lucky you...cross country with two hot guys! Too bad they're both gay, lol.*'"

Oh God.

I make an *I'm dead* sign to Bec, finger slashing throat. She cringes and makes a *Should I stay?* motion; my hands tell her *My demise needs no witnesses.* She slips away but I see her stay close, just behind a Ponderosa pine a little way back down the path.

"You lied to us," Dad says. "True or false?"

"True," I whisper. I rest my forehead on the cottonwood I'd just attacked.

"Tell us it's Abel, at least. Not someone worse."

"It's him. Or, it was. He—" My eyes fill up. "He left."

Dad makes a disbelieving *ugh* sound. "You're coming home, in case you're wondering," he says. "Right now."

"What—why?"

"*Why?*"

"There's one more convention."

"You should have thought about that before you spent five weeks lying to your parents."

"I'm not in high school anymore," I say. "It's my life."

"Well, it's my RV, kiddo," Dad says calmly. "And I want you to return it immediately. Where are you right now?"

I dig my fingernails into the bark. "Far away. Nebraska."

"All right. Fine. I want you back here tomorrow night. On Friday you can help with setup for the Funfair at St. Matt's and then you and your mother and I will have a long talk."

"I don't want to talk."

"Honey. Come on," soothes Mom.

"I'm not coming home yet!"

"Ah, okay. I see." Dad's voice goes low and taut, like it always did when he'd lecture Nat. "So this is what the Life of Brandon's all about now. No, I get it. Real cool. You walk away from church, you lie to your parents—"

"Yeah, well, why do you think I lied? What if I told you Abel was coming? There's no way you'd have said yes."

"You're damn right!"

"We're just concerned, sweetie," says Mom.

"You're just backwards, is what you are," I shoot back.

We all plunge into silence. The woods around me feel dark and cold and endless. I think of the old Family Game Nights in the St. Matt's parish hall, when Dad would school everyone in Jeopardy and Mom was reigning Pictionary Queen with a 7-layer taco dip everyone wanted the recipe for. Nat would roll her eyes when they put their goofy plastic trophies on the mantel but I thought it was great, having parents who were champions and knew just about everything.

"Do you think I *want* to be this way, Brandon?" Dad sighs. "I mean, look: I wish to God I could say 'Suuure, go ahead. Whatever you want, kiddo! Dessert for dinner! Blow off that homework! Loosey-goosey, whatever feels good...'"

Mom giggles lamely. "Loosey-goosey?"

"The *point* is," he huffs, "I'm on your side. Very much so. I want you to be happy. I want to see you fall in love, get married—"

"I can still do that."

"But the fact is, you're never, ever going to be at peace. Not like this."

I just blink.

"Greg..." my mother whispers.

"It's true. You won't, because your mom and I raised you to know what's right, and you're always going to know deep down that this isn't what God wants for you. That even if he quote-unquote 'made' you a certain way, you separated yourself from him with your choices. And if I didn't keep pointing that out to you, if I didn't give my only son every chance to fix his relationship with God—" His voice wavers. He pauses, pulls in an even breath. "— then what kind of dad would I be?"

The kind of dad I need. If hey_mamacita was real and I was in her fic, I'd say it clear and brave. I'd tell him I respected his opinion, but it wasn't mine, not anymore. I'd tell him that my beautiful boyfriend was probably still at the bus station, and if I drove fast enough I could probably still catch him.

Instead I just mumble *I gotta go.* And I hang up.

Three seconds later it rings again.

hey_mamacita says, *Answer it, baby. Stand up to him. You can do it.*

It keeps ringing.

Tell him who you are! Be Fanfic Brandon! Unleash some mayhem!

Which is easy to say, when you don't exist.

I wait for the phone to stop ringing. When it's finally quiet, I send a single pathetic text to my dad's cell. He always keeps it on his belt, even when he's home watching baseball or working in the garden. "I don't want to be fertilizing the roses when someone calls with terrible news," he likes to say.

GOING TO BALTIMORE CON
HOME SUNDAY LATEST

I hit send and shut my phone off before it can protest. The world doesn't end. The cottonwood in front of me is tall and strong and unchanged. I peel a small patch of ragged bark from its side and slip it in my pocket.

Baltimore.

Bec shuffles back down the dirt trail, drawing a line behind her with the tip of a thick walking stick.

"We're going on?" she says.

"Going on. Yeah."

My legs are going boneless. I start to shake a little.

"Here." She hands me the stick, and we start on the uphill path back to the Sunseeker.

CastieCon #6
Baltimore, Maryland

28»

BEC AND I DO OUR USUAL on the long drive east on I-80.

We put on the playlist we made together a couple years back and hum along with Fleet Foxes, Iron & Wine, Rufus Wainwright, Dylan. We argue over whether *Scott Pilgrim* is actually any good. We polish off the dregs of the snack bin: raisins, stale trail mix, packs of code-orange crackers with crumbly peanut butter filling. She props her polka-dot flip-flops on the dash and reads me ridiculous Cosmo quizzes on the right animal print for your body type and what your favorite martini says about you.

But sometimes I'll catch her eye over a diner menu or glance at her while we're stuck in bumper-to-bumper, and I know she knows that everything I say is just filling silence. That inside I'm secretly doing what Past-Tense Brandon does best: flailing wildly.

She's right. Like right this minute, on the morning of July 4th, what we're technically doing is listening to the Broken West and estimating how many crunches a day she'd have to do to get as ripped as Della Wolfe-Williams. But the whole time I'm rifling through a flipbook of options. I'll go home, straight home, and apologize to my parents. I'll call Abel, beg him for another chance. I'll find a church and talk to a priest. I'll pick up some random guy at the Baltimore con and drag him into a bathroom stall. I'll swear off sex forever and join a monastery and spend the rest of my days meditating and making thimbleberry jam.

"You miss him," Bec says, for the millionth time. We're

on 76 now, snipping the southwest corner of Pennsylvania. I'm wearing Abel's white shirt from the Castaway Ball, the sleeves rolled up to fit me and the collar still tinged with blue.

"Yeah."

"So call him."

"I can't."

"That's it." She pulls out her phone. "I'm dialing."

"No! Don't."

"Why?"

"It'll just make things worse."

"Like waiting too long won't?"

"I need a sign."

"Okay: STOP."

"No no, listen. I have a *feeling*."

She sighs. "Here we go."

I can't explain it. I try anyway. I tell her I feel like something's going to happen at the Baltimore con, at the Q&A. Like I'll absorb some of Lenny Bray's storytelling genius on this subatomic level and I'll have an epiphany, and all the confusion will dry up and I'll know exactly what to do and where to go next.

Bec nods gravely. "That's really kind of dumb."

I grip the wheel tighter and kick it up to seventy. Let her think that; I don't care. We merge onto 70 East, toward Baltimore. I direct the next part straight to God, if he's up there. *Please help me. Please find some way to speak through Leonard Bray today. Give me, once and for all, the sign I've been waiting for.*

***

WE'RE SORRY
TODAY'S Q&A WITH LEONARD BRAY

IS CANCELLED DUE TO ILLNESS
MR. BRAY SINCERELY REGRETS ANY INCONVENIENCE
NO REFUNDS

For a long time I just stare at the sign—attached to the closed door of Meeting Room 1-C with cheery mismatched thumbtacks, as if it were announcing a shortage of strawberry ice cream instead of a cruel practical joke of the universe.

"Crap," I whisper.

Bec squeezes my arm.

Outside the Q&A room in the Baltimore Dorchester, the CastieCon staff—a burly guy with a black goatee and a skinny lady with straggly brown hair—are getting absolutely jackhammered. The crowd around them gets bigger and angrier by the minute, the fans shooting out questions and threats and conspiracy theories.

"I drove my son all the way from New York! We're missing fireworks for this."

"I knew he'd pull this. He planned it, didn't he?"

"He's got stage fright, you guys. He said—"

"Bullshit! He hates us. Always has."

"Refunds or revolt, people!"

"Refunds or revolt! Refunds or revolt!"

Bec pulls me away from the chanting crowd.

"Sorry," she says. "This sucks."

"Yeah."

"What do you want to do?"

I scan the convention hall, hoping the answer will pop out. But it's all the same CastieCon stuff—the vendors and the overpriced snack stand and the trivia games and costume contests—and none of it is fun without Abel. I can't go, though. Not yet. I can't just go home to my pissed-off parents and the St. Matt's Funfair and my stupid room with the stupid solar system sheets, like the past six weeks never even happened.

"I need some time," I tell Bec. "I think maybe a long walk or something..."

"Want company?"

"Not this time. That okay?"

She nods. "I'll hang out here. I want to call Dave anyway."

"Are you sure?"

"There's a fanfic panel at 12. It might be fun and educational."

"Really."

"Plus there's a pool. Take your time."

She's snapping a little blue plastic dragonfly barrette in her hair, the kind she used to wear when we were kids and spent whole afternoons in the woods around St. Matt's with her dad's metal detector. She used to save the bottle caps for me, even that awesome vintage Orange Crush cap she probably wanted to keep.

I crush her in a hug.

"Okay, freakshow," she laughs. "Go find your epiphany."

"Thanks."

"Try the gift shop first. I think they're on sale."

I give her a raspberry and a wave.

"Bring me back a snow globe!"

***

I stick my earbuds in and call up a Sim playlist, scrolling right to the song Abel contributed ("Coin-Operated Boy" by the Dresden Dolls). I stalk the hotel lobby while the song tootles in my ears like a demented music box. I walk with purpose, even though I have none. I scan everything like there's a clue inside: the concierge, the fountains, the sleek leather armchairs, the glass chandeliers shaped like upside-down birthday cakes.

Just past the elevator banks, I spot the nun.

She's an old-school kind I've only seen in photos, with a long black veil and just a small window of face peeking through. Like a relic from Gram's day, when it was okay to throw a five-pound Latin hymnal at someone for mispronouncing *venite adoremus*. She's walking arm in arm with a young blonde woman who's dressed way older than she probably is in a dark severe pantsuit and pearls, her hair swept up and sprayed stiff. She looks familiar, the way all churchy girls do. They're probably off to some kind of youth convention, where Pantsuit Woman will pump them up with an abstinence-is-cool speech and the nun will make sure no one's secretly making out in the coat closet.

Follow them.

The weird idea presses into me. Lightly at first, then hard as a fist; they vanish around a corner and my legs jerk to action, run to catch up. Cold sweat breaks out on my neck. When you're trolling for a sign and your gut tells you *follow that nun*, you probably won't like what you get.

They turn down a narrow hallway, a dim passage with a red EXIT sign flickering at the end. I hurry past the opening, all innocent-passer-by, and then back up and duck behind the vending machine at the hall's entryway.

"He says wait here," says the nun, in a deep raspy whisper I didn't expect. "He's pulling the car around— What's that face for?"

"You look ridiculous."

"Effective, though. No one looks a nun in the eye. We'll return the costume on the way to lunch."

"Oh, geez, Lenny."

Every hair on my arms lifts straight up. Now I know where I've seen Pantsuit Woman—decorating his arm at the Emmys, shuffling shyly in a mermaid-tail gown, the forums snarking *Bray likes 'em young.*

I crouch down and sneak a quick peek.

"This is really pathetic," his wife is saying.

"Well, I'm *sorry*, Elizabeth. Some days I *can*. Some days I *cannot*. This happens to be a cannot day."

"At least be honest with them."

"I was! Illness. It's a useful word. *Crippling anxiety* slots neatly therein."

She sighs. "Crippling? C'mon, that's a little—"

"I am deep in disguise, skulking past angry throngs of fans. Would I do this unless I had to?—Yes, hello?...Uh-huh, fantastic. And it's a curtained alcove? Marvelous. We're on our way." His phone snaps shut. "Reservations at Cereza. That should cheer you up. Private room, little plates, no one to bother us."

"You break people's hearts."

"Darling, please. They just want to ogle me like a zoo animal. The only one who truly wants to see my ugly mug is you."

"Not true. You're the Genius Creator."

"Oh, tell me more."

Do it now. Talk to him. I risk another peek; Bray's yanking off the nun costume, hopping on one foot with a hand on his wife for balance, and he looks so human and approachable with his bald spot showing and his underwear peeking from the waistband of his cords that...

A sneeze sizzles up my nose and roars out of me.

"Who's there?" Bray's voice: sharp and mean, a trace of fear. I clap a hand to my mouth.

"Hello?" says Elizabeth.

"Show yourself!" I get a fanboy chill. He's doing Xaarg. I remember how he joked in that interview once, how writing the voice of God was "frighteningly easy" for him. "It's impolite to hover!"

I could run. There's a staircase three doors down; I could lose the voice of God in a heartbeat if I tried.

I close my eyes. Breathe in, breathe out.

I step into the dim hallway light.

Bray squints.

"My glasses," he whispers. Elizabeth digs in her little black purse, passes them over. He slides on a thick pair of tortoiseshell frames and sizes me up.

"What hath the heavens discharged?" He blinks theatrically. "One rumpled fool in an ill-fitting shirt."

I clear my throat. "Mr. Bray, I—"

"Oh. God. Why? Why why why do you have to know who I am?"

"Foolproof costume." Elizabeth eyerolls.

"No—" I take a step closer. He's short in person; we stand eye to eye. "No, see, I'm a fan—"

"Of course you are. Of course. You took pictures with one of those miniscule stalker-cameras, no? By day's end your Internet boards will be aflame with scandal! *Leonard Bray Ditches Q&A! Secret Nun Fetish Photos Inside!*"

"No, I won't say anything. I promise."

"Uh-huh. What a Boy Scout. I suppose you followed me to buy me pork rinds?" He gestures toward the snack machine.

"No..." I try a smile. "Do you want some?"

"Stupendous. He's a comedian, too." Lenny Bray goes off on a muttering rant, addressing the Ho-Hos in the C4 slot. I try to absorb it: the supreme creator of Sim and Cadmus, the guiding force behind everything *Castaway Planet,* the entire reason I went to bed smiling last year, is standing right in front of me and knocking his head against a vending machine.

"You'll have to excuse him," says Elizabeth. "He has... some problems."

I watch in awe. "It's okay. I do too."

"Why don't you join us for lunch?"

"What?" Bray stops the head-knocking and glares fire at her.

"Sure. We treat you to a once-in-a-lifetime afternoon with the creator of *Castaway Planet,* and you won't spread any rumors about today. Right?"

What else would I say? "Absolutely."

"Lenny?"

"Fine." He slumps against the machine and knots his arms. "He's not sitting next to me on the drive over."

29»

"LEONARD BARTHOLOMEW BRAY," Elizabeth scolds. "Will you lean in a little? He won't bite you!"

In the white curtained alcove of some fancy small-plate restaurant, Lenny Bray is protesting a photo op. Elizabeth frowns behind my phone, waving us closer together. Her pink nails are perfectly rounded and she's got a giant honker of a diamond ring on her left hand.

"He's going to post this," Bray whines. "I know it."

"Well, he said he wouldn't, and I believe him. He deserves a souvenir."

"And I deserved a day of rest. Genesis says so."

Lunch is not going exactly as planned.

I want to ask Bray a thousand questions about Sim and Cadmus and the rumors about next season and of course the cave scene, but so far opening my mouth in his presence hasn't yielded very positive results. It's like a nasty version of comedy-club improv; I toss out a random comment, he builds a complaint around it. By the time the shark fritters and goat cheese ravioli arrive, I kind of have to face it: in addition to being smart and witty and talented and even kind of cute in a pop-eyed, older-guy, sweater-vesty way, Leonard Bray is pretty much a giant jerkoff.

Once Elizabeth snaps the photo, he starts yammering again: "Oh, and *another* thing about the Loyola English department!" I made the mistake of telling him I'd be a freshman at his alma mater this year. "If Antonia Humphrey is still moldering in her corner office, don't ever take her class on The Epic. That miserable twat. I spent three days on an essay comparing Odysseus and Travis Bickle and she called it *forced and indulgent* and gave me a C minus. Meanwhile the rest of the class is stuck in preschool, decoding symbolism like good little sheep—"

"Lenny," says Elizabeth.

"What?"

"Maybe he'd like to ask you some questions about the show."

"Well, he can't. I can't say anything."

"Not spoilers. Just tidbits he might be interested in."

"Oh. Fine, fine." He sighs. "All right, Brendan. Can I interest you in any *tidbits*?"

"Sure." I fiddle with my chicken kabob. "Actually, I did have a question."

"I shall do my best."

"It's about Cadmus and Sim."

"Oh goody."

"So, I..." I gulp some water. "There's a lot of ah, fanfiction about that one scene in the crystal spider cave—"

"Terrible episode. I regret it. Derailed the whole season's momentum."

"I sort of agree, but..." I'm blushing already; there's no chance he'll take this well. "After they say that line about how the cave could swallow up your secrets and it kind of faded out? Did they, um...do anything?"

"What do you mean?"

He blinks at me. I want to vanish.

"Anything *romantic*." Elizabeth smiles.

"Did they fuck?" says Lenny Bray. "Is that the question?"

"Uh. Yeah."

"Jesus. How would I know?"

My mouth opens. Nothing comes out.

"Seriously, why even ask me that?"

"Well...ah, it's your show, and—"

"I will never, ever, for as long as I live, understand you people. Every goddamned Q&A it happens! Mr. Bray, what does this line mean? Mr. Bray, is Castaway Planet the afterlife? Can Sim fall in love? Is Xaarg good or evil?" He stuffs two ravioli in his mouth. "Apparently an *alarming* percentage of you traipse through life without a single independent thought. I thought my fans were supposed to be smart!"

"But you created the characters, so—

"Oh, so I'm God? Is that it?"

"No, but—"

"Listen, you runt. I saw that self-righteous eyeroll when you said *fanfiction*. Let me tell you something: *I fucking love fanfiction*. Why do you think I made up these characters? So I could play with dolls in public and tell everyone else 'hands off'? So I could spoon-feed you stories from on high about the mysteries of love and free will and giant alien spiders?" He shows me his palms, then the backs of his hands. "I am one man with a laptop. When I give the world my characters, it's because I don't want to keep them for myself. You don't like what I made them do? Fucking *tell me I'm wrong!* Rewrite the story. Throw in a new plot twist. Make up your own ending. *Castaway Planet* is supposed to be a living piece of *art!*" He wags a tiny fork in my direction. "I don't know you from Adam, but if you're sitting there drooling in front of the TV like I suspect you are, letting me have the Final Word every goddamned Thursday night, you frankly don't even deserve to be a fan, Brendan."

Elizabeth sighs. She's heard it before. "Lenny."

"Elizabeth."

"Come on."

He purses his lips. "What?"

"This poor kid looks up to you. Can't you give him an answer?"

Lenny Bray looks me right in the eye. He stabs another shark fritter with the little fork.

"I thought I just did," he says.

I should be crushed by all this, but I'm not. I get this calm settled feeling, like when you see where the last three pieces of a thousand-piece puzzle are supposed to go.

"I have to leave now," I tell them.

"I'm so sorry." Elizabeth touches my hand. "He's having a bad day."

"You have no idea what it's like to be me." Leonard Bray pouts and shoves a fritter in his mouth. "No one has any idea."

"That's true, sir. It was good to meet you."

"I doubt that."

Elizabeth blots her pink lips with a napkin and folds it carefully on her empty plate. She's given up saving the day; you can tell.

"At least let our driver take you back," she says to the napkin.

Outside, cabs are rattling by; the day's first fire-crackers are going off in the distance.

"That's okay." I nod to Bray, standing Sim-straight. "I'll find my own way."

***

In two months, this'll be my city.

I've been here in Baltimore a few times since I was a kid—an aquarium trip, a college tour—but never without my parents. I let myself meander. Past the tourist crowds and the glassed-in malls and the old battleships moored in the harbor, across a swarming intersection and into a homey network of narrow streets. Junk shops and bars and bookstores introduce themselves to me, murmur about new starts in new places where no one knows my name. Next year I could streak my hair with Manic Panic and go dancing at this club with the fiery wings painted on the door. I could join some Young Agnostics support group downtown or find one of those alternative churches with a rainbow-cross logo. I could watch *Castaway Planet* in a dorm bed with my boyfriend or read Thomas Merton in a tulip patch; I could sing for people in a nursing home or strum Jeff Buckley and Dylan covers on open mike nights in this café wallpapered with board games and doll heads.

Or I could do it all.

On the walk back to the Dorchester, I pass a wide patch of grass with three big abstract sculptures. Light gray concrete, shaped like smiles without a face. There's a kid on one of them, dressed for the Fourth in navy shorts and a red-and-white striped shirt, trying to see how far he can walk up the side of the smile before gravity kicks him back down. On the second one, a neo-hippie girl with blond dreads and a sunflower dress is working out some tender instrumental on a blue guitar plastered with stickers from different cities. The third smile is up for grabs.

I sit down on it gingerly, like I have no right to. The action feels familiar, and then I realize that that's how I sit down in church. Used to, at least. I swing my legs inside the smile and prop my feet up on the concrete, smoothing Abel's white shirt across my chest. The sky is thick with puffy motivational-poster clouds; I take deep breaths and watch them morph across the blue for a whole minute. Two minutes. Three. I've never looked up for this long. Ever since I was old enough to know what a sin was, I've just naturally averted my eyes from the sky. As a kid it was terrifying: a place where divine judging eyes screened everything you did, where lightning bolts were hurled in anger from a golden throne, where your dead relatives clutched their harps and scanned your dirty thoughts like a waiting-room magazine.

I wonder if other people think weird thoughts like that. It seems unavoidable. You're a kid, and how can they explain something huge and unknowable like God to a kid, so they draw a simple picture: he's like a father in the sky, watching over us. Then you see statues and paintings of God in books and museums, so old they seem like historical records and not flights of fancy from ancient dead guys. And you file those away and fill in the rest of the portrait with your own references, until your picture of God is something like mine was: Ben Kingsley in a long Michelangelo beard, enthroned in an icy castle like Superman's Fortress of Solitude and scribbling (with the angry point of his thunderbolt) a fancier version of Santa's Naughty or Nice list. You get older, but the kid's picture stays with you. And then all of a sudden you're eighteen and you've learned how to question and doubt and you think you're smart enough to draw your own grown-up picture of what God might be, but part of you is still cringing with one eye to the sky, waiting for the thunderbolt.

A cloudbank swallows the sun and the harbor cools and darkens. I keep my eyes on the shifting sky, like Sim in the operating room getting prepped for Lagarde's silver chip. I think of him three weeks post-chip, shouting on the mountaintop with Cadmus: *No one told me what doubt was like. To know how much I still don't know.* I used to feel every syllable of that line. Almost nothing hurt worse than doubt. Now it's feeling almost comfortable, like this too-big shirt of Abel's that I'll probably wear until it frays and the stitches start to unravel.

The harbor breeze rustles my shirt. I pull it tighter. I tell everything bad inside me, everything I've outgrown, to go play somewhere else for a while. I picture them all wriggling out of my head, groaning and grumbling. The clean blond boy from *Put on the Brakes!* The chalupa guy from the laundry room. Tom Shandley and Miss Maxima and my angry bearded Ben Kingsley God. Father Mike is the last to go, toting his battered guitar and an armload of little black words.

They all crowd around me. *What now?*

I close my eyes on them.

You can go anytime.

I think it softly, without anger. After a minute, I feel them shuffle off into shadows, like when Dad and I used to catch and release sunfish up the street at Tanner's Pond. They'd hover in the shallows for a second, stunned to be free, and then they'd struggle away and vanish in the murk.

Not forever, I warn myself. They'll be back, and soon. But I'll be ready.

I send a tentative prayer to my vague new idea of the maybe-God: featureless and formless, a light warm and yellow as my kitchen at home. The anti-Xaarg, like Abel said. *Help me be ready,* I say to him. Or her. *If you exist, please help.*

If you don't, I'll do it on my own.

Bright heat washes over my face. I open my eyes. The sun's shaken off the clouds again. Two kids with rocket pops are spinning themselves dizzy in the grass and Dreadlocks Girl is still hunched on her concrete smile with her blue guitar, tuning up for another song. The harbor hums with happy busy holiday noise. Alone in the midst of cute families and throngs of friends, I feel empty in the best way, cleaned out and ready to fill up on new thoughts and words.

I rest my cheek on the warm upturn of the smile, and listen.

***

Brandon set the sunflowers on the table. He took another step closer to Abel, who fixed him with a wary gaze that Brandon totally and completely deserved.

I come back to the Dorchester with my brain buzzing and my fingers itching. I call Bec and tell her I need a little more time. I don't tell her anything else. Not yet. I find a quiet corner in the coffee shop, slide my laptop out of my bag, and type for my life.

"Look, I'm probably going to be pretty screwed up for a while," Brandon admitted, his voice deep and confident. "There's a lot I haven't figured out yet. But we've got six weeks left of summer, and I think we owe it to ourselves to be screwed up together."

Brandon waited for a verdict. He braced himself for Abel's back turning on him, for the sick rumble of sunflowers in the garbage disposal.

"Is it okay to kiss you?" Abel asked.

Brandon stepped forward first. They met in the middle of the room, and their lips acted out a string of impressive adjectives as they came together.

I hop on the hotel wifi, consult thesaurus.com.

Gingerly, haltingly at first. Then ecstatically, jubilantly, hopefully.

When I'm finished with the whole scene, I don't go back and change stuff; maybe it's cheesy, but the words are all true. I address an email to amcnaughton128@gmail.com. I add a note:

See attached for the last chapter of "How to Repair a Mechanical Heart."
What do you think?

***

I find Bec sprawled on a blue plastic beach chair by the pool, her sandals kicked off and a gift-shop true-crime novel in front of her face. I sit down, pull her feet up on my lap, and dangle a big white bakery bag from the shop I passed on the walk back.

"What's this?" she grins.

"Red velvet cupcakes."

She gasps. "Why?"

"For being a good friend. Putting up with me. Having cute toes."

"You are an admirable young man." She tears the bag open. "So this text from you. Explain."

"It was a mysterious mission."

She takes a big bite of red velvet. "So you said."

"You won't believe it."

"Okay."

"I mean, you *really* won't."

"Tell me!"

I pull my phone out of my pocket, call up the Lenny Bray shot. Bec's mouth drops open.

"Is that—"

"It is."

"Oh. My God."

"That was just the beginning."

She grabs my wrist. "Start talking. Now."

"I'll tell you on the road." I pull her to her feet. "Assuming you're fine with missing the 2:00 panel on 'The Ethics of Redemption in *Castaway Planet.*'"

She grins and tosses me the keys. "Let's go home, cupcake."

Home

30»

THE ANNUAL ST. MATT'S Fourth of July Funfair is the year's third biggest deal, after the Christmas Eve Mass with the kiddie pageant and the May Procession where the Mary statue gets crowned with fake flowers and we pray for a thousand years in the hot church and one kid always passes out. My parents have been all about the Funfair since Nat and I were kids. Dad helps hammer all the game booths together and Mom decorates and arranges the food tables. The center table always holds three giant platters of her famous angel eggs, which are basically deviled eggs with cream cheese whipped into the filling and a name that won't make the organist boycott them. Every year I stuff myself with angel eggs and fried chicken and try to beat Bec at ladderball and volunteer in the dunking booth, and then we all watch the fireworks over funnel cake and frozen lemonade and Dad and I throw a ball around behind the karaoke stage.

Every year except this one.

It's after 4:00 by the time I park the Sunseeker back at my house, swap it for Mom's old Jetta, drop Bec off at her place, and make the short trek to Donovan Street. The cars of the devoted already dot the St. Matt's parking lot. Mom and Dad's Ford Focus, Mrs. Heffler's silver SUV, the Donnellys' new Camry, the beat-up blue Saturn Father Mike's had forever. I slot myself into a spot surrounded by empty spaces. I check my email for a response from Abel, like I did every five minutes on the trip home.

Nothing.

I tap my shorts pockets. Plastic Sim in the right, Plastic

Cadmus in the left. The Mom-and-Dad reunion looms like a one-on-one with Xaarg; I'm in no hurry.

Plus there's one last thing I need to do.

I haven't walked through the front doors of St. Matt's in over five months. I clutch my breath as the door creaks open, as if a horde of crystal spiders might be sleeping in the shadows inside. But when I tiptoe up the three carpeted steps, it's the same old church, everything familiar and summery. Red, white, and dyed-blue carnations on the altar, the faded tang of incense and sweat, a warm breeze wandering in through a few open windows and swaying the felt dove banners Mom helped sew.

I wander up the aisle, the same path my parents took on their wedding day. I trace a beam of light from the stained-glass Holy Spirit window to the bronze-and-oak font where I was baptized. Three tiers of red votives flicker next to it, each tiny light connecting a problem with a prayer. I'm surprised by what I don't feel, standing here alone. A rock in my stomach, a hand around my throat. Father Mike would say that this isn't peace, that I'm empty in a bad way. *Spiritually flatlined,* like he said once in a sermon. But no one's behind the altar now, and I don't have to listen.

I stop by the marble holy water font. Press a finger in the damp yellow sponge, like I did when I was a kid and St. Matt's felt like home. Now it feels like a stop on a long trip somewhere else. Until this summer that thought would have made me sad and scared, but now I can't wait to see where the road turns next.

I just wish Abel was in the seat beside me.

***

My parents are out on the Funfair field behind St. Matt's,

273

wearing matching sweats in my high school colors and hauling the ring toss platform together. Normally this is where I'd jump right in, grabbing a corner of something heavy and tacking up signs and testing extension cords. Two things stop me: the fact that they possibly want to wring my neck, and the fact that Father Mike is sitting on a stool by the ticket booth, tuning his guitar and blocking my way.

I shove my hands in my pockets and squeeze Plastic Cadmus and Plastic Sim, trying to absorb what I need. Control from Sim. Bravado from Cadmus. The rock in my throat shrinks down to a pebble.

After a minute, my legs start to walk.

"Brandon. Welcome back." Father Mike doesn't get up when he sees me coming. It's a sly calculation: assume friendly nonthreatening pose, let the lost sheep come to you.

"Hi." I nod. Neutral smile.

"Trip okay?"

"Yep, it was fine. Thanks."

"Your mom and dad thought you might show up today." He plucks the A string on his instrument—a haggard old thing with a GOT GOD? sticker on it—and twists the tuning peg. I think of the first time he passed me a guitar, showed my fingers how to shape the C and G chords. "I know they've been pretty worried. They'll be super-relieved to see you here safe."

"What'd they tell you?" I square my shoulders like Cadmus.

"Well, they—"

"Actually, it's all right. I don't want to know."

"Okay. That's okay."

"I'm gonna go talk to them."

"Want me to come along? It might help."

"No. No thank you." Sim takes over: smooth and composed. "I can do it alone."

"Sure, sure. I know. That's fine." He smiles that old *I'm-just-a-dude* smile, and my shoulders go soft. I'm not Sim or Cadmus anymore. I'm a kid, whispering fake sins to him in the face-to-face confessional, his mellow voice calming my jittering leg. hey_mamacita's mean Father X caricature pops to mind, and my face heats up. It's easy fighting villains with daggers for teeth and crosses that shoot hellfire. But he's not Father X, or Xaarg. He cares about me, the way I hope my own father still does.

"Hey Brandon?"

"Yeah."

"Give me a few minutes later on. Okay, bud? I'd like to talk to you."

I pause for a second, the fight draining out of me, and then a whole vanload of kids in matching St. Matt's Elementary t-shirts come rushing over. They've got all the usual grade-school-music-class instruments with them—triangles, egg shakers, jingle bells, probably the exact same ones I played at some point. Father Mike gives them a thumbs-up and a distracted smile. He won't let me walk without an answer.

"Sure," I mumble. I'm watching the kids. Pigtailed and sneakered, trusting and open. "I guess."

"Awesome. Meetcha back here."

I walk away. I walk fast, but his voice travels. "Hey, guys!" he's saying. "How're my SonShiners today?...Yeah? Let's try that a little louder!" He starts strumming the opening bars of that cutesy "Whatever God Wants" song that still gets stuck in my head; I don't want to glance back, don't want my brain to sing along. I look for something else to focus on. I find it across the field by the popcorn stand.

My parents, standing side by side with their arms around each other. Like instead of waiting for me to cross the field and catch up, they're watching me walk away.

***

We sit at a weathered picnic bench that's survived about fifty St. Matt's Funfairs. The bench is etched with decades of graffiti: BILL N SUE, KEVIN + KAYLA 4EVR. I trace the old names and promises, scanning my brain for the right thing to say.

Judging from past battles with Nat, I thought Dad would come down on me like the hammer of God. But he doesn't even seem angry. It would be easier if he did. He seems remote and unsettled, like an alien's replaced his son and he's approaching with caution, trying to figure out what this new thing is capable of.

"Did you remember to clean out my refrigerator?" he finally asks me.

"We did."

He ignores the *we*. "And did you empty the tanks?"

"Yes."

"The black and the gray?"

"Yeah. I returned your camping stove, too. It's back in the garage."

"I hope it's clean. If you let grease and food particles build up it can..."

He keeps going. The checklists and lectures might go on until sundown if I don't do something. I squeeze Plastic Cadmus and Plastic Sim.

"Hey. Guys?"

"I wasn't finished," Dad snaps.

"Greg. Let him talk," says Mom.

Dad bites his lip and taps the table with his fist. I take

a deep breath.

"I'm sorry I lied," I tell them. "I'm not sorry for what I did, or for anything that happened on the trip, but I'm sorry I lied. I'm not going to do that anymore. And I'm sorry I called you backwards." I catch Mom's eye. "Really."

Mom nods. Dad's eyes are shiny. He scrapes a splotch of dried mustard off the table with his thumbnail and blows the yellow dust away.

"So that's all?" he says.

"I guess. For now."

"We're glad you're home safe," says Mom. "Right, Greg?"

"I—"

Dad just sighs. He looks like he wants to say more, but I know it's not going to happen. Not today, not here. He drums at the table a couple times and then he gets up slowly and scuffs away, his ancient sneakers kicking up sad little puffs of fairground dust.

Mom watches him go.

"You were...safe, weren't you? You and..." She clears her throat. "You and him."

I blush. "Yeah. Of course."

"That's the most important thing. I don't care what you've heard—"

"Mom, I know. I know. You don't have to worry."

She exhales, long and slow. We sit there for a complicated minute.

"Your dad just—doesn't know what to say." She says it like she's apologizing for him, like she's got no problem with this at all. I watch him fix a game booth, pounding nails into loose beams. I wonder if it'll be like this all the time now, if I'll come home from college and he'll ask me if I'm passing my tests and keeping the bathroom clean and locking the doors at night, and then go off to the basement and start snipping his bonsai and hammering birdhouses together until I go to bed, and the danger of looking me in the eye has passed.

Mom, softly: "Are you in love?"

"You don't have to ask."

"I want to know."

I squirm in my seat. "I screwed everything up."

"You did?" Her eyes get big. It's cute.

"I tried to get him back. Sort of." I trace a heart carved deep in the bench's center slat. This is so weird. "But I don't really know how. I think it's too late."

"Oh." She sighs. "Honey."

A cursor blinks in the conversation. She looks like she wants to give me advice, the way she gave Nat advice before Nat shaved half her head and stopped listening, but I know she can't. Especially not here, with the big gold cross on the St. Matt's spire looming above the trees. She's probably doing the math: *Give your gay son love advice = twelve and a half years in Purgatory.*

There's nothing much else to say. I reach in my back pocket, pluck out the rolled-up David Darras head shot. I push it across the table to her.

"He couldn't sign the *TV Guide*, but I got this."

She smiles a thank you—not because of the autograph, but because I've changed the subject.

"I forgot I asked you," she says. Her glossy fingernails rake the rubber band off and the picture unrolls.

"He did sign it. It's just kind of messy."

"How was he?"

"Funny. Really nice."

"Was he just as handsome in person?"

I nod. "Even more."

She reaches across the table and grabs my hand. She pretends she's looking at the Darras photo, but really she's looking right through it. A light breeze curls the corners of the photo and ruffles her pale yellow curls. In the distance, Father Mike and the kids are running through "His Banner Over Me Is Love."

"Are you staying?" she says. "For the fair?"

"I can't."

She nods; I can tell she expected that. I watch her gaze shift to the crowded food tables and the jumble of raffle prizes. She's scrawling one of her checklists in her head, thinking about all the stuff she has to do before the Funfair starts, and if I fast-forward the future I can see her and Dad here year after year, arranging decades of gelatin stars and angel eggs and repainting the same ten game booths until the two of them are finally old and sitting side by side in their blue canvas lawn chairs, counting fireworks together.

The sun's starting to slip away. More volunteers are coming with stacks of raffle-ticket rolls, bags of game prizes. She's still holding my hand. I let her, for a long time.

Then I'm like, "Save me an angel egg?"

I squeeze her hand twice.

"I'll save you two," she says, and then she lets go.

***

I'm already in the car by the time Father Mike realizes I'm leaving. I see him with his guitar as I ride the brakes past the Funfair field: strumming another song with the kids, a whole fresh flock to teach. He looks small and breakable, like one of those ceramic saint figurines Gram keeps on her windowsill.

If this were a hey_mamacita fic, I would have confronted him before I left. The dialogue: "Bring back any nice souvenirs?" "Yeah—a *boyfriend*." That would've left him comically stewing, his face purple and steam shooting out of his ears. I remind myself he's not a cartoon. He's not even a bad guy. I don't need him now, but I don't need to hurt him, either.

He glances up, catches me idling in the car. He lifts a hand from the guitar strings and waves, like *C'mon over, bud. Come back.* I stick my hand out the open window and give him a gentle return wave. *Goodbye.*

I slip Cadmus and Sim out of my pockets and drop them both in the dashboard cupholder, their limbs tangled loosely together. Then I shift into drive and start rolling forward, down the winding road away from St. Matt's.

31»

I'VE GOT A PLAN.

Home first, to shower and change my grubby travel clothes. Francie's Florals next, for the biggest arrangement of sunflowers I can afford (which at this point isn't much). Then the candy shop in the mall—do they have cinnamon jelly beans? I call them up while I'm whizzing past the DQ, my old high school, the pizza place where I worked last summer. They do.

I'm three stoplights from my street when the phone rings.

ABEL CALLING.

This was not part of the plan.

I white-knuckle it past the post office. Plastic Sim and Plastic Cadmus shoot plastic glares of judgment from the cupholder: *Pick up, dumbass.* My thumb hovers over the Answer button. Why did I send him that stupid scene? I know exactly what I'm going to hear. *What is this fairy-tale crap? You think this fixes things? Just stay out of my life, okay?*

"It's not *completely* horrid," he says, "for your first fic."

Relief flushes through me. "Hello to you too."

"I was deeply offended by a few things, though. Number one—Where are you, by the way?"

I picture him sprawled on his fancy metal platform bed, tracing the blue and yellow squiggles on his vintage 80s sheets. "Driving home," I tell him. "From an errand."

"What kind of errand?"

"Can't tell you. So what's number one?"

"The bubble bath."

"Huh?"

"I mean, *hello*. It's humiliating. You come to my house with sunflowers, all sexy and disheveled in your dirty khakis and your black *Castaway Planet* shirt, and I'm *sulking alone in a lemon-scented bubble bath?*"

"Sorry. Is that not in character?"

"Not the point. I could at least be lifting weights or something."

I grin. "Feel free to edit."

"Oh, I have. 'Kay, number two—this is a larger issue with plotting, unfortunately."

"Let's hear it."

"Well, it's really sweet and heartwarming, having Brandon drive out to my house in a summer storm to deliver this impassioned speech and all, but at this point in the narrative it's basically Abel who's been the giant jackhole. So that whole scene kind of falls flat—no?"

I swerve to miss a squirrel. "I don't—"

"—Like, Abel's the one who broke it off the second Brandon had a relapse, right?'

"He had good reasons, though."

"What, the *Jonathan* thing? So not an excuse. What kind of self-involved assclown bails at the first sign of Catholic guilt? And then doesn't even call for like *days*, which basically forces Brandon to nut up and send him that amazing email even though the last thing Abel deserves is a grand romantic gesture."

"Abel had a point, though."

"Doesn't matter. See, when you love someone, the gentlemanly thing to do is stick with them and willfully ignore your differences and draw little valentine hearts over all their weird hangups and just be in love for as long as you possibly can because how often does that happen? And then when you finally start making each other miserable or you meet some perfect guy in your freshman philosophy class, then you can have your tearful heartrending 'it's over' phone call and a nice long satisfying wallow." He sighs. "So see, there's no way we've earned a tragic breakup yet. We didn't put in enough time. I pulled the plug too early."

My heart's going phosphorescent. *When you love someone.* "So you're saying..."

"We need a rewrite. Abel shows up at *Brandon's* house, all apologies."

"Really."

"Well, mostly apologies. Know what would really be romantic, too?"

"What's that?"

"If he'd fixed that mechanical heart he stepped on. Like if Susannah helped him glue it back together, and he wrapped it up in a little silver box and everything."

"Kind of an obvious metaphor."

"Yeah, but so? I mean, just think how sweet that scene would be."

"What if Brandon's parents were there?"

"Oh, they wouldn't be. Not in this part of the story."

"No?" I turn onto my street.

"It would be a criminally gorgeous early summer evening...Abel would be standing on the brick front steps of Brandon's white split-level..."

I brake in the middle of the street. Plastic Cadmus and Plastic Sim knock heads in the cupholder.

"...taking in a scene of awesomely adorable Americana: the birdhouse, the red geraniums, the Fourth of July wreath made of pom-poms..."

I creep forward.

"...thinking about the 'hi, we're boyfriends again' vlog post we could make from your cute little bedroom if we got back together—oh, and figure out the logistics of doing *Castaway Planet* recaps from different colleges, and draw up a shared-custody arrangement for Plastic Cadsim...Bran? You still there?"

"Keep going," I whisper.

"...so I watch a butterfly flutter around your mom's flowers, and while I practice exactly the right things to say to win you back, I watch patiently for an old blue Jetta to putter into view—it is a Jetta, right?" I spot him down the road on my front steps now, a perfect action figure in tight jeans and snakeskin boots. He's standing up, showing me the back of his head as he cranes his neck at the opposite end of the street. In his hand is a little silver box, glinting in the fading sun.

"You getting any closer, Tin Man?" he says.

I ease my foot off the brake and start the downhill coast to home. "Almost there."

Acknowledgments

Huge hugs and a bucket of cinnamon jellybeans to the following fine people:

- Jarrett and Rosie, the two main planets in my universe, for enduring a houseful of scribbled-on sticky notes and helping me to the finish line with just the right blend of tough and sweet love.
- Mom and Dad, for teaching me that brains are for using and that real love survives differences.
- Margie, Anthony, Kim, & Brett, for understanding when I vanish with my laptop.
- Mindy Dunn, cover designer extraordinaire
- Andrea Sabaliauskas, for the brilliant cover illustration of Brandon and Abel and nearly two decades of friendship, support, and B&N chats.
- The entire fantastic Twitter community of writers, including my girls Megan Joel Peterson, Nikki Godwin, and Julie Hutchings.
- Wendy Bond, my lifelong BFF, one of the first people I ever shared my writing with.
- The illustrious Dr. Maverick, my #1 fandom-enabler.
- My work pals, for being excited about this project (especially Courtney Stansbury, for A+ cheerleading).
- The magnificent geeks who invented the Internet so other magnificent geeks could find each other and perpetuate the species. Without you, fanfic would be mimeographed and mailed, this story would not exist, and people would not be skimming this acknowledgments page like "tl;dr."

About the Author

J.C. LILLIS is a veteran of eight tempestuous Internet
fandoms, three Catholic schools, and countless crushes
on fictional characters. She lives in Baltimore, where she
collects old magazines and vintage YA books. You can
contact her at jclillisbooks@gmail.com with questions,
comments, haiku, photos of gelatin-mold salads, and
Brandon/Abel steampunk fanfic.

Also by J.C. Lillis

We Won't Feel a Thing

Two teens fight forbidden love with the help of a
mysterious self-help program. Then love fights back.

www.jclillis.com

Stop by for playlists, quote graphics, general silliness, and
the continuing Adventures of Plastic Brandon and Abel.